C

English Grammar

SALZWASSER
VERLAG

C.P. Mason

English Grammar

Reprint of the original, first published in 1858.

1st Edition 2023 | ISBN: 978-3-37514-910-9

Verlag (Publisher): Salzwasser Verlag GmbH, Zeilweg 44, 60439 Frankfurt, Deutschland
Vertretungsberechtigt (Authorized to represent): E. Roepke, Zeilweg 44, 60439 Frankfurt, Deutschland
Druck (Print): Books on Demand GmbH, In de Tarpen 42, 22848 Norderstedt, Deutschland

ENGLISH GRAMMAR;

INCLUDING

THE PRINCIPLES OF GRAMMATICAL ANALYSIS.

BY

C. P. MASON, B.A.

FELLOW OF UNIVERSITY COLLEGE, LONDON.

LONDON:
WALTON AND MABERLY,
UPPER GOWER STREET, AND IVY LANE, PATERNOSTER ROW.

1858.

PREFACE.

If the difficulties of the English language bore any proportion to the number of treatises upon the grammar of it, they might well be thought rather appalling. I have before me a list, comprising the names of four hundred and thirty works of this nature. The number published since the list was made would probably raise the total to at least five hundred. The addition of one more to such a list must, under any circumstances, be regarded as a venial offence: I trust it will be found that the addition is not altogether superfluous. In the course of a protracted search after an English Grammar suitable for boys, it appeared to me that the existing works on the subject were divisible into two classes;—works displaying deep and accurate knowledge of the principles of grammar generally, and of English grammar in particular, but quite unsuited for school use; and works well adapted for use, as far as size, form, and general arrangement were concerned, but defaced by serious inaccuracies and omissions. I found that the perpetual correction of these faults was a more laborious task than the production of a systematic exposition of my own views and method; and so the present work was commenced, at first simply in the form of manuscript lessons. The design kept in view has been, to give the learner an accurate system of grammatical definitions and principles which, though applied in the first instance to English, hold good, in the main, of the other languages of the same family. If a sound knowledge of the general laws of grammatical construction be acquired through the medium of English grammar,— which is far the easiest for an English pupil,—much time may be saved that is often spent in going over and over again the same elementary principles in various and often contradictory forms.

In grammar, as in every other science, the accuracy of the *definitions* is of vital importance. They must be such that there shall be no ambiguity in their terms, and that they shall be *convertible;* that is, that the description given as a definition of the thing defined shall apply to it, *and to nothing else;* so that the definition remains true when read conversely. To say that "a square is a plane rectilinear figure with four equal sides," would not be to give a definition, because it is not true that "a (i. e. *any*) plane rectilinear figure with four equal sides is a square." No doubt, it is often difficult to give perfectly accurate grammatical definitions, and still more difficult for a pupil to understand them thoroughly; but difficulties are not surmounted by being evaded; and the clumsy, slipshod attempts at definition, with which most of the school grammars in current use abound, are worse than useless. If a rough, inexact notion of grammatical terms and principles is sufficient, the study of grammar becomes superfluous; because a reasonably intelligent pupil can make such for himself. The object of the study of grammar is to shape these rough notions into accuracy. The faults above referred to are inexcusable, because more correct statements might have been obtained from sources easily accessible. A favourite blunder is to obliterate the distinction between *things or notions* and the *words* that represent them. Thus it is repeatedly laid down that "*gender* is the distinction of *sex*," as if words were divided into males and females, as animals are; that "case is the state or condition of a noun;" that "the possessive case represents a noun in the state or case of possessing something" (that is to say, "*John's book*" implies that the *noun or name John* possesses a book); that "a noun is in the nominative case when it is the agent" (so that when we say "a horse kicked me," we are to understand that the kick was given by the *noun*—horse, which is accordingly in the nominative case); that "adjectives denote the qualities of nouns" (so that when we say *a red apple*, we mean that the *noun* is of a red colour); that *tense* is the same as *time*; that (as one writer puts it) "a preposition is a word placed before nouns and pronouns, to show the relation (of position, motion, agency, instrumentality, &c.) which they bear to each other;" or, when we say, "*he ran to the door*," the preposition *to* denotes the relation of *motion* which the pronoun *he* bears to the noun *door;* that is, the pronoun ran to the noun. Of course, this is not the only class of mistakes. One writer (of whose grammar I have the 27th edition before me), besides other eccentric modes of manipulating the conjugation of a verb, annihilates the subjunctive mood *in toto*. (It would be curious to hear him parse such a sentence as, "If it were done, then it were well it were done quickly.") Even this blunder is not too gross to have been reproduced, with others, by a recent writer, whose Explanatory Grammar has already gone through several editions. In one grammar we are told that the subjunctive mood is always preceded by a conjunction, and find for the present tense of that mood, "If I am, If thou art, &c." When the author writes a Latin Grammar, we shall of course be told that *si sum* is the subjunctive mood of *esse*. The following* are rich specimens:—"The comparative degree is that which exceeds or lessens the positive." "The superlative degree is the greatest or least quality of an adjective." "A verb is a word which *affirms what is said* of persons and things." When grammar is taught in this style, most rational persons will agree that it had better be let alone. If the above were exceptional cases, it would not be worth while to notice them; but the curious part of the matter is, that few grammars are more extensively used than those from which the preceding quotations are made.

A word or two of explanation may be necessary, on one or two points, with relation to the present work.

One of the first distinctions that a learner must get thoroughly familiar with is that between a substantive and an adjective,—between a word that can be the subject of a sentence, or be governed by a verb or preposition, and a word that cannot. I have therefore, in the first instance, introduced the learner to a considerable number of the so-called *pronouns*, under the head of *adjectives*. These last I have distributed into the three classes of Qualitative, Quantitative, and Demonstrative Adjectives. It is very perplexing to a beginner to have his notions of an adjective derived from the Qualitative class exclusively, and then to be left to deal with the rest as he best can. Indeed, many writers of grammars have perplexed themselves as much as their pupils, and have put such words as *all*, *many*, &c., and even the numerals, into the class of

* Quoted from the 4th edition of a book published in 1854.

Pronouns. For further remarks on this point the reader is referred to §§ 128—172 of the present work. I am glad to find my classification sanctioned by so high an authority as that of Mr. Morell, who in his recently published English Grammar adopts the same division :* he also agrees with me in setting down the article, not as a distinct part of speech, but as a demonstrative adjective.

In dealing with the verb, I have discarded the potential mood, for reasons given in § 186. The only fragments of it which really indicate mood (namely the combinations of *should* and *would* with the infinitive mood) may be classed under the subjunctive mood. If "I shall write" is an indicative future, there is no reason why "I should write" should not be called a subjunctive future. It is then unnecessary to invent a conditional mood, as most French and some German grammarians do. It also obviates the necessity for calling the same tense both past and future (as Mr. Morell does). The scheme of tenses which I have adopted is not an invention of my own; it will be found in an admirable fragment of a Greek grammar, printed many years ago, by Professor Malden (of Univ. Coll., London), and in Professor Key's Latin Grammar. It agrees in its main features with the classification of all the best modern grammarians. It is simpler, more exact, and in every way better than such awkward, ambiguous, and unmeaning terms as *pluperfect, prior perfect, progressive forms, first future, second future,* with which most English grammars abound. The crotchety dictum, that the English verb has only two tenses, is rejected for the reasons stated in p. 35. The comparative table of tenses in English, Latin, Greek, German, and French will be found of great service. The necessity for the recognition of a *gerund* in English is shown in §§ 97, 200. Some other details will be found, in which it is hoped an improvement has been effected.

The adverb is a part of speech which has suffered much ill usage at the hands of grammarians. Its domain has been very

* The coincidence between Mr. Morell's Grammar and my own, in this and some other innovations, is curious, as the results have been arrived at quite independently. My own work was complete, and partly in use, before Mr. Morell's Grammar was published.

improperly restricted, and many words which are genuine adverbs in their relation to verbs, adjectives, and other adverbs, have been set down as mere conjunctions. In the classification which I have adopted, I have merely endeavoured to apply carefully the acknowledged truth, that a word which indicates any of the conditions of time, place, manner, degree, cause, or circumstance under which an attributive notion is connected with an object of thought, is an adverb. Some will perhaps demur at first to the truth of the statement that such words as *than*, *as*, *therefore*, &c. are adverbs. Before they finally reject it, however, they should examine and compare what is said in §§ 260, 264, 266, 267, 292, 408, with the examples of the analysis of compound and elliptical sentences.*

In treating of conjunctions, I have ventured upon a new classification. In a note on § 286, enough has been said to justify the disuse of the stupid old names, *copulative conjunctions* and *disjunctive conjunctions*, the former of which involves an unmeaning tautology, while the latter is simply self-contradictory. The division into *co-ordinative* and *subordinative* conjunctions has at least the advantage of being based upon a well-established classification of compound sentences, of exhibiting structural distinctions which the old-fashioned division obliterates, and of presenting the only distinction which really has a *grammatical* import.†

The syntactical portion of the present work derives many of

---

* Mr. Morell admits that *why*, *wherefore*, *when*, *where*, &c., are adverbs when used interrogatively, but seems to question the propriety of their being called adverbs in clauses which are not interrogative. It is not easy to see on what principle such a distinction can be defended. *When* indicates the time of an event quite as much in the one case as in the other. Besides, the interrogative force does not really reside in the words *where*, *wherefore*, &c., but in the structure and use of the clause in which they occur (see p. 94). If *wherefore* is an adverb in an interrogative sentence, it is an adverb in every sentence ; for the definition of an adverb will equally apply to it. And if *wherefore* is an adverb, the demonstrative *therefore* is also an adverb.

† Mr. Morell has retained the terms *copulative* and *disjunctive*, subdividing the copulative conjunctions into *connective* and *continuative*, and the disjunctive into *distributive* and *adversative*. This appears to me to be needlessly complex, independently of the objections urged above. The subdivisions *connective* and *continuative* involve an obscure indication of the classification which I have adopted. In §§ 292, 408, 409, I have given reasons for excluding from the list of conjunctions many words which Mr. Morell has included.

its leading features from the principles developed by Becker in his German Grammar. The publication of that work may well be regarded as an epoch in the history of grammatical science. Its leading doctrines are incontrovertibly sound and philosophical, though the same unqualified praise is by no means to be bestowed on the details of their development. The latter abound in capricious distinctions and arbitrary generalizations. The outlines of Becker's system were presented in a very imperfect and unsatisfactory manner by the late Rev. T. K. Arnold, in his "English Grammar for Classical Schools;" but the merit of first giving a full and accurate exposition of Becker's principles, as applied to English Grammar, unquestionably belongs to Mr. Morell, whose "Analysis of Sentences" has met with great and well-deserved success. I had at first thought that any further attempt in the same direction would be superfluous, but a closer examination of the subject convinced me that some important alterations were necessary, not so much in the mode in which Becker's system had been applied to the English language by Mr. Morell, as in some subordinate but important parts of the system itself.

Becker divides words into words that express notions, and words that express the relations of notions to each other. *Notions* he subdivides into notions of things that exist (expressed by substantives), and notions of the actions or activities* of the latter (expressed by adjectives and verbs). This distribution I have disregarded, because so much of it as is true is too vague to be of any use; and because the idea that in the words *a red rose*, *red* expresses an *activity* or *action* of the *rose*, is a metaphysical subtlety, questionable in itself, and quite unintelligible to a young learner. *A fortiori*, I have passed by Becker's intricate analysis of the various relations of these *activities* to some existing thing, or to the speaker. If I might be so bold, I should pronounce the greater portion of it to be little better than rubbish.

Becker distinguishes three relations in which words stand to each other:—1. the Predicative; 2. the Attributive; 3. the Objective. About the first two of these there is no difficulty. In place of the third, I have substituted two separate relations,—the *Objective Relation* and the *Adverbial Relation*. In Becker's system, the term *object* is applied not only to what is commonly

* Thätigkeiten.

understood as the object of a verb, but also to the circumstances of time, place, manner, and causality, which are connected with the action. The first sort of object he calls the *object that completes* the predicate, the second sort the *object that extends* the predicate. There are several difficulties involved in this. It is a most arbitrary and unnatural use of the grammatical term *object*, to say that the *place*, the *manner*, nay even the *cause* of an action, is an *object* of the action (see Morell, *Analysis*, § LIII). Again, the distinction drawn between *completing* the predicate and *extending* it will not bear examination. In such sentences as "He strikes the ball," "He runs across the meadow," the verb *strikes* expresses the action referred to at least as completely as the verb *runs;* and the phrase "*across the meadow*" quite as much completes the notion in the latter case as the word *ball* does in the former.* It is therefore better to keep the term *object* for that which is commonly understood by it in grammar, namely, the word that stands for that upon which the action denoted by a transitive verb is exerted, and to treat the adverbial relation (or what Becker calls the *extending object*) as something altogether distinct. Becker's arrangement becomes perfectly absurd when we apply it to the case of an adverb qualifying an adverb. In "He writes very well," *very* certainly stands in some relation to *well;* and as that is neither the predicative nor the attributive, it must be the objective,—the same relation as that in which *ball* stands to *strikes*, in the sentence given above! Mr. Morell (*Analysis*, § LVI.) overtly classes adverbs among the words that signify *action*. I confess I do not understand the kind of *action* which is denoted by words like *yesterday, now, here*, &c.; and I am quite sure that if a young learner thought he understood it, the notion which he would have in his mind would be something very wide of the truth.

It would puzzle any one to deduce from Becker's work a distinct and accurate definition of the predicate of a sentence. The style in which the matter is dealt with may be judged of by the fact, that he classes the verb *be* and the auxiliary verbs with pronouns,

* Becker himself allows this, in a passage which contradicts his own classification.

numerals, prepositions, and adverbs, under one head as *relational words*. Mr. Morell's account of the matter (*Analysis*, § VI.) is far superior in accuracy and clearness. In § 347 of the present work I have suggested a still further simplification, for which I have given my reasons in a note. One advantage that will follow from its admission will be that we shall be able to get rid of a difficulty, which, if not quietly ignored (as is often the case in systems of grammatical analysis), is sure to lead to an anomaly. If, in the sentence *He is rich*, *rich* is the predicate, and *is* the copula, why, in the sentence *He becomes rich*, should we not call *becomes** the copula? The notion of *becoming* has quite as good a right to be considered copulative as the notion of *being*. The difficulty is removed, and the anomaly obviated, when we regard neither *be* nor *become* as a copula, but treat them both as verbs of *incomplete predication* (see § 392). And now ensues another advantage from discarding Becker's use of the term *completion of the predicate*, as applied to the object of a transitive verb. We can apply it, or some equivalent term, in the case of verbs which really do express only an incomplete notion. To avoid confusion, I have adopted the term *complement* instead of *completion*.

In the treatment of compound sentences, the chief modifications that I have introduced, as compared with Mr. Morell's Analysis, are the arrangement of co-ordinate and subordinate sentences as subdivisions of compound sentences (which is, in fact, Becker's mode of classifying them), the recognition of what I have termed *collateral* sentences, and a more thorough investigation of the construction of adverbial and elliptical sentences.

The etymological portion of the book is the result of an independent examination of the vocabulary of the language, as given in Richardson's and Webster's Dictionaries. The appendix has been added, not because its contents fall strictly within the province of grammar, but because it will be useful to the learner, and I did not know to what source to direct him for an equally complete list. I have not given a list of Anglo-Saxon roots, because, as Anglo-Saxon is rarely studied by those for whom this grammar is chiefly

---

* Arnold does so. He terms it a *strengthened copula*, a name which he also applies to *seem*, *be made*, *be called*, &c. Analysis becomes a very vague affair when we are driven to such a pass as this.

intended, it appeared that the utility of such a list would not be adequate to the labour of forming it.

Although the present work contains a great deal that must unavoidably be difficult for a beginner, it will be found that those parts of grammar that do fall within the comprehension of a young learner are expressed in a mode as simple as is consistent with accuracy. The Accidence, the Etymology, and the general principles and rules of Syntax will present no very great obstacles. It is hardly necessary to add, that the present work should be regarded as merely introductory to such treatises as those of Dr. Latham and Mr. Craik.

A brief set of exercises has been appended; in addition to which, Mr. Morell's "Graduated Exercises" (a very cheap and excellent collection) may be used with advantage.

C. P. MASON.

Denmark Hill, April, 1858.

CONTENTS.

ENGLISH GRAMMAR.

PRELIMINARY REMARKS.

1 WHEN we wish to express what is passing in our minds, we talk, or else write down certain marks or signs, which people have agreed shall stand for the sounds which we utter when we talk.

2 That which we speak with our voice, or write down to represent what we speak, is called *speech* or *language*.

3 Grammar is the science which treats about speech or language.

4 All people do not utter the same sounds, or write the same signs to express what they think. There are different languages or tongues made use of by different nations, as the English language, the French language, the Latin language, &c.; and since these differ widely from each other, it is necessary to have a separate grammar for each of them. These separate grammars, however, agree in many respects, and are all parts of the general science of grammar.

5 Speech or language is made up of words. A word is a significant combination of articulate sounds, the several parts of which are not significant. A collection of words arranged so as to convey some complete sense, is called a sentence: as, "The boy learns his lesson;" "The cat has caught a mouse."

6 The words of which a sentence is made up are of different sorts. Thus in the sentence: "The bird flies swiftly," *bird* is the name of an animal; *the* points out which bird is meant; *flies* expresses an action, which it is asserted that the bird performs; *swiftly* denotes the manner in which that action is performed. The different sorts of words which a language contains are called Parts of Speech.

7 Spoken words are made up of different sounds, and written words are made up of different signs, called *letters*, which are used to represent the different sounds of which spoken words are composed.

8 When, in writing a word, letters are used which are not sounded in speaking, those letters are said to be *mute*. Thus in the word *knot*, the *k* is mute; in the word *awe*, the *e* is mute.

9 That part of grammar which treats of the letters of which words are composed, and of the proper mode of writing and spelling words, is called Orthography.

10 That part of grammar which treats of separate words, or of the parts of speech separately, showing the mode in which they are formed and the changes which they undergo, is called Etymology.

11 That part of grammar which treats of the mode in which words are combined so as to form sentences, and sentences combined with one another, is called Syntax.

ORTHOGRAPHY.

12 The elementary sounds of the English language are represented by twenty-six letters, each of which is written in two forms, differing both in shape and in size. The large letters are called Capitals, or Capital Letters.* These letters are the following:—

A, a: B, b: C, c: D, d: E, e: F, f: G, g: H, h: I, i: J, j: K, k: L, l: M, m: N, n: O, o: P, p: Q, q: R, r: S, s: T, t: U, u: V, v: W, w: X, x: Y, y: Z, z.

13 The whole collection of letters is called the Alphabet. Alpha and Beta are the names of the first two letters of the Greek Alphabet.

14 The letters *a*, *e*, *i*, *o*, and *u* are called Vowels. They can be fully sounded by themselves.

15 The remaining letters are called Consonants. They cannot be fully sounded without having a vowel either before or after them.

16 A Diphthong is a single vowel sound, which in writing is expressed by two vowels, such as *æ* (as in Cæsar); *ai* (as in Cain); *au* (as in haul); *oi* (as in oil); *œ* (as in Phœbus); *ou* (as in house); *ea* (as in each); *ee* (as in feed); *ei* (as in neither); *eu* (as in sleuth); *ie* (as in field); *ui* (as in cruise).

17 A vowel sound which is expressed in writing by three vowels, is called a Triphthong; as *uoy* (in buoy); *eau* (in beauty); *iou* (as in anxious).

18 The letters *w* and *y* are sometimes consonants, and sometimes vowels. When they are followed by a vowel sound in the same syllable they are consonants, as in *win*, *twin*, *yon*, *yonder*. When a vowel precedes them

* Capital letters are used at the beginning of proper names, for the nominative case singular of the personal pronoun of the first person, and for any noun adjective or pronoun used for the name of the Divine Being. They may also be used at the beginning of a common noun, when it is mentioned as the principal subject of discourse. Adjectives derived from proper nouns are also written with capitals.

in the same syllable, they are vowels, and combine with the preceding vowel to form a diphthong; as *awe*, *how*, *dray*, *bey*, *buy*. Y is a vowel whenever it is followed by a consonant, (as in Yttria).

19 The letters *l*, *m*, *n*, and *r*, are called Liquids or Semi-vowels. They can be partially sounded by themselves. The other consonants are called Mutes. When sounded after a vowel, they stop the passage of the breath more completely than the liquids do.

20 A syllable is a collection of letters pronounced together, and containing only one vowel sound.

21 A word which consists of a single syllable is called a Monosyllable, such as *man*, *horse*, *hut*.

A word which consists of two syllables is called a Dissyllable; as *folly*, *learning*.

A word that consists of three syllables is called a Trisyllable, as *vanity*, *loveliness*.

A word that consists of more than three syllables is called a Polysyllable, as *singularity*.

22 When a syllable beginning with a vowel is added to a monosyllable, or a word accented on the last syllable and ending in a single consonant preceded by a single vowel, the final consonant is doubled. As *sin*, *sinner; thin*, *thinner; rob*, *robber; sit*, *sitting; begin*, *beginning; expel*, *expelled; confer*, *conferred*. But if, in a word of more than one syllable, the accent does not fall on the last syllable, the final consonant is not doubled; as *offer*, *offered; differ*, *different; visit*, *visiting*. The letter *l*, however, is generally doubled, as *travel*, *traveller; revel*, *reveller; marvel*, *marvellous*. There are also some other words in which the rule is violated, as *worshipper*.

23 When a syllable is added to a word ending in *y*, preceded by a consonant, the *y* is changed into *i*; as *happy*, *happily*, *happier; pity*, *pitiless*. When the final *y* is preceded by a vowel, it is not changed.

24 Mute *e* at the end of a word is generally omitted when a syllable that begins with a vowel is added; as *force*, *forcible; love*, *loving*: but the *e* is retained if it is required to preserve the pronunciation of the consonant, as *change*, *changeable*.

25 Mute *e* preceded by a consonant at the end of a word, is generally retained when a syllable that begins with a consonant is added, if the vowel sound of the last syllable of the word is long, as *pale*, *paleness;* but if the vowel sound of the last syllable is short, the *e* is commonly dropped, as in *judgment*, *lodgment*. It is retained, however, if necessary to preserve the pronunciation of the consonant that precedes it; as in *infringement*.

26 Mute *e* at the end of a word, and preceded by a vowel, is sometimes omitted when a syllable is added, as *true*, *truly; due*, *duly;* sometimes it is retained, as *eye*, *eyeless; true*, *trueness; blue*, *blueness*.

ETYMOLOGY.

[N.B. In conjunction with the section on Etymology it would be well for the learner to study the first few paragraphs of that on Syntax.]

PARTS OF SPEECH.

27 The words of which the English language is composed are distributed into eight parts of speech. These are: 1. Noun. 2. Adjective. 3. Pronoun. 4. Verb. 5. Adverb. 6. Preposition. 7. Conjunction. 8. Interjection.

NOUN.

28 The word *Noun* means *name* (Latin, *nomen*).

A Noun is a word used as the *name* of anything that we speak about.

29 There are two sorts of nouns—Common Nouns and Proper Nouns.

30 A Common Noun is a word that may be used as the name of each thing out of some class of things of the same sort; as *horse, man, stone, city.* A common noun distinguishes the things belonging to some class from everything which does not belong to that class. Thus, the word *horse* distinguishes the animal so called from all other sorts of things, but does not distinguish one horse from another.

31 A Proper Noun is a word used as the name of some particular person, animal, place or thing, as John, London, Bucephalus, Excalibur.

A proper noun serves to distinguish that for which it stands not only from things of a different sort, but also from other things of the same sort. Thus the name Cicero distinguishes the person who bore it, not only from a horse or a town, but from other men who did not bear that name.

Proper nouns are written with a capital letter at the beginning.

32 Proper nouns are sometimes used like common nouns, when they denote classes or collections of persons; as, the Howards, the Cæsars, the Alps.

On the other hand, some common nouns are occasionally used as the names, not of each individual in a class, but of the class *as a whole.* When we say, "Man is mortal," we mean all mankind.

33 A noun which in the singular number stands for a collection or number of things, is called a Collective Noun: as *herd, parliament, council, multitude, mob.*

34 A noun which denotes a quality or attribute, is called an Abstract Noun: as *hardness*, *prudence*, *justice*. An abstract noun always pre-supposes the existence of an adjective from which it is derived.

35 Abstract nouns are sometimes used in the *concrete* sense, that is, standing for that which possesses the quality which they denote. Thus *nobility* frequently means the whole body of persons of noble birth: *youth*, the whole class of young people, and so on.

36 Nouns admit of the three variations of Gender, Number, and Case.

Gender.

37 Living beings are divided into two classes or *sexes*, the male sex and the female sex, the individuals in the one sex corresponding to those in the other. Things without life are not of either sex. Thus all things are arranged in three classes—things of the male sex, things of the female sex, and things of neither sex.

38 In like manner, nouns are divided into three classes (called Genders), which correspond to the three classes of things just mentioned. These are the Masculine Gender, the Feminine Gender, and the Neuter Gender.

The name of anything of the male sex is called a masculine noun, or a noun of the masculine gender.

The name of anything of the female sex is called a feminine noun, or a noun of the feminine gender.

The name of anything of neither sex is called a neuter noun, or a noun of the neuter gender.

Man, king, father, horse, cock, bull, James, Henry, are masculine nouns.

Woman, queen, mother, mare, hen, cow, Mary, Jane, are feminine nouns.

Stone, tree, house, London, are neuter nouns.

39 Gender, then, may be defined to be a distinction in nouns, answering to the division of things into things of the male sex, things of the female sex, and things of neither sex.

40 Things without life are often *personified*, or spoken of as if they were living beings, and therefore either of the male or of the female sex. In this case the nouns which stand for them are treated as being of the masculine or feminine gender.

Thus, the Sun, Time, Summer, Death, &c., are looked upon as male persons, and their names are accordingly masculine.

The Moon, the Earth, Virtue, Night, a ship, countries—such as Europe, England, and many other things—are spoken of as though they were female persons, and their names are accordingly of the feminine gender.

41 **The names of animals sometimes do not indicate their sex, as *sheep, bird, parent.* Such nouns are said to be of common gender.**

42 *Sex* is a distinction between *things*, not between *names*. *Gender* is a distinction between *names*, not between *things*. It is, therefore, wrong to speak of the *masculine sex*, or the *male gender;* to speak of a noun as a *masculine being*, or to talk of *things* being of the masculine or feminine gender. *Things* may be of the male or female *sex*, but only *words* can be of the masculine, feminine, or neuter *gender*.

43 **The distinctions of gender in masculine and feminine nouns, which stand for pairs of males and females, are made in three ways.**

First Mode.—Quite different words are used: as—

Masculine.	Feminine.	Masculine.	Feminine.
Bachelor	maid or spinster	Hart	roe
Boar	sow	Horse	mare
Boy	girl	Husband	wife
Brother	sister	King	queen
Buck	doe	Lord	lady
Bull	cow	Man	woman
Bullock *or* steer	heifer	Monk	nun
		Nephew	niece
Cock	hen	Papa	mamma
Colt	filly	Sir	madam
Dog	bitch	Sire	dame
Drake	duck	Sloven	slut
Earl	countess	Son	daughter
Father	mother	Stag	hind
Gander	goose	Uncle	aunt
Gentleman	lady	Wizard	witch

44 *Second Mode.*—Different terminations are used :—

Masculine.	Feminine.	Masculine.	Feminine.
Abbot	abbess	Executor	executrix
Actor	actress	Founder	foundress
Administrator	administratrix	Giant	giantess
Adulterer	adulteress	God	goddess
Ambassador	ambassadress	Governor	governess
Arbiter	arbitress	Heir	heiress
Author	authoress	Heritor	heretrix
Baron	baroness	Hero	heroine
Beau	belle	Hunter	huntress
Benefactor	benefactress	Host	hostess
Caterer	cateress	Instructor	instructress
Chanter	chantress	Jew	jewess
Count	countess	Lad	lass
Czar	czarina	Landgrave	landgravine
Dauphin	dauphiness	Lion	lioness
Deacon	deaconess	Marquis	marchioness
Director	directrix	Master	mistress
Duke	duchess	Mayor	mayoress
Emperor	empress	Negro	negress
Enchanter	enchantress	Patron	patroness

Masculine.	Feminine.	Masculine.	Feminine.
Peer	peeress	Sorcerer	sorceress
Poet	poetess	Sultan	sultana
Priest	priestess	Testator	testatrix
Prince	princess	Tiger	tigress
Prior	prioress	Traitor	traitress
Prophet	prophetess	Tutor	tutoress
Protector	protectress	Viscount	viscountess
Shepherd	shepherdess	Votary	votaress
Songster	songstress	Widower	widow

45 *Third Mode.*—Masculine and feminine words are prefixed to nouns of common gender.

Masculine.	Feminine.
Cock-sparrow	hen-sparrow
Bull-calf	cow-calf
He-goat	she-goat
Man-servant	maid-servant

The prefix must be either a noun or a pronoun. Such combinations as *male-child* and *female-child*, do not come under this head, because the words *male* and *female* are adjectives, and do not form compounds with the nouns that follow them.

Number.

46 Number is a variation in the form of nouns, by means of which we show whether we are speaking of one of the things for which the noun stands, or of more than one.

There are two numbers, the singular and the plural.

That form of the noun which is used when we speak of one of the things for which the noun stands is called the *singular number*, as *ship, horse.*

That form which is used when we speak of more than one of the things for which the noun stands is called the *plural number*, as *ships, horses.*

47 As it is simpler to think and speak of one thing than to think and speak of several things at once, the singular is the original form of the noun. The plural form is derived from the singular by making some change in it. The process of making this change is called *inflection.*

48 The plural is derived from the singular in the following ways:—

First Mode.—By simply adding the letter *s*, as *book, books; table, tables; mother, mothers.*

49 *Second Mode.*—By adding *es* to the singular. This termination is added after the consonants *s*, *sh*, *ch* (soft), *x*, and *z*; as *gas, gases; lash, lashes; witch, witches; box, boxes; topaz, topazes;* after some words ending in the vowel *o*, as *hero, heroes; potato, potatoes; cargo, cargoes;* and after the letter *y*, when

it is preceded by a consonant. When *es* is added, the *y* is changed into *i*, as *lady*, *ladies*. When the *y* is preceded by a vowel, *s* only is added, and the *y* is not changed into *i*, as *valley*, *valleys*.

50 Many words ending in *o* have *s* only added to form the plural, as *canto*, *cantos*; *quarto*, *quartos*; *grotto*, *grottos*; *motto*, *mottos*; *solo*, *solos*.

51 Many nouns ending in *f* or *fe* have the *f* softened into *v* when the plural is formed. The plural in this case always ends in *ves*. Thus: *loaf*, *loaves*; *leaf*, *leaves*; *knife*, *knives*; *life*, *lives*. But this change is not made in nouns which end in *ff*, *rf*, *ief*, and *oof*, with the exception of *staff*, the plural of which is *staves*, and *thief*, plural *thieves*. Some other nouns also keep the *f*, as *fife*, *fifes*; *strife*, *strifes*.

52 ***Third Mode*.—By adding *en*, as *ox*, *oxen*; *brother*, *brethren*; *child*, *children*.***

The words *swine* (the plural of *sow*), and *kine* (the plural of *cow*), also belong to this class. There has been a change of the vowel sound besides the addition of the *en*.

53 ***Fourth Mode*.—By changing the vowel sound of the word, as *tooth*, *teeth*; *mouse*, *mice*; *foot*, *feet*; *goose*, *geese*.**

54 Many Latin and Greek nouns are used in English without any change of form. The plurals of these words should be made in the same way as in the languages from which they are taken. The following rules must be attended to in forming the plurals of such words:—

1. The termination *a* (in the singular), should be changed into *æ*, as *formula*, plural *formulæ*.

2. The termination *us* should generally be changed into *i*, as *tumulus*, pl. *tumuli*; *radius*, pl. *radii*.

3. The termination *um* or *on* should be changed into *a*, as *animalculum*, pl. *animalcula*; *effluvium*, pl. *effluvia*; *phenomenon*, pl. *phenomena*.

4. The termination *sis* should generally be changed into *ses*; as *analysis* pl. *analyses*; *basis*, pl. *bases*; *axis*, pl. *axes*.

5. The termination *ix* or *ex* should be changed into *ices*; as *radix*, pl. *radices*; *appendix*, pl. *appendices*.

6. The following forms should also be attended to:—

Sing.	Plur.	Sing.	Plur.
Genus	genera	Seraph (Heb.)	seraphim
Hiatus	hiatus	Bandit (Ital.)	banditti
Series	series	Beau (Fr.)	beaux
Species	species	Madam (Mrs.)	mesdames
Superficies	superficies	Mister (Mr.)	messieurs
Cherub (Heb.)	cherubim	Miasma (Gr.)	miasmata

55 The word *die* has two plurals; *dies* (stamps used for coining), and *dice* (small cubes used for gaming).

Penny has two plurals; *pennies* (a number of separate coins), and *pence* (used when we speak of a sum of money reckoned in that coin).

Genius, used in the sense of a *man of great natural ability*, has the plural

* In *brethren* there is a modification of the vowel besides the addition of *en*. *Children* is a double plural, *er* being an ancient plural termination.

geniuses. When used to denote a certain kind of supernatural beings, its plural is *genii.*

The nouns *deer, sheep, fish* (meaning the race of fishes), are the same in the plural as in the singular.

56 Names of materials or natural productions, such as *wheat, sugar, timber,* may be used in the plural number when different varieties of the article are spoken of; as *raw sugars, French wines.*

57 Names of sciences ending in *ics* (as *mechanics*) are plural as regards their form and origin, but are frequently used as if they were of the singular number.

58 It is a mistake to use a plural of the word *folk,* as it is a noun of multitude, and means *several persons.* We should write, *folk say,* not *folks say.*

59 The words *riches* and *alms* are not really plural nouns, but are generally used as if they were in the plural number. *News* is plural in form, but is used as if of the singular number. There is no sufficient reason why *means* should ever be treated as if it were of the singular number, though several good writers use such expressions as *a means.*

60 Abstract nouns, from the nature of the idea which they denote, do not generally admit of the plural number. But when they are used to denote *varieties* or *different instances* of the quality referred to, they may have plurals, as *affinities, negligences.*

61 Some nouns are used as plural in sense though the sign of plurality is not added to them, as "Ten *sail* of the line were seen off the coast;" "Two *thousand* men were slain;" "He shot three *brace* of birds;" "I bought four *pair* of gloves;" "A three *foot* rule."

Case.

62 Things of which we speak by means of nouns stand in various relations to other things, and to actions and attributes. Consequently, when these relations are expressed in language, nouns have various relations to other words in the sentences in which they are employed. In the sentence, "The horse eats the man's hay," *horse* stands for that which does the action described by the verb; *hay* stands for that upon which the action is performed; *man's* is used to indicate to whom the hay belongs. The words *horse* and *hay* have each a certain connexion with the verb *eats,* and *man's* has a certain connexion with the noun *hay.* Some languages have several different terminations which nouns are made to assume, to indicate the various relations in which they stand to other words. These different forms of the noun are called *cases.* The word *case* (Lat. *casus*) means *falling.* The ancient Greek grammarians took a fancy to represent that form of a noun in which it is used when it is the subject of a sentence, by an upright line, and compared the other forms to lines, *falling* or *sloping off* from this upright line at different angles. Hence a collection of the various forms which a noun might assume

was called the *declension* or *sloping down* of the noun. What we call the Nominative Case was called the *upright case*.

63 *Case* may be defined to be "the form in which a noun or pronoun is used, in order to show the relation in which it stands to other words."

The process of forming the different cases of a noun is called *inflection*.

64 In English there are three cases, the Nominative Case, the Possessive Case, and the Objective Case.

In pronouns these three cases are all different; in nouns the nominative and objective cases are alike.

65 The nominative case is that form in which a noun is used when it is the subject of a verb; that is, when it stands for that about which something is said by means of a verb. In the sentence, "Men build houses," the noun *men* stands for that about which something is said by means of the verb *build*. The noun *men*, therefore, is in the nominative case, because it is the subject of the verb *build*. In the sentence, "The boy was struck by his brother," the noun *boy* stands for that about which something is said by means of the verb *was struck*, and therefore the noun *boy* is in the nominative case, because it is the subject of the verb *was struck*. If the verb of the sentence be in the active voice, the subject of the verb stands for the doer of the action described by the verb. If the verb be in the passive voice, the subject of the verb stands for the object of the action described by the verb. In either case the subject stands for that about which something is said by means of the verb.

66 The noun in the nominative case is the answer to the question made by putting *who* or *what* before the verb. Thus in the above sentences: "*Who build houses?* Ans. *Men*." "*Who was struck?* Ans. *The boy*." *

67 The possessive case is that form in which a noun is used in order to show that something belongs to the person or thing for which it stands. Thus, in the sentence, "I saw John's book," the noun *John's* is in the possessive case, to denote that John possesses something (namely, a book). *John's*, then, is the possessive case of the noun *John*.

---

* Such expressions as, "The noun boy is the *nominative case* to the verb," are incorrect. *Case* is equivalent to *form*. Now a *noun* is not a *form*, nor would there be any sense in talking of the *nominative form to a* verb. The case of a noun is not its relation to a verb, but the form which indicates that relation. Of course this fundamental distinction between a noun and the form of a noun is not affected by the accident that in English the nominative and accusative cases of nouns are alike. The incorrectness of the mode of speaking above referred to is rendered evident in an amusing manner by the mistake which beginners in Latin frequently make, of explaining the accusative case which precedes an infinitive mood by ying that the noun in the accusative is the *nominative* to the verb.

68 The noun in the possessive case is said to be governed by the noun which stands for that which is possessed. In the above sentence the noun *John's* is governed by the noun *book*.

69 As what is possessed must be a person or a thing of some kind, a noun in the possessive case can only be governed by a *noun*.

70 The possessive case, in the singular number, and in those plurals which end in any other letter than *s*, is formed by adding the letter *s* with an apostrophe before it (thus, *'s*) to the nominative case; as, *John's, men's, geese's*. In those plurals which end in *s* the possessive case is indicated in writing by placing the apostrophe after the *s*, as, "the *birds'* feathers."

71 Sometimes the possessive case in the singular number of nouns that end in *s* is merely marked by placing an apostrophe after the word; as, *Æneas' son*. But this practice is now nearly obsolete, except in a few common instances; as, "for conscience' sake," "for goodness' sake."

72 In the case of a complex name, the termination of the possessive case is only affixed to the last of the names; as, "Julius Cæsar's death;" "John Thomas Smith's father." It is even usual to carry out the same principle when *one thing* is possessed by several persons; as, "John, William, and Mary's uncle;" that is, the uncle of John, William, and Mary. "John's, William's, and Mary's uncle," might imply three different persons.

73 The apostrophe in the possessive case singular marks that a vowel has been lost. The termination was anciently *es*.* It is therefore an unmeaning process to put the apostrophe after the plural *s* (as, *birds'*), because no vowel has been dropped there.

74 The meaning of the possessive case is sometimes expressed by means of the preposition *of*, with the objective case after it. Thus, for "My father's *house*," we may say, "The house of my father." But the possessive case must not be substituted for the preposition *of*, unless *possession* is implied by it.

75 The Objective Case is that form in which a noun or pronoun is used when it stands for the object of the action spoken of in some verb, or when it comes after a preposition. In the sentence, "The stone struck the boy," the act of striking is spoken of as being directed to a certain object, namely, *boy*. The word *boy*, which stands for the object of the action, is called the

---

* It is almost incredible how many persons have been induced to adopt the silly notion that the *'s* of the possessive case is an abbreviation for *his*, so that *the king's crown* is *the king his crown*. The word *his* is itself the possessive case of *he*; so that, on this principle, his=he+his=he+he+his=he+he+he+his, and so on *ad infinitum*. Moreover, *Mary's bonnet* must be explained to mean, *Mary his bonnet*. The mistake is so stupid, and shows such blank ignorance of the principles of grammatical forms, that one wonders how the notion could ever have originated.

object of the verb, and is in the objective case. In the sentence, "John was riding in a coach," the noun *coach*, which comes after the preposition *in*, is in the objective case.

76 When a noun in the objective case is governed by a verb, the noun in the objective case answers to the question formed by putting *whom* or *what* before the verb and its subject. As in the example given above, "Whom or what did the stone strike?" Ans. "The boy."

77 In nouns the objective case is the same in form as the nominative. The noun which is the subject of the verb, and therefore in the nominative case, is generally put before the verb (in assertions, not in questions): the noun which is the object of the verb is generally put after the verb. These rules, however, are by no means invariable. The former is frequently disregarded in poetry, or when an adverb or adverbial phrase is used before the verb and its subject; as, "On rushed the foe;" "By the wayside sate an old man." The second rule is also sometimes neglected for the sake of emphasis: as in such a sentence as, "The two brothers were equally guilty; John he punished, but William he forgave."

78 Strictly speaking, it ought to be said that *nouns* in English have only two cases or forms; one (such as *man*, *dog*) for which a new name would have to be invented, used indifferently for the subject and for the object of verbs; the other, the possessive case. But, as pronouns have three cases, and in other languages it is very common for the nominative and accusative cases to be alike, it does not seem worth while to alter the commonly received arrangement.

79 The following are examples of the declension of nouns in English:—

		Singular.	Plural.
Nominative Case	..	Man	Men.
Possessive Case	..	Man's	Men's.
Objective Case	..	Man	Men.
Nominative Case	..	Father	Fathers.
Possessive Case	..	Father's	Fathers'.
Objective Case	..	Father	Fathers.

ADJECTIVE.

80 When we think or speak of anything, we frequently have in mind not only the thing itself, but some quality or attribute that it possesses, or some fact or circumstance respecting it. We may think of a *rose*, and at the same time have in our minds the idea that it is *red*, and so speak of it as a *red rose*. We may be speaking about a *child*, and at the same time connect with it the idea that it is a child just spoken of or pointed to, and so speak of it as *this child*. We may speak of some birds, and at the same time indicate that there are *three* of them, and so speak of them as *three birds*. The words that are used in this way with nouns are called Adjectives.*

* Latin *adjectivus*, "capable of being annexed or attached to something," from *adjectus*, "annexed or added to something."

81 *Definition.* An Adjective is a word used with a noun to denote some quality, attribute, or fact, which we connect in thought with that for which the noun stands, without making a distinct *assertion* that the quality or attribute belongs to what we are speaking about.*

82 In the phrase *a white horse*, the word *white* is an adjective. It denotes a certain quality of the horse.

In the sentence, *I saw two men*, the word *two* is an adjective. It points out a fact respecting the men, that they were two in number.

In the sentence, *I love this child*, the word *this* is an adjective. It points out, with regard to the child spoken of, the fact that it answers to a certain designation made either by words or by pointing.

83 When placed beside the noun to which it refers, an adjective is said to be used *attributively;* as "a *red ball;*" "a *bird flying* through the air." When an adjective is placed after some part of the verb *be*, without having the substantive to which it relates expressed with it, it is said to be used *predicatively;* as "the ball is *red*," "the bird was *flying*."

84 As an adjective is not the *name* of anything, nor a word used as the substitute for a name, an adjective can never be used as the subject of a sentence, as the object of a verb, or governed by a preposition.

85 Adjectives may be distributed into the following classes:—Qualitative Adjectives, Quantitative Adjectives, and Demonstrative or Determinative Adjectives.

86 1. *Qualitative Adjectives, i.e.* adjectives which denote some *quality* or *attribute*, as *virtuous, high, white, beautiful, such,*† *same, only.*‡

Participles and verbal adjectives belong to this class.

87 2. *Quantitative Adjectives, i.e.* adjectives which denote the idea of *number* or *quantity* which we connect with that of which we speak. This class includes:—

---

* It is a mistake to call an adjective the *name* of a quality or attribute. Before we can name anything, it must be made a separate object of thought, and the *name* of anything that we can think or speak about is a *noun*. *Whiteness* is the *name* of a certain quality, and is a *noun*. *White* denotes the quality, but does not name it.

Beware of the absurdity of saying that "an adjective denotes the quality of a noun." A *noun* is a *name*. When we speak of a *red rose*, the adjective *red* does not denote a quality of the *name* rose, but of the *thing* for which the name stands. The blunder is very obvious, but is nevertheless committed in most English Grammars.

† Some Grammars contain a very silly rule (invented by L. Murray), that *such* cannot be used when there is another adjective joined attributively with the noun. Such phrases as *such wretched prejudices, such despicable characters*, are perfectly legitimate.

When *such* is used with a noun which is preceded by the indefinite article, the article comes between the adjective and the noun; as *such an event, such a sad story.*

‡ When *only* is not an adjective used attributively, it is an adverb; as "There are only four persons present." "He is only pretending." When it is not an adverb, *only* is an adjective used attributively; as "He only was saved," "My only son." *Only* is never by any chance used *instead of a noun*. It is therefore absurd to call it a *pronoun*.

a. **The Cardinal Numeral Adjectives, *one, two, three,* &c. (The words *hundred, thousand, million,* like *pair* and *dozen,* are nouns. They may be used with the indefinite article before them.)**

b. **The words *all,** *some, half, many, few, little, less, least, enough, much, more, most, both, several, whole, no* (=*not any*), *none.***

Examples. 'All men are mortal.' 'He rode all day long.' 'He sleeps all night.' 'He travelled all the next day.' 'Some men prefer this.' 'Give me some wine.' 'We had a half holiday.' 'Wait half an hour.' 'Few persons will believe that.' 'He has but little wealth, and less wisdom.' 'He has not given me the least trouble.' 'I have had enough wine.' 'Give him money enough.' 'I have much pleasure in doing this.' 'He has more sense than his neighbour.' 'Most persons admire valour.' 'He had both eyes put out.' 'They are both in fault.' 'He has eaten a whole apple.' 'Make no noise.' 'They have no more hope,' *i. e.* not any more hope. 'Give none offence.' 'Give none occasion to the adversary.'

88 **Some of these words are also used as substantives:—**

Few. 'I have a *few*† shillings.' [The phrase *a many* is equally legitimate, but is obsolete.]

Little, less, least, as 'Little was said.' 'Less will not suffice.' 'Least said, soonest mended.' 'Give me a little of that.'

Enough. 'Enough is as good as a feast.'

Much, more, most. 'Much has been said, but more remains to be told.'

Whole. 'He spent the whole of the day in playing.'

None. None are altogether without hope.'

89 *Little, less,* and *least,* when they are used before a noun and are themselves preceded by an article, are qualitative adjectives; as 'a little boy.' The comparative of *little* in this sense, when it is used attributively, is often written *lesser;* as 'the *lesser* evil of the two.'

Least, in the qualitative sense, is nearly obsolete, except in one or two phrases; as 'Not in the *least* degree.'

90 *Many* may be used with a noun in the singular,‡ provided the indefinite article be placed before the noun; as 'Many a man has lost his life by these means.'

91 *All, no, none, some, enough,* may denote either *number* or *quantity*; as 'all men,' 'all the way,' 'some pens,' 'some beer,' 'no money,' 'no friends,' &c. When *all* denotes quantity, the definite article is commonly placed between it and the noun.

92 The use of *none* before a noun is now old-fashioned. It differs from *no* as *mine* differs from *my:* i. e. *no* is used when the noun which it relates

---

* The words *all, half, little, less, least, much, more, most, enough,* are also used as adverbs; as "*all round* the world;" "*half afraid;*" "I am but *little encouraged* by that;" "he is *less careful* than his brother;" "he is the least ambitious man that I know;" "he is *much more studious* than he used to be;" "he is most anxious to succeed;" "he is *tall enough.*"

† *Few* used as an adjective involves a negation of there being *many.* "He has few friends." *A few,* when *few* is used substantively, involves a negation that there were *none;* it implies *some, but not many.*

‡ So *multus* and *plurimus* in Latin. "Plurimus in Junonis honorem, aptum dicet equis Argos."—*Horace.*

to is expressed, and *none* when the noun is not expressed; as 'I have *no* horse, and my neighbour has *none*.'

93 The quantitative numeral *one* is often used substantively, meaning a single individual of some kind already mentioned. When thus used, it may even have a plural. 'Give me another pen, this is a bad *one*;' or, 'these are bad *ones*.'

94 *Both* has the effect of directing the attention to each of two things spoken of, while at the same time the two are spoken of together. The assertion therefore is made, grammatically speaking, of the two things together, while, in sense, it is made of each separately.

95 3. *Demonstrative* or *Definitive Adjectives.*—To this class belong:—

a. The Definite Article *the*, and the Indefinite Article *an* or *a*.

b. The so-called Adjective Pronouns, or Pronominal Adjectives, comprising the following classes:—

1. The Demonstrative Pronouns, *this, these, that, those.*
2. The Relative and Interrogative Pronoun *which.*
3. The Relative and Interrogative Pronoun *what.*
4. The Distributive Pronouns, *each, every,* either, neither.*
5. The Indefinite Pronouns, *any, other, another.*†
6. The Possessive Pronouns, *mine, thine, his, hers, its, ours, yours, theirs,*‡ *own.*

c. The Ordinal Numerals, first, second, third, &c.

96 A word is known to be an *adjective* when it can be put before a noun so as to denote some attribute or fact respecting that for which the noun stands. *What* and *which* are adjectives, for we can say, *what man? which child?* *Who* is not an adjective, for we cannot say *who man?* or *whom woman?*

97 The participle ending in *ing* must be carefully distinguished from the *gerund*, or verbal substantive in *ing*. In the sentence, "I like *reading*," the word *reading* is not a participle (*i. e.* an adjective), for it does not qualify any noun expressed or understood. Whenever one of these verbals in *ing* is used as the subject or object of a verb, or after a preposition, it is a *noun*.*§

---

* *Every* is frequently classed among the pronouns in English Grammars, although under no circumstances is it ever used instead of a noun. *Any* is sometimes an adverb.

† When *other* is used substantively it may have a plural: "*Others* may believe that, but I do not."

‡ The words *my, thy, her, our, your, their,* are not adjective pronouns, but the possessive cases of personal pronouns. Writers of English Grammars are not agreed as to which of these two classes of words should be called the adjective pronouns, and which the possessive cases. The best authorities (see "Latham's Handbook," &c.), consider *my* and *our*, as equivalent to the Latin genitives, *mei* and *nostrum*, and *mine* and *ours* as corresponding to *meus* and *noster*. The forms *his* and *its* are analogous. The adjective forms, *mine, ours,* &c., are used only when the noun to which they belong is not expressed. "Whose is that hat? It is *mine*. *Yours* is in the hall." The fact that we cannot say *hers book* or *ours house*, is sufficient to show that these forms are not simple possessive cases.

§ According to some grammarians the gerund or verbal substantive in *ing*, has arisen from an old Anglo-Saxon formation of verbal nouns ending in *ung*.

98 Verbal adjectives differ from ordinary adjectives in having the idea o *action* connected with them, and in being capable of governing a noun in the objective case. The participles in *-ing* are placed after the nouns which they qualify; as, "A horse drawing a cart." When used as simple qualitative adjectives, without having any noun as their object, they are placed, like other adjectives, before the nouns that they qualify; as, "A loving child," "a convincing argument."

99 In speaking we do not always express all that we have in our thoughts, when what is expressed shows clearly enough what is to be understood as *meant*, though not expressed. One result of this is, that adjectives are very often used without having the nouns to which they relate expressed. Thus, "The *good* are happy;" *i. e.* good people. "Blessed are the *meek*;" *i. e.* meek persons. "*This* is good, but *that* is better;" *i. e.* this thing is good, but that thing is better.

"He has this character *in common* with his neighbours." "*In general* he avoids such mistakes;" "He recommended this *in particular;*" "*At least;*" "*At random;*" "*In future.*"

This is especially the case with the quantitative and demonstrative adjectives. Thus, "*Many* (persons) are called, but *few* (persons) are chosen;" "*All* (men, or persons) heard, and *some* obeyed;" "I know *that;*" "I heard *what* * you said." (See § 88.)

100 In such cases as these the adjective is said to be used *substantively*, that is, as though it were itself a substantive; the real explanation being, that the substantive to which the adjective belongs is only *not expressed*.

101 In one or two instances, however, some adjectives are used so completely as substantives, that they have the ordinary inflections of nouns. This is the case with the words, *one*, *other* (see §§ 93, 95). Even *either* and *neither* have a possessive case formed from them by some writers. But the authority for this is questionable.

102 There are several cases in which an adjective becomes, to all intents and purposes, a noun. Thus the words *subject* and *individual* are properly adjectives. They are also nouns; as when we say, "A subject's duties;" "The subjects of the Queen;" "An individual's tastes," or "Many individuals."

---

which had precisely the same force as the later formation in *ing*. The grossness of the mistake, which consists in confounding the participle with the gerund in English, is seen most palpably when beginners, who have been led astray by their English Grammars, render such phrases as "He talks about fighting," by the Latin "Loquitur de pugnante."

* When *what* and *which*, *that* and *this*, are used substantively, they are only of the neuter gender. *These* and *those* may be of any gender.

When qualitative adjectives are used in this way they generally refer to some noun in the plural which is understood, and are always preceded by the definite article: as, "The generous are loved." They may be used also without reference to a plural noun, to express an abstract idea, as, *the Sublime*, *the Beautiful*.

103 Adjectives, in English, are not declinable words. With the exception of the words *this* and *that*, which have plural forms, *these* and *those*, no adjective in English indicates gender, number, or case, by means of inflection.

104 Adjectives are generally said to *agree* in gender, number, and case, with the nouns which they qualify. But the rule is nugatory, because (with the exception mentioned above), adjectives do not admit of variations of form by which number, case, and gender can be indicated. It is better to say simply that adjectives qualify the nouns with which they are used. In other languages the case is different.

Comparison of Adjectives.

105 Adjectives admit of three varieties of form, called Degrees of Comparison. These are the Positive Degree, the Comparative Degree, and the Superlative Degree.

106 The Positive Degree of an adjective is the adjective in its simple form, used to point out some quality or attribute of that which we speak about, as "A *black* cat," "A *fine* day."

107 When we wish to indicate that one thing,* or set of things, possesses the same quality or attribute as another, but that it possesses the said quality or attribute in a greater degree than the other thing or set of things, a change is made in the form of the simple adjective to mark this. The syllable *er* (or *r* only when the adjective ends in mute *e*), is added; as "My knife is *sharper* than yours;" "John's book is pretty, but mine is *prettier*;" "Your parents are *richer* than mine;" "This soldier is *taller* than those;" "These books are *larger* than that one." In these examples, it will be seen that one thing may be compared either with one thing or with a set of things, and that one set of things may be compared either with another set of things or with a single thing.

108 The Comparative Degree of an adjective, then, is that form of it by means of which we show that one thing, or set of things, possesses a certain quality or attribute in a greater degree than another thing, or set of things.

109 It must not be imagined that the comparative degree expresses the existence of more of a certain quality in an object than the positive degree does. If we say, "William is a clever boy," and "John is

* The word *thing* means generally whatever we can *think* about, *i. e.* make a distinct object of thought, including *persons*, as well as what we commonly denominate *things*.

clеverer than Thomas," we are not to infer that *cleverer* in the second case implies the existence of more cleverness in John than the adjective *clever* implies in the case of William. The fact may be that William is cleverer than John. The positive degree is used in the one case simply because William is not compared with any one else; and the comparative degree is used in the second case because John is compared with Thomas.

110 Even the use of an adjective in the positive degree often implies some standard of comparison; as when we use such words as *high*, *great*, &c. But this results only from the meaning of the words themselves, and does not affect the grammatical use of the words.

111 The Superlative Degree of an adjective is that form of it which shows that a certain thing, or set of things, possesses some quality or attribute *in a greater degree than any other of the class to which it belongs*. It is formed by adding *st* or *est* to the simple adjective, or the adjective in the positive degree; as, *greatest*, *tallest*, *largest*. Thus, of several boys in a group, we may say, "John is *the tallest*." Of the countries of Europe we may say, "England is *the wealthiest*."

112 If we say, "John is *taller* than all the other boys in the class," we express the same relation as to height between John and the rest as if we say, "John is *the tallest* boy in the class." But in the former case John is considered *apart from* the other boys of the class, so that the *two* objects that we have in mind are *John* and *the other boys in the class*. When the superlative degree is used John is considered as *one of the group* of boys between whom the comparison is made.

113 When two things only are compared, it is usual and proper to employ the comparative degree, even when the things form one group, as such a group only admits of the comparison of *one* thing with *one* other. As, "This line is *the longer* of the two." Nevertheless, from what has been said in the last paragraph, it appears that it would not be very inaccurate to say "*the longest* of the two." Such expressions are frequently employed by good writers.

114 Many adjectives, from the nature of the ideas which they express, cannot have comparative and superlative degrees; as, *right*, *left*, *wrong*, *square*, *triangular*, together with most of the quantitative adjectives, and all the demonstrative adjectives. Sometimes, however, adjectives are used in a sense which falls short of their strict meaning, and then they admit of degrees of comparison which would not otherwise be tolerable. For example, *extreme*, *perfect*, *chief*. As when we say, "This specimen is *more perfect* than that;" "He died in the *extremest* misery;" "The *chiefest* among ten thousand."

115 In the case of some adjectives, the degrees of comparison are marked by what are commonly termed *irregular* forms. These are the following:—

Positive.	Comparative.	Superlative.
Good	better	best
Little	less	least
Much	more	most
Many	more	most
Bad	worse	worst
Late	later	latest *or* last
Nigh	nigher	nighest *or* next *
Fore	former	foremost *or* first
Old †	older *or* elder	oldest *or* eldest
Far	farther ‡	farthest ‡
[Forth]	further	furthest

116 Adjectives of more than two syllables, and most adjectives of two syllables, do not allow of the formation of comparative and superlative degrees. But the same ideas as are expressed by these degrees of comparison are denoted by prefixing the adverbs *more* and *most* to the simple adjective, or adjective in the positive degree. Thus we say, *Virtuous, more virtuous, most virtuous; Learned, more learned, most learned.* The dissyllabic adjectives which do admit of degrees of comparison are those ending in *-y* (as *merry, merrier, merriest; holy, holier, holiest*); in *-er* (as *tender, tenderer, tenderest*); and those in *-ble* (as *able, abler, ablest*).

117 It is a mistake to call such expressions as *more virtuous, most splendid,* the comparative and superlative degrees of the simple adjectives. They do not answer to the *definition* of comparative and superlative degrees; and, moreover, *less virtuous* and *least virtuous* would have quite as good a right to be called degrees of comparison of *virtuous,* as *more virtuous* and *most virtuous.*

118 It is equally incorrect to speak of phrases like *very great, very small,* as superlative degrees or their equivalents. They do not take their origin from *the same kind of comparison* as that which gives rise to the superlative degree of an adjective. They are phrases of the same class as *rather large, somewhat tedious, excessively small,* &c. They spring from the necessity for a tacit reference to some understood standard of comparison even in the use of many adjectives in the positive degree.

119 There are a few superlatives ending in *-most: hindmost, topmost, inmost, uttermost.* Most of these are derived, not from adjectives in the positive degree, but from adverbs.‖

---

* *Next* has nothing to do with the adjective *near.*

† There is an antiquated positive form, *eld.*

‡ These forms are now established in the language, but they are formed upon a false analogy. From the adverb *forth* are derived *further* and *furthest.* But there being no adjective in the positive degree except *far, further* and *furthest* were corrupted into *farther* and *farthest,* and set down as derivatives from *far.*

‖ Dr. Latham considers these to be forms in which the superlative degree is marked twice over, the letter *m* being derived from *ema,* the termination of some superlatives in Anglo-Saxon, and *ost* being a corruption of *est.*

ARTICLE.

120 One species of adjective has been classed by grammarians as a separate part of speech, namely, the Article.*

An Article is a demonstrative adjective, that is, it is a word which, when placed before a common noun, points out (with more or less distinctness), which of the things, for which the noun is a name, is spoken of.

121 There are two Articles, the Indefinite Article *an* or *a*, and the Definite Article *the*.

122 The indefinite article *an* is the same in origin as the numeral *one* (in Scotch *ane*). When placed before a noun it indicates that we are speaking of *some one* of the things for each of which the noun is a name, but does not indicate which particular individual is meant, as "*A* dog bit me;" "I saw *an* old man."

Of course the indefinite article can only be used before nouns in the singular number.

123 The form *an* is used before words beginning with a vowel sound or mute *h*, as *an apple*, *an heir*.

An drops the final *n* and becomes *a* before words beginning with a consonant, the aspirate *h*, or the letter *u* when the sound of *y* is put before the *u* in pronunciation, as *A man*, *a horse*, *a yellow ball*, *a useful book*.

124 The indefinite article is sometimes equivalent to *any* or *every*, as "Three times *a* week, i. e. *every* week;" "Half-a-crown *a* dozen, i. e. *any* or *every* dozen;" "A hundred pounds *a* year, i. e. *every* year."

125 The definite article *the* is used before a noun to define or mark out the particular individual or individuals that we are speaking of out of the class named by the noun.

125 *b*. The definite article *the* is of the same origin as the demonstrative adjectives *this* and *that*. It always points to some description, expressed or understood, by means of which the individual or individuals may be identified. When we say, "*The* Queen of England," *the* points to the words *of England*, by means of which we understand what queen is meant. When we say, "*The* brown horse kicked me," *the* points to the adjective *brown*, by means of which we identify the horse that is meant. When we say, "*The* book which I lent you," *the* points to the description, *which I lent you*. When we say, "I heard *the* end of his speech, but not *the* beginning," the application of the preceding description of the function of the article is not so obvious. But neither is the application of the ordinary definition very clear. *The end*, according to the definition, ought to signify *some particular* end. But it is evident

---

* Latin, *articulus*, "a joint;" a word used rather vaguely by the Latin grammarians

that the function of the article is not to particularize some one end in contrast with other ends. We must consider that the import of the sentence given above is, "I heard that part of his speech which was the closing part, but not that part which was the commencing part." The article points to two particular *parts* of the speech which are identified by the descriptive epithet *involved* in the words *end* and *beginning*. When we have the definite article and a noun, the noun denotes the *species*, the article points to the marks which particularize the individual meant. If we say, "The brown horse," the noun *horse* marks the *species*, the adjective *brown* particularizes the *individual* by specifying its *distinguishing mark*. When we speak of *the end* of anything, in contrast with *the beginning* of it, the words *end* and *beginning* have a double function, as they comprise both the general name and the distinguishing mark in one word: *end* being the same as *closing part; beginning*, the same as *commencing part*. The function of the definite article is still to point to the distinguishing mark by which the *individual* is separated from the rest of the *species*.

126 When a noun preceded by an article is qualified by an adjective, the adjective is generally placed between the article and the noun. But in the case of the adjective *such*, or an adjective qualified by the adverb *so*, the indefinite article comes after the adjective, as "Such an event;" "So great a misfortune." The same is the case with the definite article and the adjective *all*, as "All the day."

127 An article should only be used once before a complex description of one and the same object, as "He made a better soldier than poet." If we were to say, "He made a better soldier than *a* poet," the latter clause would mean, "than a poet would make." "He upbraided the tyrant and destroyer of his country." If we were to say "And *the* destroyer," the words *tyrant* and *destroyer* would denote two different persons.

PRONOUN.

128 *Preliminary Observations.* It would not be very easy for a learner to get a distinct idea of the part of speech called a Pronoun, by comparing what is said on the subject in different English grammars; and the difficulty would be still further increased if English grammars were compared with the best Latin and Greek grammars. The writers of many of the grammars in common use seem to have arranged under this head every kind of word that they did not know what to do with. It would be thought absurd now-a-days to give the name *Pronoun* to such words as *omnis*, *totus*, *multus*, *solus*, *talis*, *pauci*, *plus*, or the numerals. Yet the corresponding English words, and others like them, are frequently set down as pronouns, even in grammars of some repute. A pronoun is universally defined to be "a word used instead of a noun." Now, no word can be used instead of a noun, unless it is a substantive.*

* A substantive is a word which stands for some distinct object of thought, and may therefore be the subject of a proposition.

An adjective used substantively, that is, with the substantive to which it belongs *understood*, does not really become a substantive, and therefore cannot replace one; that is, it cannot be a *pronoun*. To apply the definition, in cases where the nouns are expressed, leads to a simple absurdity. In the sentence, "I esteem *this* man," we cannot say that *this* is a word used instead of a noun, for no noun could possibly be inserted in its place. Even such words as *every* are often called pronouns, though they are never used without a noun, or in place of a noun.

129 Strictly speaking, no word should be called a Pronoun unless it is a substantive. It is only in deference to the common (and it is to be feared inveterate) practice of grammars, in all languages, that the self-contradictory term Adjective-Pronoun is here introduced. It must be allowed, however, that in the case of two or three of the demonstrative adjectives, the noun understood is commonly so entirely lost sight of,* that it is convenient to call them pronouns, though, strictly speaking, they have no right to the appellation.

130 A Pronoun † is a word used instead of a noun, as when we say, "John has come in: *he* is very tired," instead of "John has come in: John is very tired."

Pronouns are divided into two classes, Substantive Pronouns and Adjective Pronouns.

131 The Substantive Pronouns are the following:—

A. The Personal Pronouns, *I, thou, he, she, it, we you*, or *ye, they*.

B. The Relative and Interrogative Pronouns, *who* ‡ and *what*.

C. The Relative Pronoun *that*.

D. The Interrogative Pronoun *whether*.

E. The Indefinite Pronoun *one*.

F. The Reflective Pronoun *self*.

132 The Adjective Pronouns are the following:—

G. The Demonstrative Pronouns *this* (plural *these*), *that* (plural *those*).

H. The Relative and Interrogative Pronoun *which*.

I. The Relative and Interrogative Pronoun *what*.

J. The Distributive and Indefinite Pronouns, *each, either, neither, any, other* (plural *others*).

K. The Possessive Pronouns *mine, thine, his, hers, its, ours, yours, theirs*.

These words should be called Pronouns only when used substantively. When the nouns to which they relate are expressed, they should be called *Demonstrative Adjectives*.

---

* See also § 101, 103.

† Latin *pronomen*: *pro* for, *nomen* noun.

‡ The real identity between the Relative and the Interrogative pronoun, and the nature of the apparent difference between them will be found treated of in the introductory part of the Syntax (§ 356).

SUBSTANTIVE PRONOUNS.

A.—Personal Pronouns.

133 Personal Pronouns are of three kinds. 1. Those of the First Person. 2. Those of the Second Person. 3. Those of the Third Person.

134 1. The Pronoun which is used when a person speaks of himself singly, or of himself in conjunction with one or more others, without mentioning any names, is called the Personal Pronoun of the First Person. It is declinable, and has the following forms:—

		Singular.	Plural.
Nominative Case	..	I	We
Possessive Case	..	My	Our
Objective Case	..	Me	Us.

The Nomimative Case *I* is always written with a Capital letter.

135 The Pronoun which is used when a person speaks to another person singly, or to two or more persons together, is called the Personal Pronoun of the Second Person. It is declinable, and has the following forms:—

		Singular.	Plural.
Nominative Case	..	Thou	You or Ye
Possessive Case	..	Thy	Your
Objective Case	..	Thee	You or Ye.*

The plural forms of this pronoun (except *ye*) are commonly used when speaking to a single person.

136 The plural forms of the pronouns of the first and second persons are not etymologically derived from the singular forms. In fact the notion involved (for example) in *we* is not related to that expressed by *I* in the same way that the idea expressed by *men* is related to that expressed by *man*. *We* does not imply a simple repetition of *I*. The notion involved in the word *I* does not admit of plurality.

137 The Pronouns of the first and second persons do not mark distinctions of gender, because when a person speaks of himself or to another person, the sex, being evident, does not need to be marked in language by differences of gender, and the plural forms must of necessity be ambiguous, as *we* and *you* may include persons of different sexes.

---

* Several grammarians maintain that *ye* is exclusively *nominative*; but the best writers in the language use *ye* as an objective case. As, "Comfort *ye*, comfort *ye*, my people." "His wrath, which one day will destroy *ye* both." (*Milton*). "The more shame for *ye*, holy man I thought *ye*." (*Shakspere*).

138 The pronoun which is used when a person speaks of one or more other persons or things, without describing them by a noun, is called the Personal Pronoun of the Third Person. It admits of the distinctions of number, case, and gender. It has the following forms:—

		Singular.	
	Masculine.	Feminine.	Neuter.
Nominative Case ..	He	She	It
Possessive Case ..	His	Her	Its
Objective Case ..	Him	Her	It.

	Plural.	
Nominative Case ..	They	For all genders.
Possessive Case ..	Their	
Objective Case ..	Them	

139 The plural forms must be ambiguous as to gender, because they may be used when speaking of persons of different sexes, or of persons and things together.

140 The possessive case *its* is of comparatively modern origin. It is not found in the English Bible. *His* was formerly used for the neuter as well as for the masculine. As, "If the salt have lost *his* savour," &c. *Its* is found in Shakspere, but even there *his* is much more common as the possessive case of *it*.

141 The possessive cases of the above pronouns are frequently set down as possessive pronouns, that is, as *pronominal adjectives*. This is a mistake. When we say *My book*, *my* is not an adjective qualifying the noun *book*, but a possessive case governed by the noun book, just as the word *John's* is in *John's book*. It follows from this that it is perfectly correct to say, "Pity my sorrows, who am bereaved of my children," "I bewail thy fate, who art so poor." Nevertheless such expressions as the above are unusual.

142 Originally, *mine* was the possessive case of *I*; *thine* of *thou*. In old-fashioned English the *mine* and *thine* are found before words beginning with a vowel; but this distinction is now abandoned. (See § 95, note.)

143 The possessive cases of the personal pronouns differ from the possessive cases of nouns in this respect, that they cannot be used without a noun. We can say, "This knife is John's," but we cannot say, "This knife is my."

B.—The Relative and Interrogative Pronoun WHO.

144 The Relative Pronoun is a word used instead of a noun, and referring to some noun or pronoun which has been already used to mark the person or thing spoken about, and which is called the *antecedent* of the Relative. Thus, in the sentence, "He is reading about Harold who was slain at Hastings," *who* refers to the noun *Harold*, and *Harold* is called the antecedent to the relative. In "I have found the sheep which I had lost," *which* refers to the noun *sheep*, and *sheep* is called

the antecedent to the pronoun *which*. In "He who is contented is rich," *who* refers to the pronoun *he*, and *he* is called the antecedent to *who*. When a common noun in the singular number is the antecedent to a relative, it is always accompanied by some demonstrative adjective; as "He is *the man* whom I was speaking about;" "I found *a bird* which had been shot." In such cases there is always a reciprocal relation. The relative points us to the demonstrative word which accompanies the antecedent, while the demonstrative word in its turn points us to the relative, by means of which its own signification is made clear.

145 The relative pronoun, however, differs from the definite article and the demonstrative adjectives *this* and *that* by having at the same time a *grammatically connective* force. *Who* is equivalent to *and he*, or *and she*, &c.

146 The pronoun *who* is used only when *persons* are spoken of. It does not mark the distinctions of *number* and *gender*, but it has the distinctions of case. It is thus declined:—

Nominative Case	..	Who
Possessive Case	..	Whose
Objective Case	..	Whom.

147 When a thing, or an animal, is referred to by means of a relative, the pronoun *which* is used. It is wrong, however, to call *which* the neuter of *who;* for *which* is an adjective pronoun,* and not necessarily neuter. In old-fashioned English it is found instead of *who;* as, "Our Father *which* art in Heaven." At present, however, it is never used substantively as a relative, except with reference to *things*. The proper neuter of *who* is *what*, which is still preserved when this pronoun is used interrogatively.

148 In place of *of which* (implying possession) many good writers use *whose*. Thus:—"The question *whose* solution I require." (*Dryden.*) "I could a tale unfold, *whose* lightest word," &c. (*Shakspere.*) There is the more justification for this, as *hwaes* in Anglo-Saxon was neuter as well as masculine. But it is a mistake to call *whose* the possessive case of *which*. The pronoun *which*, being an adjective, is not declined.

149 The pronoun *who* is also used interrogatively; as, "*Who* did this?" "*Whose* book is that?" As an interrogative pronoun *who* has a neuter *what*. The neuter *what* is not declined.

C.—The Relative Pronoun THAT.

150 The relative pronoun *that* is a substantive. It may be used

---

* *Which* (in Scotch, *whilk* or *quhilk*) is of the same origin as the German *welcher*. *Who* and *what* are connected with *wer* and *was*.

either of persons or of things. It is never placed *after* prepositions, and is governed by a preposition only when the preposition is placed at the end of the clause. It has no variations in form to mark number, gender, or case. *Examples.* "The horse *that* I rode, fell." "He to-day *that* sheds his blood with me, shall be my brother." "This is the man *that* I spoke of."

151 *That* cannot be used in all cases where *who* can be used. It can be used only when the relative clause is required to give to the antecedent its full signification. We cannot use *that* when the antecedent is a proper name, or when the antecedent noun has with it a demonstrative adjective which sufficiently defines the thing or person spoken of. We cannot say, "Thomas *that* died yesterday, was my brother;" or "I have heard from my father, *that* is in America." The words *Thomas* and *my father* explain perfectly by themselves who is meant. (See § 166.)

152 The relative pronoun is frequently *understood*, that is implied, but not expressed. As, "He has not returned the book I lent him," for "the book which I lent him." "That is the person I spoke of," for "the person whom (or that) I spoke of." But the relative can be omitted only when, if expressed, it would be in the objective case.

D.—The Interrogative Pronoun WHETHER.

153 The pronoun *whether* is used with reference to two persons or things. It was formerly an adjective; as, "Whilst thus the case in doubtful balance hung, unsure to *whether* side it would incline." (*Spenser.*) This pronoun is now nearly obsolete. When used at all it is a substantive; as, "*Whether* of them twain did the will of his father?"

E.—The Indefinite Pronoun ONE.

154 This pronoun is not the same as the numeral adjective *one*. It is a substantive, and is the same word as the French *on*, which is derived from the Latin *homon*.*

The pronoun *one*, from its meaning and derivation, can be used only in the singular number. It has a possessive case, *one's*. *Examples.* "One cannot be too careful." "One's reputation is at stake." "You might as well tell one what is the matter."

F.—The Reflective Pronoun SELF.

155 *Self* † (plural *selves*) is used with either the possessive or the objective case of the personal pronouns. It is preceded by

* Compare the German *man* and the noun *mann*.

† *Self* was originally an adjective, meaning *same* (German *selber*). It still preserves that force in the compound *self-same*.

the possessive case of the personal pronouns of the first and second persons, and by the objective case of the pronouns of the third person, *myself, thyself, ourselves, yourself, yourselves, himself, herself, itself, themselves.*

156 The pronoun *self* may also be used with the possessive case of a noun, especially along with the adjective *own;* as, "A man's own self." "Men's own selves."

157 The pronoun *one* is generally treated as being on a par with the pronouns of the third person; so that we write *oneself,* not *one's self.*

158 Although *self* is a substantive, *myself, ourselves, thyself, yourself, yourselves,* are never considered to be of the third person, but of the first and second respectively, as, "Myself am hell." These compounds, however, when used as the subjects of sentences, are generally preceded by the personal pronouns, as, "I myself saw him;" or, "I saw him myself." Even *himself* is used in apposition to *he.* "*He himself* told me;" or, "He told me *himself.*"

ADJECTIVE PRONOUNS.

G.—The Demonstrative Adjectives THIS and THAT.

159 *This* has a plural, viz. *these.* *That* has a plural, viz. *those.* *This* refers to what is near the speaker (*near me*) in position; *that* refers to what is at a distance from the speaker. As "*This* apple is ripe, *that* is not." In this sense *this* and *that* are called *real* demonstratives, or words that point to *things* (Latin *res*).

160 *This* and *that* are also used to point, not to things themselves, but to some description of what we are speaking about, as, "The general was in command of a large force. *This* force consisted of infantry and artillery." "They remained one day at Rome. *That* day passed without any remarkable event." When thus used, *this* and *that* are called *logical* demonstratives. When two things which have been already mentioned are referred to, *this* refers to what has been mentioned last, *that* refers to what was mentioned before it; as, "Virtue and vice offer themselves for your choice: *this* leads to misery, *that,* to happiness." *This* is also used to refer to something which is going to be mentioned, as, "*This* is my hope and prayer, *that* my children may grow up in the fear of the Lord."

161 *This* and *that* (in the singular) are not used substantively to stand for persons, except as subjects of the verb *be* when the latter is followed by a noun as the predicate; as, "This is my brother;" "that is John." We cannot say, "This did the deed," meaning "this man;" or, "That shall be punished," meaning "that person." This restriction does not

apply to the plural: "*These* are not drunken, as ye suppose;" "Upon *those* did Solomon levy a tribute." But this use of the plural is now almost obsolete.

H.—The Relative and Interrogative Pronoun WHICH.

162 *Which* is, properly speaking, an adjective.

As an adjective it is used both relatively and interrogatively; as, "The doctrine of the Nicolaitans, *which* thing I hate;" "Wait till to-morrow, on *which* day I shall be with you;"* "He employed his money unsparingly, by *which* means he succeeded;"* "*Which* dress are you going to wear?"

Which, when used interrogatively, asks for *one out of a definite number*.

Respecting *which*, used substantively as a relative, see § 147.

I.—The Relative and Interrogative Pronoun WHAT.

163 *What* is properly the neuter of *who*. When used interrogatively it is sometimes a substantive, and sometimes an adjective; as, "*What* did you say?" "*What* events happened in that year?"†

164 When used as a relative also *what* is both a substantive and an adjective; but it has a peculiar force. It never has an antecedent expressed, so that it seems to be equivalent to an antecedent and a relative combined in one word; as, "*What* I said was this," that is, "That which I said," &c.; "*What* time I am afraid, I will trust in thee," that is, "At that time at which I am afraid," &c.

165 It is a mistake, however, to parse the word *what* as though it were made up of *that which*. In such a sentence as, "I know *what* is correct," it is wrong to say that *what* is in any sense governed by the verb *know*. *What* is the subject of the verb *is*, and is in the nominative case. The object of the verb *know* is the whole clause, *what is correct*.

166 The pronoun *that* used to be employed in the same sense as *what*: "I am *that* I am;" "We speak *that* we do know, and testify *that* we have seen."

167 The relative pronouns *who*, *which*, and *what* are compounded with *ever* and *soever*. *Whosoever* is declined—

Nominative Case	..	Whosoever, *or* whoever.
Possessive Case	..	Whosesoever.
Objective Case	..	Whomsoever.

Whosever and *whomever* are not used.

---

* In such a sentence as this, *which* has not any one substantive as an antecedent, but refers to the whole preceding clause.

† When *what* is a substantive it is used only with reference to *things*, not with reference to persons.

168 *Whoever* and *whatever* have the same peculiar force as *what*. (See § 164). They also give the notion of universality to the antecedents that are implied; thus, "*Whoever* does this shall be punished," is equivalent to "Every one (or any one) who does this," &c.; "*Whosesoever* sins ye remit, they are remitted," is equivalent to "The sins of every one whose sins ye remit, are remitted."

J.—The Distributive and Indefinite Pronouns EACH, EITHER, NEITHER, ANY, OTHER.

169 These pronouns are used adjectively and substantively. *Any*, when it refers to a singular noun, implies *quantity*; when it refers to a plural noun, it implies *number*, as, "This food is bad; I will not eat *any*;" "There were some apples on that tree; did you pluck *any*?"

170 *Other*, when used as a substantive, has the ordinary inflections of a noun.

		Singular.	Plural.
Nominative Case	..	Other	Others
Possessive Case	..	Other's	Others'
Objective Case	..	Other	Others.

When *an* is used before *other* the two words are usually written together—*another*.

171 In such phrases as, "They loved each other;" "They hated one another;" the words *each* and *other*, and *one* and *other*, have a reciprocal relation to each other; but it is a mistake to call them compound pronouns (as though equivalent to the Greek *alleloi*). They are independent pronouns, having separate and different constructions in the sentences where they occur. In "They loved each other," *each* is in the nominative case, in apposition with *they*, which it distributes in sense; *other* is in the objective case, governed by the verb *loved*. In "They heard each other's voice," *each* is in the nominative case, in apposition with *they*; *other's* is in the possessive case, governed by the noun *voice*. Such phrases as *to each other*, *from one another*, &c., are corruptions, made upon a false analogy. In old-fashioned and *correct* English we find *each to other*, *one from another*. The expressions now in common use are anomalous and ungrammatical.

K.—The Possessive Pronouns.

172 These words have already been considered. (See §§ 95, 142.) The word *own* has no pretensions to be considered as a pronoun.

VERB.

173 **A Verb* is that part of speech by means of which we are able to make an assertion about something.**

174 **That word in the sentence which stands for what is spoken about is called the subject of the verb (or of the sentence). A verb expresses with regard to what is spoken about, that it *is something*, that it *does something*, or that it *is the object of some action*.**

175 When an adjective is prefixed to a noun, the notion of some quality, attribute, or fact is connected with our notion of that which is spoken about. If we say a *red apple*, the notion of *red* is connected with that of *apple*. The same end is attained by the use of a verb, with this difference, that when we prefix an adjective to a noun, the connexion between the two notions is spoken of as *already existing;* the use of a verb *effects* the union of the two notions. When we say *a blue coat*, the connexion between the object of thought and its attribute is presupposed. When we say *the coat is blue*, the verb *is* effects the union of the two notions. [The different kinds of sentences that result from the use of verbs are treated of in the Syntax.]

176 Verbs are divided into two classes—Transitive† and Intransitive Verbs.

A Transitive Verb is one which denotes an action or feeling which is directed towards some object; as, *strike*, "He *strikes* the ball;" *love*, "He *loves* his father."

An Intransitive Verb is one which denotes a *state* or *condition*, or an action or feeling which is not directed towards or exerted upon an object; as, *to be*, *to dwell*, *to stand*, *to sit*, *to rejoice*, *to run*. Verbs of this kind are sometimes called Neuter Verbs.

177 Many verbs which denote actions are used sometimes as transitive verbs, sometimes as intransitive verbs; as, "He *rolls* a ball; the ball *rolls*." "He *ran* away; he *ran* a thorn into his finger." "The child *speaks* already. He *speaks* several languages." In all such cases there is not only a difference of use, but a real difference of meaning. Thus, *roll* (transitive), "to give a rotary motion to a body;" and *roll* (intransitive), "to move with a rotary motion." *Speak*, "to utter articulate sounds" (intransitive); *speak*, "to use (a language) as the means of expressing ideas" (transitive). Sometimes the intransitive use of a verb may be explained by understanding the reflective pronoun after it; as, "The earth *moves* (itself)." "The needle *turns* (itself) towards the pole." But this explanation will not apply in all cases.

---

* Latin, *verbum*, "word;" the verb being emphatically the *word* of the sentence.

† Latin, *transire*, "to go across;" the action passes over, as it were, from the doer of it to the object of it.

178 Verbs admit of the following modifications:—Voice, Mood, Tense, Number, and Person.

Voice.

179 There are two Voices, the Active Voice and the Passive Voice.

The Active Voice is made up of those forms of a verb which denote that the subject of the sentence stands for the doer of the action described by the verb; as, "The boy *strikes* the ball." "The cat *killed* the mouse."

The Passive Voice is made up of those forms of a verb which denote that the subject of the sentence stands for the object of the action described by the verb; as, "The ball *is struck* by the boy." "The mouse *was killed* by the cat."

180 We may speak of one and the same action by means either of a verb in the active voice, or of a verb in the passive voice; but then the word that is the *object* of the active verb must be the *subject* of the passive verb, as in the above examples.

181 It is clear that only transitive verbs can properly be used in the passive voice. There is, however, a remarkable exception to this principle in English in the case of such phrases as "He *was laughed at*;" "The boy *was run over*."

The intransitive verb, with the preposition that follows it, is treated as being equivalent to a transitive verb.

182 The Passive Voice of a verb is formed by prefixing the various parts of the verb *be* to the perfect participle of the verb. The perfect participle of a transitive verb is *passive* in meaning.

183 Some intransitive verbs have their perfect tenses formed by means of the verb *be*, followed by the past or perfect participle;* as, "I *am* come;" "He *is* arrived;" "He *is* fallen." Great care must be taken not to confound these with passive verbs. The sign of the passive voice is not the verb *be*, but the *passive participle* that follows it.

Mood.

184 Moods (that is, *modes*) are certain variations of form in verbs, by means of which we can show the *mode* or *manner* in which

* Some grammarians are pleased to order us to alter these forms into "I *have* come," "He *has* arrived," &c. They had better at the same time mend the French and German languages, which at present still tolerate the forms, *Je suis venu*, *Ich bin gekommen*.

the attribute or fact indicated by the verb is connected in thought with the thing that is spoken of.

185 In English there are four moods :—1. The Infinitive Mood. 2. The Indicative Mood. 3. The Imperative Mood. 4. The Subjunctive Mood.

186 To these moods many grammarians add the *Potential Mood*, meaning by that mood certain combinations of the so-called auxiliary verbs *may*, *might*, *can*, *could*, *would*, *should*, *must*, with the infinitive mood. This is objectionable—1. Because such a way of forming a mood is different from what we find in the case of the other moods, which depend upon inflection. 2. Because the said potential mood would need to be itself subdivided into Indicative forms and Subjunctive forms. The sentences, "I *could* do this at one time, but I cannot now," and "I *could* not do this, if I were to try," do not contain the same parts of the verb *can*. In the first sentence, *could* is in the indicative mood; in the second it is in the subjunctive mood. 3. Because no grammatical analogy justifies us in calling these compound expressions moods. *I can write*, and *I must go*, are no more *moods* of the verbs *write* and *go*, than *possum scribere* is a mood of *scribo* in Latin; or *Je puis écrire*, *Ich kann schreiben*, and *Ich muss gehen*, moods of the verbs *écrire*, *schreiben*, and *gehen* in French and German. The potential mood seems to have been invented, because grammarians did not know what to do with an infinitive mood that is not preceded by *to*.

1.—The Infinitive Mood.

187 The Infinitive Mood is that form of the verb which is used when the action or state that is indicated by the verb is spoken of without reference to person, number, or time. The infinitive mood has the force of a substantive. It is used (sometimes with, sometimes without the preposition *to*) either as the subject or as the object of some other verb. Thus, "*To rise* early promotes health." *To rise* is the subject of the verb *promotes*. "I love *to read* good books." *To read* is the object of the verb *love*. "I dare not *do* this." *Do* is the object of the verb *dare*.

188 It is impossible to make an assertion by means of the Infinitive Mood. Hence the Infinitive Mood can never have a substantive as its subject.

189 The preposition *to*, which commonly precedes the infinitive mood, *is no part of the mood itself*. An infinitive mood is complete without it. After many verbs (such as *may*, *can*, *shall*, *will*, *must*, *let*, *dare*, *do*, *bid*, *make*, *see*, *hear*, *feel*, *need*) *to* is not required before the infinitive that follows. As, "I bid you *go* away." "He made me *turn* out of my way." "I feel the shock *vibrate* through my nerves." "Let me *depart*." "How dare you *tell* such a lie?" &c. As the verbs

in Italics are all in the infinitive mood, it follows that the preposition *to* is not necessary to form an infinitive.*

190 The preposition *to* which commonly precedes the infinitive, properly implies that the feeling or action spoken of in the preceding verb tends towards some object or end. Thus: "I wish *to* depart;" that is, my wishes are directed towards departing. "I love *to* hear sweet music;" that is, my love is directed towards hearing sweet music. Not unfrequently the *to* has a still stronger force, and introduces the purpose or consequence of some action or state of being expressed by a verb or adjective. Thus: "I am come *to release* you." "This danger is *to be feared.*" (The danger is such that its being feared should follow.) "This water is good *to drink.*" In old-fashioned English this idea was still more distinctly marked by the use of *for*. As, "This is Elias, which was *for to* come." (*Matt.* xi. 14.) "The thief cometh not but *for to* steal, and to kill, and to destroy." (*John* x. 10.) The use of *to* before the infinitive, when it is the subject of a sentence, is an example of that false analogy which is frequently to be traced in grammatical idioms.

2.—The Indicative Mood.

191 The Indicative Mood comprises those forms of a verb, by means of which a simple assertion can be made without reference to any other fact or event; as, "He *struck* the ball." "I *love* my parents." "We *shall set out* to-morrow."

3.—The Imperative Mood.

192 The Imperative Mood includes those forms of the verb by means of which we utter a command—(requests and exhortations are only weaker kinds of commands;) as, "*Give* me that book." "*Go* away." From its nature the imperative mood can only be used in the second person.

4.—The Subjunctive Mood.

193 The Subjunctive Mood includes those forms of the verb by means of which a fact or event is spoken of, not simply and unconditionally, but as a supposition, or as contingent upon some other action or event.

194 A verb in the Subjunctive Mood is generally (but not always) preceded by one of the conjunctions,† *if*, *that*, *though*, *unless*, *except*, either expressed or understood; as, "If he *were* here,

---

* The case is exactly analogous in German. The preposition *zu* precedes the infinitive mood after all verbs except such as answer to the English verbs after which *to* is not required. But no one would dream of writing down *zu lesen* as an infinitive mood. The infinitive mood of the verb is *lesen*.

† It is necessary to caution the learner that the conjunction is no part of the mood itself. He may meet with English grammars in which *If I am* is set down as the subjunctive mood of the verb *be*. On the same principle we shall next be told that *si sum* is the subjunctive mood of the verb *esse*.

I should see him." "Would that this *were* so." "The sentence is, that he *be* imprisoned for life."

195 It must be observed that the indicative mood follows most of these conjunctions quite as often as the subjunctive.

196 Some of the contingent or dependent modes in which a fact or event is viewed, which in other languages are expressed by the subjunctive mood, are expressed in English by certain parts of some verbs, which are called *auxiliary*, or *helping verbs*.

Participle.

197 Participles are verbal *adjectives*, differing from ordinary adjectives in this, that the active participle can take a substantive after it as its object.

198 There are two participles formed by inflection, the Imperfect Participle, and the Perfect Participle. The Imperfect Participle is always *active*, the Perfect Participle is always *passive*, provided the verb be a transitive verb. As, "I saw a boy *beating* a dog." "*Frightened* by the noise, he ran away." Even in the perfect tenses, as "I *have written* a letter," the origin of the construction is, "I have a letter written," where *written* is an adjective agreeing with *letter*; in Latin, *Habeo epistolam scriptam*. (In French the participle agrees with the object in some constructions, as "Les lettres que j'ai écrites.")

199 Besides the participles formed by inflection, there are the following compound participles:—

Active Perfect Participle—*Having struck*.

Active Perfect Participle of continued action—*Having been striking*.

Passive Indefinite Participle—*Being struck*.

Passive Perfect Participle—*Having been struck*.

Gerund.

200 Besides the participles (which are *adjectives*), most verbs in English have a *noun* ending in *-ing* formed from them, called the *gerund*. A gerund is like an imperfect participle in form, but is totally unlike it in construction. As the verbs *have* and *be* have gerunds, there are also certain compound forms, which may be called *compound gerunds*, made up of the gerunds of these verbs combined with participles; as, *Having gone, being loved, having been writing, having been struck*.

201 Gerunds are used either as the subjects or objects of verbs, or after prepositions; as, "I like *reading*." "He is fond of *studying*." "He is desirous of *being distinguished*." "After *having been writing* all the

morning, I am tired." "Through *having lost* his book, he could not learn his lesson." The English gerunds (like the Latin gerunds) may govern a noun in the objective case; as, "I like *hearing music*."

202 Participles (being adjectives) are never used as the subjects or objects of verbs, or after prepositions. It must be observed, too, that in all such compounds as *a hiding-place*, *a walking-stick*, &c., it is the gerund and not the participle which is used. If the latter were the case, *a walking-stick* could only mean *a stick that walks*.

Tense.

203 **Tense (Latin *tempus*, time) is a variation of form in verbs, indicating partly the time to which an action or event is referred, and partly the completeness or incompleteness of the event at the time indicated.**

204 The term *variation of form* is here used in an extended sense, meaning not only changes produced by inflection, but also combinations of auxiliary verbs with participles and infinitive moods. In perfect strictness it ought to be said that *a verb in English has only two tenses*, the present and the past, because these alone are formed by inflection.*

205 There are three divisions of time to which an event or a state may be referred,—the Present, the Past, and the Future. Hence, if the *time* of an event were the only thing to be considered, there could not be more than three tenses. But, besides the time of an action, there are three ways in which an action or event may be viewed:—

1. It may be spoken of as incomplete, or still going on. A tense which indicates this is called an *imperfect* tense.

2. It may be spoken of as complete. A tense which indicates this is called a *perfect* tense.

3. It may be spoken of without distinct reference to its completeness or incompleteness. A tense in which an action is thus spoken of is called an *indefinite* tense. The indefinite tenses are employed when an action or event is spoken of as one whole, without reference to its duration; as, "He *strikes* the ball." "He *fell* to the ground." "He *will break* his neck."

206 An action may be viewed in these three ways, with reference either to past, to present, or to future time. We thus get nine primary tenses.

---

* But as it would be thought needlessly rigid to deny that *monitus sum* is a *tense* of the Latin verb *moneo*, and as it is all but universal in the grammars of other languages to include compound forms under the name *tense*, and the rejection of this practice in English would entail excessive inconvenience in the comparison of English idioms with those of other languages, the limitations insisted on by certain purists are here discarded. It is curious that grammarians who deny that *have written* is a *tense*, because it is not formed by inflection, have no difficulty in accepting *may write*, or *must write*, as a *mood*, or *am struck* as a passive voice.

A.

1. The Past Imperfect, showing that at a certain past time an action was going on; as, *I was writing.*

2. The Past Perfect, showing that at a certain past time an action was complete; as, *I had written.*

3. The Past Indefinite, speaking of the action as one whole referred to past time; as, *I wrote.*

B.

1. The Present Imperfect, showing that an action is going on at the present time; as, *I am writing.*

2. The Present Perfect, showing that at the present time a certain action is complete; as, *I have written.*

3. The Present Indefinite, speaking of the action as one whole, referred to present time; as, *I write.*

C.

1. The Future Imperfect, showing that at a certain future time an action will be going on; as, *I shall be writing.*

2. The Future Perfect, showing that at a certain future time an action will be complete; as, *I shall have written.*

3. The Future Indefinite, speaking of an action as one whole, referred to future time; as, *I shall write.*

207 From this table it appears at once that *perfect* and *past* are not the same. A tense is past, present, or future, according to the *time* with reference to which an action is spoken of, not according to the completeness or incompleteness of the action at that time. When we say, "*I have written*," although the act of writing took place in past time, yet the *completeness* of the action (which is what the tense indicates) is referred to *present time*. Hence the tense is a *present* tense, although it speaks of an action that is completed. To justify us in using this tense, it is necessary that the state of things brought about by the action should still exist at the present time. We may say, "England has founded a mighty empire in the East," because the empire still lasts: but we cannot say, "Cromwell has founded a dynasty," because the dynasty exists no longer.

208 The *indefinite* tenses are often *imperfect* in sense. Thus, "I *stood* during the whole of the performance." "While he *lived* at home he was happy." The verbs in such cases would have to be rendered into the past *imperfect* tense in French, Latin, or Greek.

209 As every tense of the verb *be* may be followed by an imperfect participle, besides the primary tenses given in § 206, we have the following:—

The Present Perfect of continued action:—I *have been* writing.

The Past Perfect of continued action:—I *had been* writing.

The Future Perfect of continued action:—I *shall have been* writing.

210 The Present Indefinite Tense is used not only of what takes place now, but also of what frequently or habitually takes

place; as, "John often *goes* to the theatre." "He *writes* beautiful poems." "It *rains* here almost every day." It is also used of what is universally true; as, "Virtue *is* its own reward." "Honesty *is* the best policy"

211 A Substantive has no relation to any time in particular. The Infinitive Mood is virtually a substantive. Hence the Infinitive Mood does not indicate time.* It admits only of the distinctions in tense, called Imperfect, Perfect, and Indefinite. "[To] *be* writing" is an Imperfect tense, but it may refer either to present, or to future time. In "I *ought to be* writing my letters now," it refers to present time; in "I *shall be* travelling to-morrow," it refers to future time.

212 The tenses of the English verb are made partly by inflection, partly by the use of auxiliary verbs.

The Present Indefinite and the Past Indefinite are the only two tenses formed by inflection.

The Imperfect tenses are formed by the indefinite tenses of the verb *be*, followed by the imperfect participle.

The Perfect tenses are formed by means of the indefinite tenses of the verb *have*, followed by the perfect particle.

The Future tenses are formed by means of the auxiliary verbs *shall* and *will*, followed by the infinitive mood; *shall* being used for the first person, *will* for the second and third, (except after such conjunctions as *if*, *when*, &c., when the verb *shall* is used for all three persons; as, "If it *shall* be proved." "When they *shall* turn unto the Lord.") See § 219.

213 All moods and tenses in the Passive Voice are made by means of auxiliary verbs; the Passive Voice of a verb consisting of its perfect participle, preceded by the various moods and tenses of the verb *be*.

Number.

214 Number is a modification of the form of a verb, by means of which we show whether the verb is spoken of one person or thing, or of more than one. There are therefore two numbers in verbs, corresponding to the two numbers in substantives.

Person.

215 Person is a modification of the form of verbs, by which we indicate whether the speaker speaks of himself, or speaks to

* The same is the case with the Participles. They express *imperfect* and *perfect*, but not *past* or *present*.

some person or persons, or speaks of some other person or thing. There are three persons, the First Person, the Second Person, and the Third Person.*

The First Person includes those forms of the verb which are used when the speaker speaks of himself either singly or with others.

The Second Person includes those forms of the verb which are used when the speaker speaks to one or more others.

The Third Person includes those forms of the verb which are used when the speaker speaks of some one or more other persons or things.

DEFECTIVE VERBS.

216 Several verbs in English are *defective*, that is, have not the full complement of moods and tenses. These are *shall*, *will*, *may*, *must*, *can*, *ought*.

SHALL.

217 No Infinitive Mood. No Participles.

Indicative Mood.

Present Indefinite Tense.

Singular.	Plural.
1. [I] shall	1. [We] shall
2. [Thou] shalt	2. [You] shall
3. [He] shall	3. [They] shall

Past Indefinite Tense.

Singular.	Plural.
1. [I] should	1. [We] should
2. [Thou] shouldst	2. [You] should
3. [He] should	3. [They] should

Subjunctive Mood.

Past Indefinite Tense.

Singular.	Plural.
1. [I] should	1. [We] should
2. [Thou] shouldest *or* shouldst	2. [You] should
3. [He] should	3. [They] should

218 In the first person of the present indicative and past subjunctive, this verb simply indicates *futurity*. In the second and third persons of

* Observe that the *subject* of the verb forms no part of the *person* of the verb. The first person of the present tense of the verb *be* is *am*, not *I am*. In *thou writest*, *writest* (without *thou*) is the second person of the verb. It is usual, however, to conjugate verbs with a subject expressed, for the sake of clearness.

these tenses, and in all the persons of the past indicative, the idea of a moral necessity or compulsion, depending on the will of the speaker, is involved in addition. As the verb makes no complete sense by itself it is always followed by some other verb in the infinitive mood, but without the preposition *to*. For example: "I *shall* die;" "Thou *shalt* not steal;" "He *shall* not do that."

219 In questions, however, and in reported speeches, the force of this verb is the same in the second and third persons as it would be in the answer, or as it was in the direct speech: "*Shall* you be present?" "I *shall*." "I *shall* not set out to-morrow;" "I said I *should* not set out to-morrow;" or, "John said that he *should* not set out to-morrow."

WILL.

220 *Infinitive Mood*, [*To*] *will*.

Imperfect Participle, Willing.

Perfect Participle, Willed.

Compound Perfect Participle (active) Having willed.

The infinitive mood and the participles of this verb are only used when it has the stronger of its two senses.

Indicative Mood.

Present Indefinite Tense.

Singular.	Plural.
1. [I] will	1. [We] will
2. [Thou] wilt	2. [You] will
3. [He] will *or* wills*	3. [They] will

Past Indefinite Tense.

Singular.	Plural.
1. [I] would	1. [We] would
2. [Thou] wouldst *or* wouldest	2. [You] would
3. [He] would	3. [They] would

Subjunctive Mood.

Past Indefinite Tense.

Singular.	Plural.
1. [I] would	1. [We] would
2. [Thou] wouldest *or* wouldst	2. [You] would
3. [He] would	3. [They] would

The verb *will* is followed by the infinitive, without the preposition *to*; as, "I *will* strive;" "He *will* not obey."

---

* This form is used only when the verb is used in its strong sense.

221 This verb, beside being used as a mere auxiliary for forming future tenses in the second and third persons, is used to express determination or intention. It has this force in all its persons; as, "Not as I *will*, but as thou *wilt*;" "In spite of warning, he *will* continue his evil practices." When used in the strong sense of "having a determination" to do something, the verb *will* may be conjugated like an ordinary regular verb; but in this case the preposition *to* must be used with the infinitive that follows it.

222 The Past Indefinite tense of the indicative mood of this verb is used to express the frequent repetition of an action; as, "When he was irritated he *would* rave like a madman."

MAY.

223 No Infinitive Mood. No Participles.

Indicative Mood.

Present Indefinite Tense.

Singular.	Plural.
1. [I] may	1. [We] may
2. [Thou] mayest *or* mayst	2. [You] may
3. [He] may	3. [They] may

Past Indefinite Tense.

Singular.	Plural.
1. [I] might	1. [We] might
2. [Thou] mightest	2. [You] might
3. [He] might	3. [They] might

Subjunctive Mood.

Past Indefinite Tense.

Singular.	Plural.
1. [I] might	1. [We] might
2. [Thou] mightest	2. [You] might
3. [He] might	3. [They] might

224 The notion involved in this verb is that of *permission* or *liberty* to do something. It is also used to express *possibility* or *concession*; as, "That *may* be so, but I scarcely believe it." This sense of *may* is expressed in Latin, French, and German, by the verbs which answer to the English *can*. When placed before its subject, this verb expresses a wish; as, "*May* he be blessed;" "*Might* I but see him."

225 The Past Tense of the indicative mood is scarcely ever used, except in the reported form of the present. Thus, "You *may* go" (direct); "He told me that I *might* go," *i. e.* that it *was permitted* me to go (reported). "He *might* [not];" "I *might* [not];" &c., are sometimes used (especially in poetry) for "He was [not] permitted;" "I was [not] permitted," &c.

226 The verb *may* is followed by the infinitive mood without the preposition *to*.

MUST.

227 No Infinitive Mood. No Participles.

This verb is only used in the indicative mood, sometimes as a present, sometimes as a past tense; but there is no difference of form to mark tense, number, or person. It is followed by the infinitive without *to*. It denotes, 1. Being *obliged* or *compelled*, "He *must* do as he is bid." 2. Compulsion arising from the inability to control the desire or will: hence a *fixed determination* to do something; as, "I *must* and will have my own way;" "So you *must* always be meddling, *must* you?" 3. *Certainty*, or the idea that a thing cannot but be as is stated; "He surely *must* have arrived by this time;" "It *must* be so; Plato, thou reasonest well."

CAN.

228 No Infinitive Mood. No Participles.

Indicative Mood.

Present Indefinite Tense.

Singular.	Plural.
1. [I] can	1. [We] can
2. [Thou] canst	2. [You] can
3. [He] can	3. [They] can

Past Indefinite Tense.

Singular.	Plural.
1. [I] could	1. [We] could
2. [Thou] couldest *or* couldst	2. [You] could
3. [He] could	3. [They] could

Subjunctive Mood.

Past Indefinite Tense.

Singular.	Plural.
1. [I] could	1. [We] could
2. [Thou] couldest *or* couldst	2. [You] could
3. [He] could	3. [They] could

This verb is followed by the infinitive mood without *to;* as, "I can *speak* Greek."

HAVE.

229 **Infinitive Mood.**

Indefinite Tense, [To] have. *Imperfect Tense,* [To] be having. *Perfect Tense,* [To] have had.

Participles.

Imperfect Participle, Having. *Perfect Participle* (passive), Had. *Compound Perfect Participle* (active) Having had.

Indicative Mood.

Present Indefinite Tense.

Singular.	Plural.
1. [I] have	1. [We] have
2. [Thou] hast	2. [You] have
3. [He] hath *or* has	3. [They] have

Present Perfect Tense.

Singular.	Plural.
1. [I] have had	1. [We] have had
2. [Thou] hast had	2. [You] have had
3. [He] has had *or* hath had	3. [They] have had

Past Indefinite Tense.

Singular.	Plural.
1. [I] had	1. [We] had
2. [Thou] hadst	2. [You] had
3. [He] had	3. [They] had

Past Perfect Tense.

Singular.	Plural.
1. [I] had had	1. [We] had had
2. [Thou] hadst had	2. [You] had had
3. [He] had had	3. [They] had had

Future Indefinite Tense.

Singular.	Plural.
1. [I] shall have	1. [We] shall have
2. [Thou] wilt have	2. [You] will have
3. [He] will have	3. [They] will have

Future Perfect Tense.

Singular.	Plural.
1. [I] shall have had	1. [We] shall have had
2. [Thou] wilt have had	2. [You] will have had
3. [He] will have had	3. [Thou] will have had

Imperative Mood.

Singular.	Plural.
Have [thou]	Have [you *or* ye]

Subjunctive Mood.

Present Indefinite Tense.

(Used after *if, that, lest, unless,* &c.)

Singular.	Plural.
1. [I] have	1. [We] have
2. [Thou] have	2. [You] have
3. [He] have	3. [They] have

Present Perfect Tense.

(Used after *if, that, unless,* &c.)

Singular.	Plural.
1. [I] have had	1. [We] have had
2. [Thou] have had	2. [You] have had
3. [He] have had	3. [They] have had

Past Indefinite Tense.

(Used after *if, that, unless,* &c.)

Singular.	Plural.
1. [I] had	1. [We] had
2. [Thou] hadst	2. [You] had
3. [He] had	3. [They] had

Past Perfect Tense.

(Used after *if, that, unless,* &c.)

Singular.	Plural.
1. [I] had had	1. [We] had had
2. [Thou] hadst had	2. [You] had had
3. [He] had had	3. [They] had had

Future Indefinite Tense.

Singular.	Plural.
1. [I] should have	1. [We] should have
2. [Thou] shouldst *or* wouldst have	2. [You] should *or* would have
3. [He] should *or* would have	3. [They] should *or* would have

Future Perfect Tense.

Singular.	Plural.
1. [I] should have had	1. [We] should have had
2. [Thou] shouldst *or* wouldst have had	2. [You] should *or* would have had
3. [He] should *or* would have had	3. [They] should *or* would have had

230 The verb *have* often has the sense of *to keep* or *to hold.* In this case it may have the *imperfect* tenses, and may be used in the passive voice, like an ordinary verb.

Indicative Mood.

Present Imperfect Tense.

Singular.	Plural.
1. [I] am having	1. [We] are having
2. [Thou] art having	2. [You] are having
3. [He] is having	3. [They] are having

Past Imperfect Tense.

Singular.	Plural.
1. [I] was having	1. [We] were having
2. [Thou] wast having	2. [You] were having
3. [He] was having	3. [They] were having

Future Imperfect Tense.

Singular.	Plural.
1. [I] shall be having	1. [We] shall be having
2. [Thou] wilt be having	2. [You] will be having
3. [He] will be having	3. [They] will be having

Present Perfect of continued action.

Singular.	Plural.
1. [I] have been having	1. [We] have been having
2. [Thou] hast been having	2. [You] have been having
3. [He] has been having	3. [They] have been having

Past Perfect of continued action.

Singular.	Plural.
1. [I] had been having	1. [We] had been having
2. [Thou] hadst been having	2. [You] had been having
3. [He] had been having	3. [They] had been having

Future Perfect of continued action.

Singular.		Plural.	
[I] shall have been	having	1. [We] shall have been	having
2. [Thou] wilt have been		2. [You] will have been	
3. [He] will have been		3. [They] will have been	

Subjunctive Mood.

Present Imperfect Tense.

(*If, that, though,* &c.) I be having, &c.

Past Imperfect Tense.

(*If, that, though,* &c.) I were having, &c.

Future Imperfect Tense.

(*If, that, though,* &c.) I should be having, &c.

231 For the formation of the Perfect Tense of continued action in the subjunctive mood, and for the passive forms of the verb, see (further on) the conjugation of the verb *Smite*.

Example:—"I am *having* my dinner." "At one o'clock he will be *having* his likeness taken." "This fact will be *had* in remembrance." "I have been *having* a ride," and so on.

BE.

232 ### Infinitive Mood.

Indefinite Tense.—[To] be.

Perfect Tense.—[To] have been.

Imperfect Participle.—Being. *Perfect Participle.*—Been.

Compound Perfect Participle.—Having been.

Indicative Mood.

Present Indefinite Tense.

Singular.	Plural.
1. [I] am	1. [We] are
2. [Thou] art	2. [You] are
3. [He] is	3. [They] are

Present Perfect Tense.

Singular.	Plural.
1. [I] have been	1. [We] have been
2. [Thou] hast been	2. [You] have been
3. [He] has been	3. [They] have been

Past Indefinite Tense.

Singular.	Plural.
1. [I] was	1. [We] were
2. [Thou] wast *	2. [You] were
3. [He] was	3. [They] were

* Some writers use *wert* for *wast*, especially in poetry. This is ungrammatical, the only excuse for the practice being that *wert* is more euphonious than *wast*.

Past Perfect Tense.

Singular.	Plural.
1. [I] had been	1. [We] had been
2. [Thou] hadst been	2. [You] had been
3. [He] had been	3. [They] had been

Future Indefinite Tense.

Singular.	Plural.
1. [I] shall be	1. [We] shall be
2. [Thou] wilt be	2. [You] will be
3. [He] will be	3. [They] will be

Future Perfect Tense.

Singular.	Plural.
1. [I] shall have been	1. [We] shall have been
2. [Thou] wilt have been	2. [You] will have been
3. [He] will have been	3. [They] will have been.

Imperative Mood.

Singular.—Be (thou). *Plural.*—Be (ye *or* you).

Subjunctive Mood.

Present Indefinite Tense.

(After *if*, *that*, *though*, *lest*, &c.)

Singular.	Plural.
1. [I] be	1. [We] be
2. [Thou] be	2. [You] be
3. [He] be	3. [They] be

Present Perfect Tense.

(After *if*, *that*, *though*, *unless*, &c.)

Singular.	Plural.
1. [I] have been	1. [We] have been
2. [Thou] have been	2. [You] have been
3. [He] have been	3. [They] have been

Past Indefinite Tense.

(After *if*, *that*, *though*, *unless*, &c.)

Singular.	Plural.
1. [I] were	1. [We] were
2. [Thou] wert	2. [You] were
3. [He] were	3. [They] were

Past Perfect Tense.

(After *if*, *that*, *though*, *unless*, &c.)

Singular.	Plural.
1. [I] had been	1. [We] had been
2. [Thou] hadst been	2. [You] had been
3. [He] had been	3. [They] had been

Future Indefinite Tense.

Singular.	Plural.
1. [I] should be	1. [We] should be
2. [Thou) wouldst be	2. [You] would be
3. [He] would be	3. [They] would be

Future Perfect Tense.

Singular.	Plural.
1. [I] should have been	1. [We] should have been
2. [Thou] wouldst have been	2. [You] would have been
3. [He] would have been	3. [They] would have been

233 The verb *be* is a most important verb for the right understanding of the etymology and syntax of verbs in general, because it has distinct forms for the past indefinite in the indicative and subjunctive moods. In no other verb is there a corresponding difference of *form*, though there is a real difference of *mood*. This identity of form, concealing a real difference of construction, is a fact of very common occurrence in English; as in the nominative and objective cases of nouns, the three different persons in the plural of verbs, &c. The verb *be*, therefore, is a *test* verb. By substituting it in place of any other verb in a sentence where the construction is doubtful or difficult, we can see directly what part of the verb it is that is really used. In such sentences as, "He *would* not come when I called him;" "He *could* not lift the weight when he tried;" "Ye *would* not come unto me that ye might have life" (*i. e.* Ye did not choose to come); "He told me that I *might* go" (*i. e.* that it *was* permitted me to go); "You *should* not have done that" (*i. e.* it *was your duty* not to have done that); the verbs *could*, *would*, *might*, are in the indicative mood: the sentences are simple assertions. On the other hand, in such sentences as these:—"I *could* not do it if I *were* to try;" "I *should* not have said that, if you *had* not asked me;" "I *would* not tell you if I *could*;" "He *might* have done it if he *had* liked;"—the verbs which are in Italics are in the subjunctive mood.

DO.

234 *Do* is one of the verbs which do not require the preposition *to* before the infinitive mood which follows them. It is not defective, and has nothing peculiar in the formation of its moods, tenses, &c. They are made like those of the verb given at full length (see § 237).

235 The conjugation of any English verb is known when we know the infinitive mood, the past indefinite tense, and the perfect participle, all other parts being formed from these according to fixed rules.* The following table exhibits the personal *inflections* that are made use of. Let a single stroke (——————) stand for the infinitive mood (without *to*), and a double stroke (══════) for the first person singular of the past indefinite tense.

Imperfect Participle. ———ing.

Indicative Mood.

Present Indefinite Tense.

	Singular.			Plural.
1.	——————		1.	——————
2.	——————	est *or* st.	2.	——————
3.	——————	eth, th, *or* s	3.	——————

Past Indefinite Tense.

	Singular.			Plural.
1.	══════		1.	══════
2.	══════	est *or* st	2.	══════
3.	══════		3.	══════

Subjunctive Mood.

Present Indefinite Tense.

	Singular.		Plural.
1.	——————	1.	——————
2.	——————	2.	——————
3.	——————	3.	——————

Past Indefinite Tense.

The same as in the Indicative Mood.

236 Verbs ending in a mute *e* drop the *e* before the suffixes *ing*, *est*, and *eth*. *Do* takes *th*, not *eth* in the present tense (*doth*: *doeth* is obsolete). The suffix *eth* is now seldom used except in poetry. (See § 22.)

The learner must analyse the following verb, and ascertain how the compound tenses are formed. It will then be unnecessary to set down the rules at full length.†

---

* It must be observed that verbs ending in *o* add *es* for the third person singular, not *s*, as, *goes*, *does*. Verbs in *ie* form the imperfect participle with *y* instead of *ie*; as, *die*, *dying*; *tie*, *tying*. The verb *dye* retains the mute *e* (*dyeing*), to distinguish it from *dying*.

† It will not be easy to make mistakes in the verb which is here given. There is not a large choice of verbs which are transitive, denoting a single action which may be prolonged or repeated, having the past indefinite tense and the perfect participle different, and making some reasonable sense when conjugated through all varieties of voice, mood, and tense. Most grammars follow the very objection-

237 CONJUGATION OF A VERB.

SMITE.

ACTIVE VOICE.

Infinitive Mood.

Indefinite Tense.—[To] smite.
Imperfect Tense.—[To] be smiting.
Perfect Tense.—[To] have smitten.
Perfect of continued action.—[To] have been smiting.

Participles.

Imperfect.—Smiting.
Perfect.—Having smitten.
Perfect of continued action.—Having been smiting.

Indicative Mood.

Present Indefinite Tense.

Singular.	Plural.
1. [I] smite	1. [We] smite
2. [Thou] smitest	2. [You] smite
3. [He] smites *or* smiteth	3. [They] smite

Present Imperfect Tense.

Singular.	Plural.
1. [I] am smiting	1. [We] are smiting
2. [Thou] art smiting	2. [You] are smiting
3. [He] is smiting	3. [They] are smiting

Present Perfect Tense.

Singular.	Plural.
1. [I] have smitten	1. [We] have smitten
2. [Thou] hast smitten	2. [You] have smitten
3. [He] has smitten	3. [They] have smitten

Present Perfect of continued action.

Singular.	Plural.
1. [I] have been smiting	1. [We] have been smiting
2. [Thou] hast been smiting	2. [You] have been smiting
3. [He] has been smiting	3. [They] have been smiting

able plan of giving as a model some verb in which the past indefinite tense and the perfect participle are the same in form. If a dozen beginners were set to analyse such a verb, three-fourths of them would probably pronounce the present perfect tense to be made up of *have* and the past indefinite tense.

Past Indefinite Tense.

Singular.	Plural.
1. [I] smote	1. [We] smote
2. [Thou] smotest	2. [You] smote
3. [He] smote	3. [They] smote

Past Imperfect Tense.

Singular.	Plural.
1. [I] was smiting	1. [We] were smiting
2. [Thou] wast smiting	2. [You] were smiting
3. [He] was smiting	3. [They] were smiting

Past Perfect Tense.

Singular.	Plural.
1. [I] had smitten	1. [We] had smitten
2. [Thou] hadst smitten	2. [You] had smitten
3. [He] had smitten	3. [They] had smitten

Past Perfect of continued action.

Singular.	Plural.
1. [I] had been smiting	1. [We] had been smiting
2. [Thou] hadst been smiting	2. [You] had been smiting
3. [He] had been smiting	3. [They] had been smiting

Future Indefinite Tense.

Singular.	Plural.
1. [I] shall smite	1. [We] shall smite
2. [Thou] wilt smite	2. [You] will smite
3. [He] will smite	3. [They] will smite

Future Imperfect Tense.

Singular.	Plural.
1. [I] shall be smiting	1. [We] shall be smiting
2. [Thou] wilt be smiting	2. [You] will be smiting
3. [He] will be smiting	3. [They] will be smiting

Future Perfect Tense.

Singular.	Plural.
1. [I] shall have smitten	1. [We] shall have smitten
2. [Thou] wilt have smitten	2. [You] will have smitten
3. [He] will have smitten	3. [They] will have smitten

Future Perfect of continued action.

Singular.		Plural.	
1. [I] shall have been	smiting	1. [We] shall have been	smiting
2. [Thou] wilt have been		2. [You] will have been	
3. [He] will have been		3. [They] will have been	

Imperative Mood.

Singular.—Smite [thou]. *Plural.*—Smite [you *or* ye].

238 Subjunctive Mood.

Present Indefinite Tense.

(After *if, that, though, lest, unless,* &c.)

Singular.	Plural.
1. [I] smite	1. [We] smite
2. [Thou] smite	2. [You] smite
3. [He] smite	3. [They] smite

Present Imperfect Tense.

(After *if, that, though, lest,* &c.)

Singular.	Plural.
1. [I] be smiting	1. [We] be smiting
2. [Thou] be smiting	2. [You] be smiting
3. [He] be smiting	3. [They] be smiting

Present Perfect Tense.

(After *if, though, unless,* &c.)

Singular.	Plural.
1. [I] have smitten	1. [We] have smitten
2. [Thou] have smitten	2. [You] have smitten
3. [He] have smitten	3. [They] have smitten

Present Perfect of continued action.

(After *if, though, unless,* &c.)

Singular.	Plural.
1. [I] have been smiting	1. [We] have been smiting
2. [Thou] have been smiting	2. [You] have been smiting
3. [He] have been smiting	3. [They] have been smiting

Past Indefinite Tense.

(After *if, though, unless,* &c.)

Singular.	Plural.
1. [I] smote	1. [We] smote
2. [Thou] smotest	2. [You] smote
3. [He] smote	3. [They] smote

Past Imperfect Tense

(After *if, that, though, unless,* &c.)

Singular.	Plural.
1. [I] were smiting	1. [We] were smiting
2. [Thou] wert smiting	2. [You] were smiting
3. [He] were smiting	3. [They] were smiting

Past Perfect Tense.

(After *if, though, unless,* &c.)

Singular.	Plural.
1. [I] had smitten	1. [We] had smitten
2. [Thou] hadst smitten	2. [You] had smitten
3. [He] had smitten	3. [They] had smitten

Past Perfect of continued action.

(After *if, that, though, unless,* &c.)

Singular.	Plural.
1. [I] had been smiting	1. [We] had been smiting
2. [Thou] hadst been smiting	2. [You] had been smiting
3. [He] had been smiting	3. [They] had been smiting

Future Indefinite Tense.

Singular.	Plural.
1. [I] should smite	1. [We] should smite
2. [Thou] wouldst smite	2. [You] would smite
3. [He] would smite	3. [They] would smite

Future Imperfect Tense.

Singular.	Plural.
1. [I] should be smiting	1. [We] should be smiting
2. [Thou] wouldst be smiting	2. [You] would be smiting
3. [He] would be smiting	3. [They] would be smiting

Future Perfect Tense.

Singular.		Plural.	
1. [I] should have	smitten	1. [We] should have	smitten
2. [Thou] wouldst have		2. [You] would have	
3. [He] would have		3. [They] would have	

Future Perfect of continued action.

Singular.	Plural.
1. [I] should have been smiting	1. [We] should have been smiting
2. [Thou] wouldst have been smiting	2. [You] would have been smiting
3. [He] would have been smiting	3. [They] would have been smiting

239 PASSIVE VOICE.

Infinitive Mood.

Indefinite Tense.—[To] be smitten.
Imperfect Tense.—[To] be being smitten.
Perfect Tense.—[To] have been smitten.

Participles.

Indefinite Participle.—Being smitten.
Perfect Participle.—Smitten.
Compound Perfect Participle.—Having been smitten.

Indicative Mood.

Present Indefinite Tense.

Singular.	Plural.
1. [I] am smitten	1. [We] are smitten
2. [Thou] art smitten	2. [You] are smitten
3. [He] is smitten	3. [They] are smitten

Present Imperfect Tense.

Singular.	Plural.
1. [I] am being smitten	1. [We] are being smitten
2. [Thou] art being smitten	2. [You] are being smitten
3. [He] is being smitten	3. [They] are being smitten

Present Perfect Tense.

Singular.	Plural.
1. [I] have been smitten	1. [We] have been smitten
2. [Thou] hast been smitten	2. [You] have been smitten
3. [He] has been smitten	3. [They] have been smitten

Present Perfect of continued action.

Singular.	Plural.
1. [I] have been being smitten	1. [We] have been being smitten
2. [Thou] hast been being smitten	2. [You] have been being smitten
3. [He] has been being smitten	3. [They] have been being smitten

Past Indefinite Tense.

Singular.	Plural.
1. [I] was smitten	1. [We] were smitten
2. [Thou] wast smitten	2. [You] were smitten
3. [He] was smitten	3. [They] were smitten

Past Imperfect Tense.

Singular.	Plural.
1. [I] was being smitten	1. [We] were being smitten
2. [Thou] wast being smitten	2. [You] were being smitten
3. [He] was being smitten	3. [They] were being smitten

Past Perfect Tense.

Singular.	Plural.
1. [I] had been smitten	1. [We] had been smitten
2. [Thou] hadst been smitten	2. [You] had been smitten
3. [He] had been smitten	3. [They] had been smitten

Past Perfect of continued action.

Singular.	Plural.
1. [I] had been being smitten	1. [We] had been being smitten
2. [Thou] hadst been being smitten	2. [You] had been being smitten
3. [He] had been being smitten	3. [They] had been being smitten

Future Indefinite Tense.

Singular.	Plural.
1. [I] shall be smitten	1. [We] shall be smitten
2. [Thou] wilt be smitten	2. [You] will be smitten
3. [He] will be smitten	3. [They] will be smitten

Future Imperfect Tense.

Singular.		Plural.	
1. [I] shall be being	smitten	1. [We] shall be being	smitten
2. [Thou] wilt be being		2. [You] will be being	
3. [He] will be being		3. [They] will be being	

Future Perfect Tense.

Singular.		Plural.	
1. [I] shall have been	smitten	1. [We] shall have been	smitten
2. [Thou] wilt have been		2. [You] will have been	
3. [He] will have been		3. [They] will have been	

*Future Perfect of continued action.**

Singular.	Plural.
1. [I] shall have been being smitten	1. [We] shall have been being smitten
2. [Thou] wilt have been being smitten	2. [You] will have been being smitten
3. [He] will have been being smitten	3. [They] will have been being smitten

---

* It may be doubted whether many examples of the passive perfects of continued action can be found in actual use.

Imperative Mood.

Singular.	Plural.
Be [thou] smitten.	Be [ye] smitten.

240

Subjunctive Mood.

Present Indefinite Tense.

(After *if, that, though* &c.)

Singular.	Plural.
1. [I] be smitten	1. [We] be smitten
2. [Thou] be smitten	2. [You] be smitten
3. [He] be smitten	3. [They] be smitten

Present Imperfect Tense.

(After *if, that, though*, &c.)

Singular.	Plural.
1. [I] be being smitten	1. [We] be being smitten
2. [Thou] be being smitten	2. [You] be being smitten
3. [He] be being smitten	3. [They] be being smitten

Present Perfect Tense.

(After *if, that, though*, &c.)

Singular.	Plural.
1. [I] have been smitten	1. [We] have been smitten
2. [Thou] have been smitten	2. [You] have been smitten
3. [He] have been smitten	3. [They] have been smitten

Present Perfect of continued action.

[I] have been being smitten, &c.

Past Indefinite Tense.

(After *if, that, though*, &c.)

Singular.	Plural.
1. [I] were smitten	1. [We] were smitten
2. [Thou] wert smitten	2. [You] were smitten
3. [He] were smitten	3. [They] were smitten

Past Perfect Tense.

The same in form as the Past Perfect Indicative.

Past Perfect of continued action.

The same in form as the Past Perfect of continued action in the Indicative Mood.

Future Indefinite Tense.

Singular.	Plural.
1. [I] should be smitten	1. [We] should be smitten
2. [Thou] wouldst be smitten	2. [You] would be smitten
3. [He] would be smitten	3. [They] would be smitten

Future Imperfect Tense.

Singular.	Plural.
1. [I] should be being smitten	1. [We] should be being smitten
2. [Thou] wouldst be being smitten	2. [You] would be being smitten
3. [He] would be being smitten	3. [They] would be being smitten

Future Perfect Tense.

Singular.	Plural.
1. [I] should have been smitten	1. [We] should have been smitten
2. [Thou] wouldst have been smitten	2. [You] would have been smitten
3. [He] would have been smitten	3. [They] would have been smitten

Future Perfect of continued action.

I should have been being smitten, &c.

241 The Indefinite Tenses and the Indefinite Participles of the Passive Voice are a little ambiguous in meaning. They may refer either to the *action* indicated by the verb, or to the *results* of the action. In the latter case they are not strictly *tenses* of the passive voice, but the participle that follows the verb *be* is used as an adjective. In "He *was terrified* at the sight," *was terrified* is a past indefinite tense of the passive voice of the verb *terrify*. It represents an action exerted upon a certain person. In "He *was terrified*, so that he could not speak," the verb of the sentence is *was*, and *terrified* is a mere adjective.* In "Every house is built by some man," *is built* is a present indefinite tense passive of the verb *build*. In "This house is built of stone," *is* is the verb, and *built* is used as an adjective. So also the indefinite participle may be either perfect or imperfect in tense. If we say, "Being warned of the danger, he turned aside," *being warned* is strictly a participle. If we say, "Being distracted with pain, he could not sleep," it is better to treat *being* as the participle, and *distracted* as an adjective. In "I saw a sheep being killed," *being killed* is a compound *participle*, denoting the *action* of killing. In "He is a wretched man, being hated by everybody," it is better to separate *hated* from *being*, and call *hated* an adjective, and *being* a participle of the verb *be*, rather than to call *being hated* a compound passive participle of the verb *hate*.

242 There is a peculiar use of the gerund, which must not be confounded with any part of the passive voice of a verb, or with the imperfect

---

* This distinction can be easily marked in Greek and in German. "The letter is written" may be rendered either "ἡ ἐπιστολὴ γράφεται," and "Der Brief wird geschrieben," or, "ἡ ἐπιστολὴ γεγραμμένη ἐστι," and "Der Brief ist geschrieben."

tenses of the active voice. In old-fashioned English we find such expressions as "While the ark was a (i. e. *at*) preparing;" "Forty and six years was this temple in building;" "I lay a thinking." There is no difficulty about the construction of such sentences. The word in *-ing* is a gerund, governed by a preposition. But in modern English it has become usual to omit the preposition, leaving the gerund without any grammatical construction: so that we get such phrases as "The temple was building," that is, "was being built."

243 When it is requisite to make an emphatic assertion or command, the verb *do* is employed, followed by the infinitive mood, as, "I do love you;"* "Yes, he did say so;" "Do go." This use of *do* is not admitted in the case of the compound tenses, or the passive voice.

244 Interrogative sentences are formed in two ways. 1st. By placing the verb before its subject, as, "Said he not so?" "Went they not this way?" In the present and past indefinite tenses of the active voice this mode is now not used in ordinary prose, except in the case of the verbs *may, can, must, shall, will, have, be.* With any of the compound tenses a question is asked by placing the subject of the verb after the auxiliary verb, as, "Shall we begin?" "Have you dined?" "Must we go?"

2. By using the verb *do,* followed by the infinitive mood, provided the verb in the affirmative form of the sentence would be in the present or past indefinite tense, indicative mood, of the active voice: "Do you hear?" "Did you learn your lesson?"

245 But the verb *do* is never employed when the sentence begins with an interrogative pronoun, provided that pronoun is the *subject* of the verb, or when it begins with an interrogative word which qualifies either the subject of the sentence, or an adjective attached to the subject of the sentence, as, "Who broke the window?" "Which boy did this?" "How many persons were present?" But "Whom did you see there?" "How far did you walk?"

246 In poetical language, when an *inflected* tense is used, a sentence is made negative by simply putting *not* after the verb; as, "He went not forth;" "I heard not his voice." In ordinary prose the verb *do,* with the infinitive mood, is employed; as, "I do not understand;" "He did not reply." But *do* is never used in this way to replace a compound tense of the active voice, or any tense of the passive voice; nor is it used at all with the verbs *have, be, may, can, must, shall, will.*

---

* It is quite a mistake to set down such an expression as *do go* as a *tense* of the verb *go.*

247 Comparative Table of Tenses in English, Latin, French, German, and Greek.

ACTIVE VOICE.

INDICATIVE MOOD.

		English.	Latin.	Greek.	French.	German.
Present	*Indefinite*	He writes	scribit	γράφει	il écrit	er schreibt
	Imperfect	He is writing	scribit	γράφει	il écrit	er schreibt
	Perfect	He has written	scripsit	γέγραφε	il a écrit	er hat geschrieben
Past	*Indefinite*	He wrote	scripsit	ἔγραψε	il écrivit	er schrieb
	Imperfect	He was writing	scribebat	ἔγραφε	il écrivait	er schrieb
	Perfect	He had written	scripserat	ἐγεγράφει	{il avait écrit / il eut écrit}	er hatte geschrieben
Future	*Indefinite*	He will write	scribet	γράψει	il écrira	er wird schreiben
	Imperfect	He will be writing	scribet	γράψει	il écrira	er wird schreiben
	Perfect	He will have written	scripserit	..	il aura écrit	er wird geschrieben haben
Perfect of continued Action		He has been writing, &c.	..	..	..	..

PASSIVE VOICE.

INDICATIVE MOOD.

		English.	Latin.	Greek.	French.	German.
Present	*Indefinite*	It is written	scribitur	γράφεται	il est écrit	es wird geschrieben
	Imperfect	It is being written	scribitur	γράφεται	———	es wird geschrieben
	Perfect	It has been written	{ scriptum est / scriptum fuit }	γέγραπται	il a été écrit	es ist geschrieben worden
Past	*Indefinite*	It was written	{ scriptum est / scriptum fuit }	ἐγράφθη	il fut écrit	es wurde geschrieben
	Imperfect	It was being written	scribebatur	ἐγράφετο	. .	es wurde geschrieben
	Perfect	It had been written	{ scriptum erat / scriptum fuerat }	ἐγέγραπτο	{ il avait été écrit / il eut été écrit }	es war geschrieben worden
Future	*Indefinite*	It will be written	scribetur	γραφθήσεται	il sera écrit	es wird geschrieben werden
	Imperfect	It will be being written	scribetur	γράψεται	. .	es wird geschrieben werden
	Perfect	It will have been written	scriptum erit	γεγράψεται	il aura été écrit	es wird geschrieben worden seyn

248 From the preceding table it will be seen that the English language admits of greater accuracy than any other in the expression of all the shades of meaning that are involved in *tense*. In other languages the same form often has to do double duty.

249 The *Present Indefinite Tense* is often equivalent to (or rather used in place of) a future indefinite or future perfect tense after such words as *if*, *when*, *whenever*, *however*, &c. As, "If he *does* this, he shall be punished." "When he *leaves* me, I shall feel desolate." "Whatever he *does*, he will never redeem his character." "Whoever *wins* the game will receive the stakes."

250 English verbs are commonly divided into two classes, *Regular* and *Irregular*, the *regular* verbs being those in which the past indefinite tense and the perfect participle are formed by the addition of *d* or *ed* to the infinitive mood; as, *call*, *called*; *love*, *loved*. These verbs are called *regular*, because they are all formed according to *one* rule. Verbs in which the past indefinite tense and the perfect participle are formed in any other mode, are commonly called *irregular*, not that they do not conform to certain rules, but because they are not all formed according to *one* rule. The so-called irregular verbs may be divided into classes, in each of which classes the formation is *regular*, as far as that class is concerned. The only reason for the common division is, that the *regular* verbs are by much the most numerous, and that all new verbs introduced into the language are formed after that fashion. Some grammarians call the regular verbs verbs of the *weak* conjugation, and the irregular verbs verbs of the *strong* conjugation.* It is more accurate to call the regular verbs verbs of the *new* formation, and the rest, verbs of the *old* formation.

251 The chief mark of the *old* formation is, that the past indefinite tense and the perfect participle are formed either by a change of the vowel sound of the verb (the participle sometimes taking a suffix in addition), or by a modification of the final consonant. These verbs are almost always monosyllabic. In the following table, the vowel changes are indicated at the head of each class.

---

* There does not seem to be much sense in such a use of the words *weak* and *strong*. It explains nothing, and is little more than a piece of affectation.

252 A. Verbs in which the vowel sound is changed, but no suffix is added in the past indefinite tense.

	Present.	*Past Indefinite.*	*Perfect Participle.*
1.	ā	ō	ō
	awake	awoke *or* awaked	awoke
2.	ea	a *or* o	o *with suffix* n *or* ne
	bear (carry)	bare *or* bore	borne
	bear (bring forth young)	bare *or* bore	born
	break	brake *or* broke	broken
	swear	sware *or* swore	sworn
	tear	tare *or* tore	torn
	wear	wore	worn
3.	ā	oo	a *with suffix* en
	forsake	forsook	forsaken
	shake	shook	shaken
	take	took	taken
4.	ă	ŭ	ŭ
	hang	hung *or* hanged	hung *or* hanged
5.	ēā *or* ee	ĕă *or* ĕ	ĕă *or* ĕ
	bleed	bled	bled
	breed	bred	bred
	feed	fed	fed
	lead	led	led
	meet	met	met
	read	read	read
	speed	sped	sped
6.	ēā	ēā *or* ā	ēā *with suffix* en
	beat	beat	beaten
	eat	ate	eaten
7.	ēā	ā *or* ō	ō *with suffix* n *or* en
	cleave	clave *or* clove	cloven
	freeze	froze	frozen *
	heave	hove	
	shear	shore *or* sheared	shorn *or* sheared
	speak	spake *or* spoke	spoken
	steal	stole	stolen
	weave	wove	woven
8.	ĕă *or* ĕ	ă *or* ŏ	ŏ *with suffix* en
	get	gat *or* got	gotten *or* got
	forget	forgat *or* forgot	forgotten *or* forgot
	tread	trode *or* trod	trodden

* In some provincial dialects they use the forms *squeeze, squoze, squozen.*

	Present.	*Past Indefinite.*	*Perfect Participle.*
9.	ī	ĭ	ĭ *with suffix* en
	bite	bit	bitten *or* bit
	chide	chid	chidden *or* chid
	hide	hid	hidden *or* hid
	slide	slid	slidden *or* slid
10.	ĭ	ă	ŭ *sometimes with suffix* en
	begin	began	begun
	drink	drank	drunk *or* drunken
	ring	rang	rung
	shrink	shrank	shrunk *or* shrunken
	sink	sank	sunk *or* sunken
	sling	slang *or* slung	slung
	spin	span *or* spun	spun
	spring	sprang	sprung
	stink	stank	stunk
	swim	swam	swum
11.	ĭ	ă *or* ŭ	ŭ
	cling	clung	clung
	dig	dug	dug
	fling	flung	flung
	sling	slang *or* slung	slung
	spin	span *or* spun	spun
	stick	stuck	stuck
	sting	stung	stung
	strike	struck	struck *or* stricken
	string	strung	strung
	swing	swung	swung
	win	won (*pronounced as if* wun)	won
	wring	wrung	wrung
12.	ĭ	ă	ă
	sit	sat *or* sate	sat
	spit	spat	spat *or* spit
13.	ĭ	ă *or* ā	ĭ *with suffix* en
	bid	bade	bidden
14.	ī	ō *or* ŏ	ō *or* ŏ
	abide	abode	abode
	shine	shone	shone
15.	ī *or* ĭ	ā	ĭ *with suffix* n *or* en
	drive	drave *or* drove	driven

	Present.	*Past Indefinite.*	*Perfect Participle.*
	ī *or* ĭ	ā	ĭ *with suffix* n *or* en
	lie	lay	lien *or* lain
	give	gave	given
16.	ī	ō	ĭ *with suffix* n *or* en
	drive	drove *or* drave	driven
	ride	rode	ridden
	rise	rose	risen
	arise	arose	arisen
	smite	smote	smitten
	stride	strode	stridden
	strive	strove	striven
	thrive	throve	thriven
	write	wrote	written
17.	ī	ou	ou
	bind	bound	bound *or* bounden
	find	found	found
	fight	fought	fought
	grind	ground	ground
	wind	wound	wound
18.	ow	ew	own
	blow	blew	blown
	crow	crew	[crowed]
	grow	grew	grown
	know	knew	known
	throw	threw	thrown
	show	[shew]* *or* showed	shown *or* showed
	[fly]	flew	[flown]
19.	u (*or* o *sounded like* u)	ă *or* ā	u (*or* o *sounded like* u)
	run	ran	run
	come	came	come
	become	became	become
20.		*Unique Forms.*	
	awake	awoke	awoke
	choose	chose	chosen
	draw	drew	drawn
	fall	fell	fallen
	hang	hung	hung
	hold	held	holden *or* held
	see	saw	seen

* A provincial form.

Present.	*Past Indefinite.*	*Perfect Participle.*
seethe	sod	sodden
shoot	shot	shot
slay	slew	slain
stand	stood	stood

253 B. Verbs in which, besides the change of the vowel sound, *d* or *t* is added as a suffix in the past indefinite tense and the perfect participle. These verbs are sometimes called *mixed* verbs, because they are conjugated partly according to the *old* and partly according to the *new* formation.

Present.	*Past Indefinite.*	*Perfect Participle.*
1. ee *or* ēā.	ĕă *or* ĕ + d *or* t	ĕ + d *or* t
bereave	bereft	bereft
creep	crept	crept
deal	dealt	dealt
dream	dreamt *or* dreamed	dreamt *or* dreamed
feel	felt	felt
flee	fled	fled
hear	heard	heard
keep	kept	kept
leave	left	left
mean	meant	meant
sleep	slept	slept
sweep	swept	swept
weep	wept	wept
2. ee *or* ea	ou *or* au (*pronounced alike*) + d *or* t	ou *or* au (*pronounced alike*) + d *or* t
beseech	besought	besought
seek	sought	sought
teach	taught	taught
3. ĕ	ō + d	ō + d
sell	sold	sold
tell	told	told
4. o *or* oe (*sounded like* oo)	ŏ + d *or* t	ŏ + d *or* t
lose	lost	lost
shoe	shod	shod
5. ing *or* ink	ought	ought
bring	brought	brought
think	thought	thought

6. Unique forms.

Present.	*Past Indefinite.*	*Perfect Participle.*
buy	bought	bought
can	could	———
catch	caught	caught
clothe	clad *or* clothed	clad *or* clothed
do	did	done
may	might	———
owe	ought	———
say	said	said
shall	should	———
will	would	———
work	wrought	wrought

254 C. Verbs which have the past indefinite of the new formation, and the perfect participle of the old formation.

Present.	*Past Indefinite.*	*Perfect Participle.*
[en]grave	[en]graved	[en]graven
hew	hewed	hewn *or* hewed
lade	laded	laden
load	loaded	laden
mow	mowed	mown
rive	rived	riven *or* rived
saw	sawed	sawn
shape	shaped	shapen *or* shaped
shave	shaved	shaven *or* shaved
shew	shewed	shewn
sow	sowed	sown *or* sowed
strew	strewed	strewn, strown, *or* strewed
swell	swelled	swollen *or* swelled
wash	washed	washen *or* washed
wax	waxed	waxen *or* waxed

255 D. Verbs in which there is a modification of the final consonant, but not of the vowel sound.

Present.	*Past Indefinite.*	*Perfect Participle.*
bend	bent	bent
build	built *or* builded	built *or* builded
gild	gilt *or* gilded	gilt *or* gilded
gird	girt *or* girded	girt *or* girded
lend	lent	lent
rend	rent	rent
send	sent	sent
spend	spent	spent
wend	went *or* wended	wended

256 E. Verbs in which there is no change.

Present.	*Past Indefinite.*	*Perfect Participle.*
burst	burst	burst
cast	cast	cast
cost	cost	cost
cut	cut	cut
hit	hit	hit
hurt	hurt	hurt
knit	knit	knit
let	let	let
put	put	put
rid	rid	rid
set	set	set
shed	shed	shed
shut	shut	shut
slit	slit	slit
split	split	split
spread	spread	spread
thrust	thrust	thrust

257 F. Anomalous Verbs.

Present.	*Past Indefinite.*	*Perfect Participle.*
am	was	been
dare	durst *or* dared	dared
go	[went*]	gone
have	had (i. e. *haved*)	had
make	made (i. e. *maked*)	made

258 In some of the regular verbs the *d* at the end of the past indefinite and perfect participle is sounded like *t*, and sometimes replaced by *t*, as *spilt* for *spilled*, *dwelt* for *dwelled*, *learnt* for *learned*, *leapt for leaped*, *pent* for *penned*.

In the verbs *lay*, *say*, and *pay*, *laid* is written for *layed*, *said* for *sayed*, and *paid* for *payed*.

ADVERB.

259 When we think of an event that takes place, or of a quality that exists in anything, we may either consider it simply and absolutely (as when we say, "The bird *flies*;" "A *large* house"); or we may also take into consideration the conditions or circumstances under which the event or quality is viewed, such as *time* (as, "The man died *yesterday*"); *place* (as "He lives *here*"); *manner* (as "The bird flies *swiftly*"); *degree* (as "The house is *very* large," "The distance is *too*

* Really derived from *wend, to wend one's way.*

great"). The words by which these conditions or circumstances are marked are called *adverbs.**

260 *Definition.* An adverb is a word which is used with verbs, adjectives, or other adverbs, to mark the conditions of time, place, manner, degree, cause, effect, &c., under which an event or attribute is viewed.

261 Adverbs are said to *modify* the meanings of the words with which they are used, that is, to mark the *mode* or *manner* in which the meaning of the words is applicable. We may express the definition conversely by saying that any word which thus modifies a verb, adjective, or adverb, is itself an adverb.

262 Adverbs are of two kinds:—1. Simple Adverbs; 2. Relative or Conjunctive Adverbs.

263 A *simple* adverb is one which does nothing more than modify the word with which it is used, as *yesterday* ("We arrived yesterday"); *now* ("I hear him now"); *hither* ("He is coming hither").

264 A *relative* or *conjunctive* adverb is one which not only modifies the meaning of some verb or adjective, but connects the clause in which it occurs with the rest of the sentence; as *when* ("Come when you are ready"); *whither* ("I know not whither he has gone").

265 A relative adverb always refers to some demonstrative word, expressed or understood, which stands to it in the same sort of relation that the *antecedent* does to a *relative pronoun*, as, "Come (*then*) *when* you are ready;" "This is *the place where* the battle was fought;" "There are (*certain*) times *when* we need help."

266 Care is necessary to distinguish connective *adverbs* from connective words which are not adverbs. Many conjunctions refer to time, place, cause, &c.; but *they do not refer to these conditions in connexion with any verb or adjective of the clause which they introduce;* but the whole of the subordinate clause has the force of an adverb attached to some word in the principal clause of the sentence, as, "He said that, *because* he believed it." Here *because* does not, by itself, modify either the verb *believed* or the verb *said*, but the clause *because he believed it* is an adverbial clause modifying the verb *said*.

267 The following words are *conjunctive* or *connective* adverbs: *When, while, where, whither, whence, why, wherein, whereby, whereon, whereat, whereout, whereafter, wherever, than,*† *as*

---

* From Latin *ad* (*to, near,* or *by*), *verbum* (word).

† *Than* and *as* are difficult words to deal with. It is a gross blunder to call *as* a relative *pronoun*. Such a sentence as "His conduct is not such as I can approve," is elliptical. At full length it would be, "His conduct is not such as (conduct would be which) I can approve." Here the adverb *as* qualifies *would be;* the adverb *as* with the verb *be* being equivalent to an adjective. The *mode* or *manner* in which a thing *is*, may represent some quality which it possesses (compare

(when it answers to *so*, *such*, or the demonstrative *as*), *that* (in some of its uses, as, "He arrived there the day *that* I left"). See also § 289.

268 Most of the relative adverbs are also used interrogatively, as, "*Where* do you live?" "Whence do you come?"

269 From the adverb *where* are formed the compounds *elsewhere*, *anywhere*, *somewhere*, *nowhere*, which have not the relative force of *where*.

270 There is an adverbial use of *the*: as, "*The* more you learn, *the* wiser you will become." Here *the* in the first clause qualifies *more*, and *the* in the second clause qualifies *wiser*. It is not clear whether *the* in the first clause should be regarded as a relative adverb (answering to *quo* in Latin), or whether the two clauses should be regarded as *co-ordinately* demonstrative, like such sentences as the proverb, "So many men, so many minds."

271 Both simple and relative adverbs admit of being classified according to the ideas of time, place, &c., which they indicate.

1. *Adverbs of Time.* Now, then, after, before, presently, immediately, when, while, as (in such sentences as "*As* I was returning, I met him)."

2. *Adverbs of Place and Arrangement.* Here, there, where, whither, wherever, whithersoever, thence, whence, wherein, whereat, whereupon, within, inside, without, backwards, firstly, secondly, &c.

3. *Adverbs of Repetition.* Once, twice, &c.

4. *Adverbs of Manner.* Well, ill, badly, how, however, than, as.

To this class belong the numerous adverbs formed from adjectives by the suffix *ly*, as, *rightly*, *virtuously*, *badly*, &c.

Terence *Phorm.* iii: 2, 42. *Sic sum. Ego hunc esse aliter credidi. Ego isti nihilo sum aliter ac fui*). Writers who make *as* a pronoun, would have to do the same with *wie* and *als* in German, and *que* in French. (*Ein solcher wie er*). It need hardly be added that sentences like, "He is the man as did this," "That is the horse as I saw yesterday," are utter abominations.

Than is commonly set down as a *conjunction*. This is a mistake. It is a conjunctive *adverb*. Compare it with the words that answer to it in other languages. *As* is the same as *als* in German, and *als* means both *as* and *than*. *Als* is unquestionably an adverb. *Quam* in Latin is an adverb, whether used interrogatively or relatively. It is the exact correlative, in form and force, of the adverb *tam*. Whether we say, *Non tam dives est quam ego*, or *Ditior est quam ego*, *quam* is the same word, and had the same force to a Roman in each case; in one case we translate it by *as*, in the other by *than*. *Que*, in French, means both *as* and *than*. All this shows that *as* and *than* are to be treated exactly on the same footing. If we say, "He writes better than I write," *than* clearly refers to *the manner* in which I write. It is therefore an adverb qualifying the verb *write*. In such a sentence as, "He does not behave as I wish him to behave," there is no difficulty. *As* of course refers to the *manner* in which I wish him to behave. It is therefore an *adverb*, qualifying the verb *behave*. The demonstrative *as* qualifies only adjectives and adverbs.

5. *Adverbs of Degree.* Very, nearly, almost, quite, much, more, most, little, less, least, all, half, any, only. (See § 87.) These are only a particular kind of Adverbs of Manner.

6. *Adverbs of Affirmation and Negation.* Yes, yea, aye, no, not.

7. *Adverbs of Cause and Effect.* Therefore, wherefore, why.

272 Adverbs are often identical in form with adjectives. Thus: "A *hard* bed," and "He hits *hard*," "*hard* by," "A *fast* runner," "He runs *fast*;" "A *quick* step," and "My pulse beats *quicker* than yours;" "A *right* action," and "It passes *right* through."

273 Some participles are occasionally used in such a way as to seem adverbs. As *exceeding great*, *passing strange*. They were originally strictly participles: and the adjective that follows them was used substantively, and was governed by them. "*Passing* strange" meant "*Passing* (surpassing) what is strange."

274 Adverbs are sometimes used after prepositions, so as to appear as if they were substantive words, as, "I have heard that *before now*," "He has changed *since then*." These must be treated as compound adverbial expressions, like *deinde* in Latin.

Comparison of Adverbs.

275 Some adverbs (like adjectives) admit of degrees of comparison.

The comparative degree of an adverb is that form of it which indicates that of two actions or qualities which are compared together, one surpasses the other with respect to some circumstance of manner or degree by which they are both attended, but in different degrees. Thus: "John reads *ill*, but Thomas reads *worse*;" "I was but *little* prepared for that event, but he was *less* prepared."

The superlative degree of an adverb is that form of it which indicates that out of several actions or qualities which are compared together one surpasses all the rest with respect to some circumstance of manner or degree by which they are all attended, but in different degrees; as, "Of all these boys, William writes the *worst*;" "John was less cautious than I, but Thomas was the *least* cautious of the three."

276 Comparative and superlative adverbs are the same in form as the corresponding adjectives. It is only some adverbs of *manner* and *degree* which admit of degrees of comparison. Adverbs in *-ly* do not form degrees of comparison, but may be qualified by *more* and *most*, like adjectives.

PREPOSITION.

277 Prepositions are words placed before substantives, by means of which we show the relation in which things, and their actions and attributes, stand to other things. In the sentence, "I saw a cloud in the sky," *in* is a preposition, and marks the relation (of place) in which the *cloud* stands to the *sky*. In the sentence, "Tuesday comes after Monday," *after* is a preposition, and shows the relation (of time) in which the *coming* of Tuesday stands with respect to Monday. In "He struck the dog on the head," *on* is a preposition, and denotes the relation of the act of *striking* to the *head*. In "The cup is full of water," *of* is a preposition, and marks the relation of the attribute *fulness* to *water*.

278 The principal relations which prepositions indicate are those of *time*, *place*, and *causality*.*

279 Things † and their actions and attributes, can only bear these relations to other *things*. Therefore a preposition can only be placed before a word that stands for a *thing*, that is, a *substantive*. (See *Introduction to Syntax*.)

280 The word *preposition* implies *placed before* (Latin, *prae*, before; *positus*, placed).

The substantive which follows a preposition is in the objective case, and is said to be governed by the preposition.

281 A preposition can connect the substantive which follows it only with a substantive, a verb, or an adjective, since these alone stand for things and their actions and attributes.

282 The following is a list of prepositions :—

abaft	along	aslant	beneath
above	amid	astride	beside
about	amidst	at	besides ‡
across	among	athwart	between
adown	amongst	atween	betwixt
afore	anent	before	beyond
after	around	behind	but §
against	round	below	by

---

* By *causality* is meant the *cause*, *reason*, or *purpose* of any action or event. When we say, *full of water*, *of* marks the *cause* of the *fulness*.

† Whatever can be made a separate object of thought is a *thing*.

‡ *Beside* has reference to place; as, "A house beside a river." *Besides* means *in addition to*; as, "Besides the profit, there is the honour."

§ Many grammars ignore this preposition, which is a genuine old word, not yet obsolete, an abbreviation of the Anglo-Saxon *butan*, = *without*. In Chaucer we find

"But meat or drinke she dressed her to lie
In a dark corner of the house alone."

The conjunction *but* used to be written *bot*. The preposition *but* is worth noticing

despite	near	since	under
down	next	through	underneath
during	nigh	throughout	up
[except]	of	till	upon
for	off	until	with
from	on	to	within
in	over	unto	without
inside	outside	toward	withal
into	[save]	towards	

283 Words like *concerning*, *respecting*, *regarding*, &c., are not prepositions. They are participles constructed elliptically to agree with some substantive understood, or else constructed impersonally.

284 Many of the above words are adverbs as well as prepositions. The mode in which they are used will always determine which part of speech they are. When they are prepositions there is always a substantive, expressed or understood, which they govern. (But compare § 274.) In, "He laid one book above the other," *above* is a preposition. In, "One was below, the other above," *below* and *above* are adverbs. *But*,* *except*, and *since*, are also used as conjunctions. *Except* and *save* are verbs in the imperative mood.

CONJUNCTION.

285 Words which unite other words or sentences are called *connective* or *conjunctive* words. Connective words are found among various parts of speech. *Who* is a connective word which is a substantive. *Which* is a connective word which is an adjective. *Whither* is a connective word which is an adverb. The name *conjunction* is applied to a particular class of connective words.

286 Conjunctions are connective words which are neither substantives, adjectives, nor adverbs.

Conjunctions may be divided into two classes:—1. Coordinative Conjunctions; 2. Subordinative Conjunctions.†

287 Co-ordinative Conjunctions are those which unite either co-ordinate clauses, that is, clauses which stand in the same relation to the entire sentence (§ 402), or words which stand in the same relation to some other word in the sentence.

---

because it is the only preposition except *to* which may be followed by the infinitive mood; as, "He did nothing *but laugh*." *But* being a preposition, it follows that such phrases as *none but he* are ungrammatical. A preposition must have the accusative case after it.

* It is not quite certain that the conjunction *but* is of the same origin as the preposition *but*. It used to be spelt *bot*.

† Most grammarians distribute conjunctions into *copulative* and *disjunctive* conjunctions. A *copulative conjunction* is *a joining word which couples together*. A *disjunctive conjunction* is a *joining word which disjoins*. A person need be very keen-sighted to see the sense or utility of this classification.

The co-ordinative conjunctions are *and*, *either*, *or*, *neither*, *nor*, *but*.

288 2. Subordinative conjunctions are those which unite *subordinate* clauses (see § 412) to the *principal* clause of a sentence. They never couple *words* only.

The Subordinative Conjunctions are *for*, *since* (expressing a reason); *as* (in the sense of since, in such a sentence as,—"*As you say so, I must believe it*), *whereas*, *because*, *if*, *whether*, *though*, *although*, *albeit*, *unless*, *but*,* *except*, *lest*, *that* (in some of its meanings), *until*.

For the further illustration of this classification the learner is referred to the Syntax.

289 The words *before*, *since*, *after*, are usually set down as conjunctions, but it is better to class them among the adverbs. In such sentences as, "He arrived before I did;" "He left soon after I did;" the conjunction *that* has in reality been omitted. We find it expressed in old-fashioned English; as, "Before that certain came from James, he did eat with the Gentiles." (*Galat*. ii. 12.) "Surely after that I was turned I repented, and after that I was instructed I smote upon my thigh." (*Jerem*. xxxi. 19.) Such constructions agree exactly with the use of *now* and *that;* as, "Now that you have come, I may take my leave." Here *now* is an adverb qualifying the verb *may* ("I may now take my leave") and *that you have come* is an adverbial clause qualifying and explaining *now*. So, in the above sentences, *after* and *before* are adverbs qualifying the main verb of the sentence, and the clause beginning with *that* (expressed or understood) is itself an adverbial clause qualifying the *after* or *before*. The construction of Latin sentences with *antequam* and *priusquam* is precisely analogous.

290 Conjunctions and adverbs occasionally appear to be correlatives, but this is only in appearance, for one part of speech cannot be the correlative of another. Thus: "*Though* you say so, *yet* I do not believe it;" *though* is a subordinative conjunction, and *yet* is an adverb qualifying the verb *believe*. In such cases the subordinative conjunctions introduce adverbial clauses, the sense of which is repeated in the adverb, and so attached more closely to the verb.

291 Some conjunctions are correlatives; as, *neither—nor*, *either—or*, *whether*.

292 Many words, which are frequently set down as conjunctions, are really simple adverbs, not having even a connective force, except in so far as every demonstrative word, which refers to something that has already been said, causes a connexion in thought,† though a mere demonstrative is not, *grammatically speaking*, a connective word. Such words as, *therefore*, *still*, *yet*, *nevertheless*, *notwithstanding*, *consequently*, *however*, *hence*, *accordingly*, *likewise*, *also*, are *adverbs*, inasmuch as they indicate

* *But*, when it is a subordinative conjunction, has a meaning different from what it has as a co-ordinative conjunction. It approaches more nearly in meaning to the preposition *but*=*without* or *except;* as, "He never tried any plan but it succeeded."

† As, "He suddenly lost all his fortune. *This* was a great blow to him."

some of the conditions or circumstances under which the predicate of the clause to which they belong is asserted of the subject.* (See further in the Syntax, under the head of *collateral sentences*, § 408.)

INTERJECTION.

293 Interjections are words which are used to express some emotion of the mind, but do not enter into the construction of sentences; as, "*Oh! O! Ah! Ha! Alas! Fie! pshaw! Hurrah! Lo!*" &c.

In written language interjections are usually followed by what is called a mark of admiration (!)

* A proper attention to the nature and use of adverbs will enable us to correct mistakes on the subject which are to be found in the grammars of most languages. Even the best Latin and Greek grammars are not free from them. Thus, *quum* in Latin is an adverb, not a conjunction, even when, for the sake of convenience, we translate it by *since*. The explanation is not that *quum* is sometimes an adverb and sometimes a conjunction, but that the Romans used a word meaning *when* in cases where we use the word *since*. *Quum* is in form and meaning the correlative of *tum*, and, like it, refers both to *time* and to *attendant circumstances*. So *ut=as, ut=how, ut=that, ut=when*, is the same part of speech in all these uses, and to a Roman ear conveyed in all cases the same fundamental meaning. The adverbial force of *ut* may be indicated by treating it as other relatives are often treated in translation; namely, by substituting for it a demonstrative with a conjunction. As *qui=and he*, so *ut=and so*. Thus, *tam validus est ut nemo eum superare possit*, "he has such and such a degree of strength, *and so* no one can overcome him." The *ut* refers to the *circumstances under which* the verb *possit* is affirmed of the subject.

COMPOSITION AND DERIVATION.

294 The words of which the English language is composed may be divided into two classes, *primary* words, and *secondary* or *derivative* words.

295 A word is a *primary* word when it does not admit of being resolved into simpler elements; as, *man*, *horse*, *run*.

A word is a *secondary* word when it is made up of significant parts, which exist either separately or in other combinations.

296 Secondary words are formed partly by *Composition*, partly by *Derivation*.

COMPOSITION.

297 A word is a *compound* word when it is made up of two or more parts, each of which is a significant word by itself; as, *apple-tree*, *tea-spoon*, *spend-thrift*.

298 All compounds admit of being divided primarily into two words; but one of these may itself be a compound word, so that the entire word may be separated into three or four words; as, *handicraftsman* (made up of *man* and *handicraft*, *handicraft* being itself made up of *hand* and *craft*); *midshipman* (made up of *man* and *midship*, *midship* being itself made up of *mid* and *ship*). In such cases the subordinate compound is usually the first of the two words into which the whole is divisible.

299 In a compound word it is the first word which modifies the meaning of the second. (The second denotes the *genus*, the first distinguishes the *species*.) *Rosebush* means a particular kind of *bush*, namely, one that bears roses. A *haycart* is a certain kind of *cart*, namely, one for carrying hay.

A.—Compound Nouns.

300 Compound Nouns may be divided into the following classes:—

1. Those which consist of a noun preceded and modified by a noun, as *haystack*, *inkstand*, *teaspoon*, *cornfield*, *turning-lathe*, *milking-stool*, *riding-whip*.*

---

* The word ending in *ing* in these compounds in the *gerund*, not the imperfect participle. (See § 200.)

2. Those which consist of a noun preceded and modified by an adjective, as *roundhead*, *bluebeard*, *freeman*, *halfpenny*, *blackbird*, *quicksilver*, *Northampton*, *Eastham*, &c.

3. Those which consist of a noun preceded by a verb, as *stopgap*, *makeweight*, *daredevil*, *spitfire*, *turncock*, &c.

This class of words is peculiar. The verb does not *modify the meaning* of the noun which follows it, but *governs* it.

4. Those which consist of a verb, preceded by a noun, as *godsend* (very rare).

5. Those which consist of a noun preceded by an adverb, as *forethought*, *foretaste*, *foresight*, *afterthought*, *afteract*, *forenoon*, *afternoon*, *afterpart*, *forepart*, *aftertaste*.

301 Such combinations as *standstill*, ("everything was at a *standstill*,") are not proper compounds, but *phrases* used as nouns. (Compare *pis-aller*, *laisser-aller*, in French.) So "an *everyday* occurrence;" "an *extempore* speech."

B.—Compound Adjectives.

302 Compound Adjectives may be arranged in the following classes:—

1. Those consisting of an adjective preceded by a noun, as *sky-blue*, *fire-new*, *pitch-dark*, *blood-red*, *grass-green*, *ankle-deep*, *ell-long*, *breast-high*, *head-strong*, *sin-ful*, *hope-ful* (and other compounds of *full* written with one *l*), *child-like*, *war-like*.

2. Verbal Adjectives formed by the suffix *d* or *ed* from compounds made up of (*a*) a noun preceded by a noun, or (*b*) an adjective preceded by a noun; as, (*a*) *hare-brained*, *ox-eyed*, *bull-necked*, *pigeon-breasted*, (*b*) *wry-necked*, *faint-hearted*, *blue-eyed*, *fair-haired*, *hot-headed*.

3. Compounds consisting of an imperfect participle, preceded by its object; as, *truth-telling*, *tale-bearing*, *all-seeing*, *heart-rending*, *wine-bibbing*, *peace-making*, *time-serving*.

4. Compounds consisting of an adjective or participle, preceded by an adverb; as, *all-powerful*, *red-hot*, *close-grained*, *up-right*, *down-right*, *ill-favoured*, *under-done*, *over-done*, *over-fed*, *well-meaning*, *out-spoken*, *new-born*.

5. Compounds consisting of a passive participle preceded by a noun, which stands to it in a kind of adverbial relation; as, *thunder-riven*, *bed-ridden*, *heart-broken*, *tempest-tossed*, *sea-borne*. (Compounds of this kind are of frequent occurrence in poetry).

6. Compounds formed by prefixing a numeral to the noun *fold*: *twofold*, *threefold*, *manifold*, *&c.*

C.—Compound Verbs.

303 Compound Verbs consist of—

1. Compounds consisting of a verb preceded by a separable adverb; as, *over-do, under-stand, over-lie, over-lap, under-go.*

2. Compounds consisting of a verb preceded by a noun, which in fact stands in the objective relation to it; as, *back-bite, ham-string.* Compounds formed on this principle are most common in the participial form. (See § 302-3.)

D.—Compound Adverbs.

304 These consist of—

1. Adverbs followed by prepositions; as, *herein, thereto, wherefore, whereby.*

2. Nouns preceded by adjectives; as, *sometimes, straightway.*

3. Nouns preceded by prepositions; as, *peradventure.*

4. Adverbs preceded by adverbs; as, *thereabout, thenceforward, whereas.*

5. Adverbs preceded by adjectives; as, *somewhere, nowhere.*

6. Some adverbs are a sort of amalgamated phrases; as, *nevertheless, moreover, howbeit, although.*

E.—Compound Prepositions.

These consist of two prepositions; as, *into, upon, throughout, within.*

DERIVATION.

305 A word is a *derived word,* or a *derivative,* when there exists some simpler word or *root,* out of which it has been formed by certain changes of letters, by the addition of prefixes or suffixes which have not an independent existence as separate words, or by the operation of both the above modes of formation at the same time.*

306 When two words are related to each other, it is sometimes evident from the form alone, which is the primary and which the derived form. Prefixes and affixes mark *derivatives,* as derivatives are not formed by the *omission* of elements already existing in a word. Thus we see at once that *bestir* is derived from *stir,* and *bondage* from *bond.*

307 But the connexion is not always so obvious. We could not tell *à priori* from the form alone whether *bond* was derived

* In the present work, this analysis is not carried to any great extent beyond the limits of the English language itself.

from *bind*, or *bind* from *bond*; whether *advice* was derived from *advise*, or *advise* from *advice*. In such cases we must be guided partly by analogy, and partly by a consideration of *the relation of the ideas represented*. Thus, as the act of *binding* precedes the existence of the *bond*, *bond* is a derivative from *bind*. As the act of *speaking* precedes and produces *speech*, the noun is derived from the verb, not the verb from the noun.*

Derived Nouns.

308 Derived Nouns are formed (A) from other nouns, (B) from adjectives, (C) from verbs.

A.—Nouns derived from Nouns.

309 (*a*) Nouns are derived from nouns by the following prefixes:—

1. *dis*; as, distaste, disfavour, disproof.

(*Dis*, though of Latin origin, has become thoroughly naturalized in English, retaining, as an English prefix, only that meaning which it has in such Latin words as *dissimilis*, *displiceo*, i. e. it negatives the meaning of the following word.)

2. *un*; as, unrest.

3. *mis*; as, misdeed, mistrust, mischance, misconduct, misrule.

This prefix (connected with the verb *to miss*) implies error or fault in the action indicated by the other part of the compound.

310 (*b*) Nouns are formed from nouns by the following suffixes:—

1. *-dom*; as, kingdom, serfdom, Christendom, earldom, thraldom, dukedom, martyrdom.

Freedom and *wisdom* are derived from adjectives.

Nouns in *-dom* are properly abstract nouns, indicating the state or condition that is implied by the primary word.

2. *-ship*; kingship, lordship, sonship, worship (i. e. *worth*ship), friendship. These are abstract nouns denoting the state or condition of the person represented by the root-noun.

3. *-hood*; manhood, knighthood, wifehood, babyhood. This termination has much the same force as the last.

4. *-red*; kindred, hatred. Abstract nouns denoting the condition or feeling implied by the primary noun.

---

* Some grammarians lay down the principle that the noun is always the primary word. This is clearly wrong. That will be named first in language which exists first in thought.

5. *-age;* bondage, mileage, village (Fr. *ville*), herbage, pottage (from *pot*), tonnage, poundage, vassalage, pilotage, vintage, bandage. (See § 316. 13.)

6. *-yer;* sawyer, lawyer, bowyer. This termination marks a person who carries on some trade or profession.

7. *-ier*, or *eer;* brigadier, grenadier (properly, a soldier who throws *grenades*), pioneer, bombardier (one who throws *bombards*, i. e. large hollow shot), musketeer, cannoneer. Words of this sort are generally military terms, and of French origin.

8. *-ry*, or *ery;* cookery, slavery, husbandry, misery, eyry (i. e. *eggery*), buffoonery, rookery, hostelry, scullery, napery (*nap-kin*), drapery (Fr. *drap*), lottery, scenery.

A few nouns of this formation are derived from adjectives; as, bravery, finery, pleasantry.

Nouns in *ry* or *ery* have a kind of *collective* force.

9. *-try;* pantry (a place for *bread*, Fr. *pain*), peltry (from *pellis=skin*), poultry (Fr. *poule*).

10. *-y;* smithy, deputy, folly (from *fool*), bastardy, baby, daddy, mammy. Some of these are diminutives.

A more numerous class of nouns in *-y* consists of those derived from nouns in *-er* or *-ar*, being usually abstract names for the act indicated by the primary noun; as, bakery, soldiery, farriery, beggary, mockery, pottery, gunnery, archery, foundry, brewery.

11. *-ion* (not Latin); million, billion, &c.; bullion, scullion, stanchion, pillion.

12. *-ow;* window (an aperture to let in *wind* or *air*), meadow, shadow.

13. *-ing* (not the gerund suffix); morning, evening.

14. *-en;* garden (connected with *yard*), maiden, kitchen (from *cook*).

15. *-el* or *le* (sometimes forming diminutives); satchel (from *sack*), kernel, hostel, barbel, trammel, spaddle (from *spade*), nozzle (from *nose*).

16. *-kin* (forming *diminutives;* that is, words which denote *a small sort* of that for which the primary noun stands); lambkin, napkin, pipkin (a little *pipe;* as, "a *pipe* of wine"), firkin (from *four*), mannikin. Also in proper names: Perkin, *i. e.* Peterkin, little Peter), Tomkin, Wilkin (from Will-iam), Hawkin (from *Hal*), Watkin (*Wat*, an abbreviation of Walter).

17. *-ling* (forming diminutives); duckling, gosling (a little *goose*), yearling, dumpling, kidling, witling, stripling (a little *strip* or *stripe*).

A few noun of this formation are derived from adjectives,

as, darling (from *dear*), fatling, firstling. *Suckling* is derived from a verb (Germ. *Säugling*).

18. *-et* (forming diminutives); billet, couplet, blanket (properly a *white* covering), owlet, jacket, pocket (a little *pock* or *poke*; Fr. *poche*), bullet (a little *bulla* or *ball*), ticket, plummet (a little piece of *lead*—*plumbus*), socket, puppet (a little *doll*; Fr. *poupée*), lancet, lappet, mallet, packet, cricket (so called from the *cricks* or *crutches* (A. S. *cricce*), i. e. *stumps* with which it is played), crotchet (from *crook*).

19. *-ock* (forming diminutives); bullock, hillock, paddock.

20. *-let* (forming diminutives); armlet, bracelet (Fr. *bras*), cutlet, streamlet, tartlet.

21. *-ess*. Feminine nouns are formed from masculine nouns by this termination:—Deaconess, shepherdess, duchess, abbess.

22. *-ine* (forming feminines); heroine, landgravine.

B.—Nouns derived from Adjectives.

311 Nouns are derived from adjectives by the addition of the following suffixes:—

1. *-ness*; dearness, redness, goodness, weakness, &c. Almost any adjective may have a noun formed from it by this suffix, which forms an abstract noun denoting the quality indicated by the adjective.

2. *-dom*; wisdom, freedom (see § 310. 1).

3. *-ship*; hardship (see § 310. 2).

4. *-hood*; likelihood (*likely*), hardihood (from *hardy*) (see § 310. 3).

5. *-th* or *-t*; dearth (*dearness*), wealth, truth, strength (from *strong*), breadth (from *broad*), length (from *long*), width, health (from *heal* or *whole*—Germ. *heil*), height (properly *highth*, from *high*), mirth (from *merry*). These are abstract nouns.

Guilt is from a noun, *guile*.

In the word *month*, *th* is not a suffix, but is radical. Comp. Germ. *Monat* and *Mond*.

6. *-ling* (see § 310. 16).

7. *-ard*; drunkard, dullard, sluggard (*sluggish* implies an adjective with a guttural at the end), wizard (from *wise*).

8. *-ry* or *-ery*; finery, bravery, pleasantry (see § 310. 8).

C.—Nouns derived from Verbs.

312 Nouns are derived from verbs (*a*) by a modification of the vowel sound (*b*) by a modification of the final consonant; (*c*) by a modification both of the vowel sound and of the final consonant; (*d*) by suffixes, with or without a change of the vowel sound.

313 *a.* **Nouns derived from verbs by a change in the vowel sound, as:—**

bond	*from*	**bind**	**food**	*from*	**feed**
stroke	„	**strike**	**dole**	„	**deal**
song	„	**sing**	**brood**	„	**breed**
drove	„	**drive**	**knot**	„	**knit**
bliss	„	**bless**	**writ**	„	**write**
scrap	„	**scrape**	**bit**	„	**bite**

314 *b.* **Nouns derived from verbs by a modification of the final consonant; as:—**

ditch	*from*	dig	advice	*from*	advise
belief	„	believe	speech	„	speak
proof	„	prove	strife	„	strive
use	„	use	girth	„	gird
abuse	„	abuse			

315 *c.* Nouns derived from verbs by a modification both of the vowel sound, and of the final consonant.

woof	*from*	weave	loss	*from*	lose
dike	„	dig	breath	„	breathe
choice	„	choose	web	„	weave
life	„	live	breach	„	break
batch	„	bake			

316 *d.* Nouns are derived from verbs by the addition of the following suffixes:—

1. *-er* (denoting the agent by whom an act is performed); digger, cutter, runner, seeker, finder, preacher, idler, &c.

2. *-ar* or *or* (having the same force as *-er*); sailor, grantor, lessor, tailor, beggar, liar.

3. *-ster* (denoting the agent, and originally a feminine termination); Brewster, Baxter or Bagster (from *bake*) spinster, gamester, punster, trickster.

One or two of this class are derived from nouns; as webster, barrister (*bar*).

4. *-ee* (marking the object of an action); nominee, assignee, lessee, committee, grantee, and feoffee.

Grandee, settee, guarantee, have a different meaning. The termination *-ee* is of French origin.

5. *-ard* or *art;* laggard, lollard, blinkard, stinkard, braggart, pollard, coward (from the verb *to cow*, as "His courage was cowed").

Nouns of this formation mostly imply a person by whom something is habitually done. They have also generally an *opprobrious* meaning.

6. *-en* or *-n;* heaven (from *heave*), main (from *may*—"might and main"), token (from a root found in German, *zeig-en*), warden.

7. *-th;* growth, stealth, ruth (from the verb *to rue*), blowth, filth (*de-file*), birth (from *bear*).

8. *-t* (often with a modification of the vowel sound).

feint (from *feign*)	weft (*weave*)
frost (*freeze*)	theft (*thieve*)
blast (German *blas-en*)	cleft (*cleave*)
sight (*see*)	drift (*drive*)
flight (*flee* or *fly*)	thrift (*thrive*)
graft (*graff*)	shrift (*shrive*)
restraint	gift (*give*)

9. *-el*, *-l*, or *-le*.

shovel	*from*	shove	shuttle	*from*	shoot
prickle	„	prick	puzzle	„	pose
treddle	„	tread	bundle	„	bind
spindle	„	spin	nipple	„	nip
spittle	„	spit	stopple	„	stop
cripple	„	creep	girdle	„	gird

10. *-ter;* laughter.

11. *er* (not denoting the agent); supper, dinner, dower (*en-dow*).

Platter (from a noun *plate*), stranger (from an adjective).

12. *-m;* team (from *tow*), seam (from *sew*), qualm (from *quail*), bloom (from *blow*).

13. *-age* (see also § 310. 5); breakage, leakage, brewage, tillage, coinage, salvage, demurrage, pillage (from the verb *pill* or *peel*, meaning to *strip*), stowage. Nouns of this formation are names either of the *act* which the verb indicates, or of what is produced by it.

14. *-y;* delivery, recovery, embroidery.

15. *-ment* (a termination of Latin origin, but naturalized in English); bewilderment, punishment, estrangement, instalment, defilement, encroachment, judgment, banishment.

16. *-lock* or *-ledge;* wedlock, knowledge.

17. *-et;* hatchet (from *hack*).

11. *-ing;* Gerunds.

Derived Adjectives.

317. Adjectives are derived (A) from nouns; (B) from other adjectives; (C) from verbs.

318. A. Adjectives are derived from nouns by means of the following suffixes:—

1. *-ed;* ragged, wretched, wicked (perhaps from *witch*, = *witched*), left-handed, long-legged, &c. (See § 302. 2).

2. *-en* or *-n* (generally denoting the *material* of which a thing is made); wooden, golden, leathern, brazen, earthen, woollen, waxen, &c.

3. *-ern:* northern, southern, eastern, western.

4. *-eous;* beauteous, duteous, bounteous, righteous, courteous, piteous.

5. *-ish;* slavish, swinish, Romish, thievish, Spanish, Gaulish, Turkish.

6. *-less;* heedless, thriftless, senseless, useless, lawless, penniless, pitiless. Adjectives of this kind are extremely common. They denote the absence of that which is indicated by the noun.

7. *-ly* (a softened form of *-like*); manly, heavenly, earthly, godly, lively, ghostly, ghastly (from *ghost*, German *geist*), beastly.

8. *-some;* quarrelsome, frolicsome, troublesome, handsome. Adjectives of this kind indicate the presence of a good deal of that which the noun denotes.

9. *-th;* the ordinal numerals, fourth, fifth, &c.

10. *-ty;* the cardinal numerals, twenty, thirty, &c.

11. *-y* (or *-ey* after a word ending in *-y*); airy, lofty, balmy, feathery, downy, dreamy, bony, clayey, hairy, stormy, earthy.

12. *-ward;* awkward (from *auke*, the left hand, a word found in old writers; as, for example, in Holland's translation of Plutarch. Aukely = awkwardly, is found in Fuller). It is doubtful, however, whether *-ward* or *-ard* is the right termination. Dryden uses *awkard*, which is also a common provincial pronunciation of the word.

Southward, northward. (It is doubtful whether these are genuine adjectives.)

319 B. Adjectives are formed from adjectives partly by prefixes, and partly by suffixes.

1. By the prefix *un* (negative); unwise, unlikely, untrue, unimpressible, unkind, &c.

2. By the prefix *-dis;* as disloyal, dishonest.

3. By the suffix *-ish* (having a diminutive force); blackish, whitish, dullish, smartish, brackish.

4. By the suffix *-some* (see § 318. 8); lightsome, wearisome, fulsome, blithesome, darksome.

5. By the suffix *-ly;* likely, southerly (*i. e.* southernly), northerly (*i. e.* northernly).

320 C. The most important class of adjectives derived from verbs consists of participles. When a participle is used as a

mere attributive adjective, it is placed *before* the noun which it qualifies; as, "A pleasing tale," "A tiring walk."

321 Adjectives are also formed from verbs:—

1. By the suffix *-y;* as sticky, sundry (from *sunder*, to separate), flabby (from *flap*).

2. By the suffix *-some* (see § 319. 4; 318. 8); tiresome, irksome, winsome.

3. By the suffix *-able;* eatable, bearable.

4. By the suffix *-tive;* talkative.

The last two suffixes are of Latin origin, but naturalized.

Derived Verbs.

322 Verbs are derived (A) from nouns, (B) from adjectives, (C) from other verbs.

A.—Verbs derived from Nouns.

Verbs are formed from nouns (*a*) by prefixes, (*b*) by suffixes, (*c*) by a modification of the vowel sound, or (*d*) by a modification of the final consonant.

323 *a.* Verbs are formed from nouns by the following prefixes:—

1. *A;* abut (from *butt*); alarm (German *Lärmen*); amuse, abash (from the root of *bashful*).

2. *Be;* becloud, befool, befriend, beguile, belie, befleck (from *fleck*, a spot), belabour, bedew, behead.

3. *En* (*em* before a labial); empower, embody, encase, encamp, encourage, encompass, enact, enslave, enshrine, enthral, &c. (This prefix is of Latin origin, but has been naturalized, so that it is used before words of Saxon origin.)

4. *Dis* (implying the removal of that which the noun indicates); disburden, disguise, dismask.

5. By the prefix *un;* unbosom, unkennel, unsex, untile.

324 *b.* Verbs are formed from nouns by the suffix *-l* or *-le*.

muffle *from* muff		nestle *from* nest	
quibble ,, quip		scribble ,, scribe	
kneel ,, knee		curdle ,, curd	
freckle ,, freck		whittle ,, whit*	
sparkle ,, spark		boggle ,, bog (perhaps)	

325 *c.* Verbs are formed from nouns by a modification of the final consonant.

calve *from* calf	bathe *from* bath
halve ,, half	soothe ,, sooth

* Used in the phrase "Not a whit," *i. e.* "Not a chip.

bulge	*from*	bulk	grease	*from*	grease
dredge	„	dregs (pl.)	prize	„	price
ap-pease	„	peace	shelve	„	shelf
delve	„	delf (*a pit*)			

326 *d.* Verbs are formed from nouns by a modification of the vowel sound; as graze (*from* grass), glaze (*from* glass), hitch (*from* hook).

B.—Verbs derived from Adjectives.

327 *a.* By the following prefixes:—

1. *en* or *em;* enable, empurple, emboss (boss = hollow), endear, embitter (see § 323. 3).
2. *be;* bedim, begrime (*from* grim).

b. By the suffix *-er;* bewilder (*from* wild), linger (*from* long).

C.—Verbs derived from Verbs.

328 *a.* Verbs are formed from verbs by the following prefixes:—

1. *a;* awake, await, abear, abide, amount, arouse, arise, amend.
2. *be;* bestride, besmear, bedabble, bedaub, befall, befit, bestir, bestow, betake, beseech (*from* seek).

The effect of this prefix is to convert an intransitive verb into a transitive one.

3. *dis;* disembody, disband, disbelieve, dispraise, disenthral, displease, disseize, distrust (see § 323. 4).
4. *mis* (see § 309. 3); mislead, misstate, misspend, misgive, misjudge.
5. *un* (negative); undo, untie, unstring, unbind.

In the case of verbs *un* is not merely a negative, but implies the *reversal* of an act already done.

6. *fore* (German *ver;* not the same as the following); foredo, forego, forbid, forgive, forswear, forget, forsake.
7. *fore* (= Lat. *prae* or *pro*); foretell, forebode, forecast, foreknow, forerun, forestal.
8. *gain* (German *gegen*, root of *against*); gainsay, gainstand, gainstrive.
9. *with* (German *wider;* not the preposition *with*); withstand, withdraw, withhold.
10. *re;* retouch, regild, rebind, rebuild (a Latin prefix, but naturalized.)

329 *b.* Verbs are formed from verbs by the following suffixes:—

1. *-er* (giving a combined diminutive and frequentative form to the verb.*

* That is, implying that the action is repeated in a petty form.

glimmer	*from*	gleam	slobber	*from*	slop
swagger	„	swag *or* sway	fritter	„	fret
			batter	„	beat
sputter	„	spit	patter	„	pat
be-spatter	„	spit	wander	„	wend.

2. *-le* or *-el* (having much the same force as *-er*).

dazzle	*from*	daze	gamble	*from*	game
settle	„	set	waddle	„	wade
snivel	„	sniff	snuffle	„	snuff
straddle	„	stride	swaddle	„	swathe
shuffle	„	shove	startle	„	start
grapple	„	grab *or* gripe	nibble	„	nip
grovel	„	grope	draggle	„	drag
dribble	„	drip	crumple	„	crimp
wrinkle	„	wring	crackle	„	crack.

3. *-on.* Reckon, blazon.
4. *-ish.* Burnish, banish.
5. *-y.* Sully (*from* soil), worry (*from* wear).

330 *c.* Verbs are formed from other verbs by a modification of the final consonant; as, wrench (*from* wring), drench (*from* drink), dredge * (*from* drag), watch (*from* wake), dodge (*from* dog, "to *dog* a person's steps"), hatch (*from* hack).

331 *d.* Verbs are formed from other verbs by a modification of the vowel sound.

fell	*from*	fall	roost	*from*	rest
raise	„	rise	lay	„	lie
set	„	sit	drip	„	drop
chip	„	chop	droop	„	drop
sip	„	sop	dun	„	din.
sniff	„	snuff			

Collateral Forms.

332 In the case of nouns, adjectives, and verbs, we often find collateral forms, differing slightly, but not (apparently) derived one from the other; as:—

smash	*and*	mash	hurl	*and*	whirl
splash	„	plash	scuffle	„	shuffle
swag	„	wag	scabby	„	shabby
smelt	„	melt	skirt	„	shirt
squash	„	quash	mark	„	march (*a boundary*)
squench	„	quench			
screech	„	creak	lurk	„	lurch

* See also § 325, where a different etymology is suggested.

stumble	*and*	tumble	pouch	*and*	poke (*or* pocket)
slash	„	lash	scot (*in* *scot free*)	„	shot
bark	„	barge	pick	„	peck
bank	„	bench	seek	„	beseech
stench	„	stink	beam	„	boom
clot	„	clod	desk	„	dish (*discus*, *G. Tisch*)
sneak	„	snake	state	„	estate
stop	„	estop	strange	„	estrange
spy	„	espy	crimp	„	shrimp
stark	„	starch			

Derived Adverbs.

333 1. Adverbs are formed from nouns or adjectives by the prefix *a*. Abed, asleep, aboard, aground, ahead, astern, adrift, afloat, afoot, agape, aghast (*from* ghost), astride, awry, aloud, astray, along. Some of the above seem to be compounds of the preposition *at* and a noun.

2. Adverbs are formed by the prefix *be;* as, *betimes*.

3. Adverbs are formed from nouns by the prefix *to* (meaning *this*.) To-night, to-day, to-morrow.

4. Adverbs are formed from adjectives by the suffix *-ly*. Largely, sweetly, softly, slowly, sharply, &c. &c.

5. A few adverbs are formed by the suffix *-ward* or *-wards*. Northwards, forward, backward.

6. Adverbs of repetition are formed from numerals by the suffix *-ce*. Once, twice, thrice.

Derived Prepositions.

334 Derived Prepositions are formed by means of the following prefixes :—

1. *a*. Amid, among (*mingle*), along, around, against.

2. *be*. Besides, behind, before, beneath (*nether*), below, between (i.e. *by two*).

LATIN PREFIXES.

335 The following prefixes are found in words of Latin origin. Most of them are prepositions or adverbs :—

1. *a*, *ab*, *abs* (from or away). Avert, abduction, abstract.

2. *ad* (to), found also in the forms *ac*, *al*, *an*, *ap*, *as*, *at*, according to the consonant that follows it. Accede, allude, announce, appear, assent, attend, aspect, aspire.

3. *am* or *amb* (round). Amputate, ambiguous.

4. *ante* or *anti* (before). Antediluvian, antecessor, anticipate.

5. *circum* or *circu* (round). Circumlocution, circuit.

6. *con* (with), or (when modified by the next consonant) *com*, *col*, *co*. Conduct, contend, compact, compare, collusion, coheir.

7. *contra* (against), often Anglicized into *counter*. Contravene, counteract.

8. *de* (down, from). Denote, describe, descend.

9. *di*, *dis*, or *dif* before *f* (apart, in different directions). Dilute, dissent, differ.

10. *ex*, *e*, *ec*, or *ef* (out of). Extrude, educe, effusion.

11. *extra* (beyond some boundary, outside). Extravagant, extradition.

12. *in* (in, into, on, *or* against), sometimes modified into *im*, *il*, or *ir*. Induct, impel, illusion, irruption.

13. *in* (not), modified as above. Insecure, improper, illegitimate, irrational.

14. *inter* (among, between). Interest, interpose.

15. *intro* (within). Intromit, introduce.

16. *ob* or *obs* (against), modified into *oc*, *op*, *of*. Obdurate, obstinate, occur, offend.

17. *per* or *pel* (through). Perpend, pellucid.

18. *post* (after). Postpone.

19. *prae* or *pre* (before). Praelection, precentor, presume.

20. *praeter* (past). Praetermit.

21. *re* or *red* (back). Relent, reduce, reduction.

22. *retro* (backwards). Retrograde, retrospect.

23. *se* (apart). Seduce, separate.

24. *sub* (under), modified to *suc*, *suf*, or *sur*. Subdue, suffuse, succeed, re-surrection.

25. *subter* (beneath). Subterfuge.

26. *trans* or *tra* (across *or* beyond). Translate, tradition.

27. *ultra* (beyond). Ultramontane.

GREEK PREFIXES.

336 The following prefixes are found in words of Greek origin :—

1. *a* or *an* (not). Anarchy.

2. *amphi* (on both sides, *or* round). Amphibious, amphitheatre.

3. *ana* (up). Anabasis, anatomy, analogy.

4. *anti* (against). Antithesis, antipathy.

5. *apo* (from). Apogee, apology.

6. *cata* (down). Catalepsy, catastrophe.

7. *dia* (through, among). Diameter, diaphanous.

8. *en* or *em* (in *or* on). Emphasis, enema.

9. *endo* (within). Endosmose.
10. *epi* (upon). Epilogue, epitaph.
11. *ec* or *ex* (out of). Exodus, ecstatic.
12. *exo* (outside). Exosmose.
13. *hyper* (over). Hyperbolical.
14. *hypo* (under). Hypotenuse, hypothesis.
15. *meta* (implying change). Metamorphosis.
16. *para* (beside). Parabola, paraphrase.
17. *peri* (round). Peristyle, perimeter.
18. *syn* (with, together), modified into *sym* or *syl*. Syndic, syntax, symbol, syllogism, syllable.
19. *eu* (well). Euphony, eulogy.

LATIN SUFFIXES.

337 The following suffixes are found in words of Latin origin:—

a.—Noun Suffixes.

1. *acy* (Lat. *acia*). Fallacy.
2. *aster* (forming diminutives). Poetaster.
3. *ance* or *ancy* (Lat. *antia*). Constancy, constance, parlance.
4. *ency* or *ence* (Lat. *entia*). Credence.
5. *olence* or *ulence* (Lat. *olentia* or *ulentia*). Violence, virulence, corpulence, somnolence.
6. *ion* (Lat. *io*, in nom. case). Religion, legion.
7. *tion* or *sion* (Lat. *tio* or *sio*, in nom. case, derived from perfect participles). Scansion, detention, election, monition.
8. *tude* (Lat. *tudo*). Latitude, fortitude.
9. *ture* or *sure* (Lat. *tura* or *sura*, derived from perfect participles). Juncture, tonsure.
10. *ice* (Lat. *itia* or *itium*). Justice, solstice.
11. *ty* or *ity* (Lat. *tas* or *itas*). Dignity, security, ability.
12. *ment* (Lat. *mentum*). Discernment.
13. *mony* (Lat. *monia*). Parsimony, acrimony.
14. *or* or *our* (Lat. *or*). Amour, ardour, clamour.
15. *t* or *te* (Lat. *tum*). Fact, date, com-pact.
16. *bule* (Lat. *bulus* or *bulum*). Vestibule.
17. *cule*, *cle*, *ule*, or *le*. (Lat. *culus*, *cula*, or *culum*, *ulus*, *ula*, *ulum*, *lus*, *la*, *lum*), forming diminutives. Animalcule, corpuscule, part-i-cle, radicle, globule.
18. *ple* (Lat. *pulus*). Maniple.
19. *sor*, *tor*, and *trix*, *f.* (marking the agent). Sponsor, victor, executrix.

338 **b.—Adjective Suffixes.**

1. *al* (Lat. *alis*). Carnal, venal, regal.
2. *ar* (Lat. *aris*). Solar, polar.
3. *ary* (Lat. *arius*). Binary, plenary, auxiliary.
4. *an* or *ane* (Lat. *anus*). Pagan, urban, mundane.
5. *ene* (Lat. *enus* and *oenus*). Terrene, obscene.
6. *ine* (Lat. *inus*). Vaccine, marine.
7. *ian* (Lat. *ianus*). Christian.
8. *ible* or *ble* (Lat. *ibilis, bilis*). Forcible, amiable, able.
9. *id* (Lat. *idus*). Fervid, horrid.
10. *ic* (Lat. *icus*). Gastric, concentric.
11. *il* or *ile* (Lat. *ilis*). Civil, futile.
12. *y* (Lat. *ius*). Amatory, cursory, illusory.
13. *ous* or *ose* (Lat. *osus*). Gibbous, curious, verbose.
14. *aceous* (Lat. *aceus*). Herbaceous, crustaceous.
15. *olent* or *ulent* (Lat. *olentus* or *ulentus*). Virulent, turbulent, violent.
16. *tive* or *sive* (Lat. *tivus* or *sivus*). Cursive, furtive.
17. *ant* or *ent* (Lat. *ans, ens*, nom. case, participle). Extant, verdant, ardent.
18. *te* or *se* (Lat. *tus* or *sus*, pass. part.) Irate, concrete, erudite, sparse, diffuse.

c.—Verb Suffixes.

339 There are two principal modes in which verbs are formed in English from Latin verbs. One mode is by taking simply the crude form of the infinitive mood or present tense, without any suffix; as *intend, defend, manumit.* Sometimes mute *e* makes its appearance after a long vowel, as in *incline, opine, revise.* The second mode is to adopt as a suffix the termination of the perfect participle passive (slightly modified), *t, s, ate*, or *ite* (Lat. *tus, sus, atus, itus*); as create (from *creatus*), conduct (from *conductus*), credit (from *creditus*), expedite (*expeditus*), incense (from *incensus*).

GREEK SUFFIXES.

340 The following suffixes mark words of Greek origin :—

a.—Noun Suffixes.

1. *sm* or *ism.* Sophism, spasm, aneurism.
2. *st* or *ist.* Iconoclast, panegyrist, sophist.
3. *sis.* Crisis, phthisis, emphasis.
4. *e.* Catastrophe.
5. *y.* Anatomy, analogy, monarchy.

6. *ic* or *ics*, or *tic*. Logic, rhetoric, ethics, arithmetic.
7. *ad* or *id*. Iliad, Aeneïd, Thebaïd, Troad.
8. *isk* (diminutives). Asterisk, obelisk.
9. *ma*. Diorama, enema.
10. *tre* or *ter*. Centre, meter, theatre.

b.—Verb Suffix.

ize. Baptize, criticise.

341 The following examples will illustrate the way in which groups of derivatives cluster round a common origin.

Root, mun-us (*share, portion*).

munition
muniment
commune
communicate
communicant
communicable
communicability
communication
communicative
communicativeness
communicator
communion
community
excommunicate
incommunicable
immunity.

Root, fac-io (fec *or* fic, *make*).

defect
defection
defective
defectively
deficient
deficiency
effect
effective
effectively
effectless
effector
effectual
effectually
effectuate
efficacy
efficacious
efficaciously
efficient
efficiently
efficiency
infect
infectious
infection
sufficient
sufficiency
proficient
proficiency, &c.

SYNTAX.

342 The word *syntax* means *arrangement.* (Greek *syn*, together, *taxis*, arrangement). The rules of syntax are statements of the various ways in which the words of a sentence are related to each other.

343 A sentence is a collection of words of such kinds, and arranged in such a manner, as to make some complete sense.

By "making some complete sense" is meant, that *something is said about something.*

344 It is plain, therefore, that every sentence must consist of two essential parts: 1st, that which stands for what we speak about: 2nd, that which is said about that of which we speak.

345 The word which stands for that about which we speak, is called the *subject* of the sentence, or the *subject of a sentence* is the word that stands for the *subject of discourse.* (Note.—The *subject of a sentence* is a *word*; the *subject of discourse* is a *thing*).

346 That part of a sentence which consists of what is said about the subject of discourse consists of two portions or elements. One part represents some idea which we attach in thought to the subject of discourse. This is called the Predicate: the other part consists of the means by which the predicate is connected with the subject. This part is called the copula (or *link*). That act of the mind by which the notion expressed by the predicate is joined to the notion expressed by the subject, is called a *judgment.* The result of a judgment is a *thought.* The expression of a thought is a *sentence.*

347 The grammatical copula in every sentence consists of the *personal inflections* * of the verb. In the sentence, "Time flies," the subject is *Time;* that which is predicated or asserted of *time*, is *flying:* the personal termination of the verb *flies* unites this idea to the subject. In the sentence, "The rose is red," the subject is *rose;* that which is predicated of the rose is, *being red;* the personal inflection by which *is* becomes a third person singular, is the copula. If we say, "The journey was pleasant," what we assert of the journey is its

* That is, the inflections by which number and person are marked, and by which the verb is made a *finite* verb.

having been pleasant, it being clear that the notion of *time* belongs to the predicate.

Inasmuch as the personal terminations of a verb have no existence apart from the verb itself, it is usual (and convenient) in grammar to treat the copula as a part of the predicate. Thus in the sentence, "Time flies," *time* is called the subject, and *flies* the predicate. In the sentence, "The rose is red," *rose* is called the subject, and *is red* the predicate. This mode of speaking is slightly inaccurate (at least with reference to the use of the word *predicate* in *Logic*); but it must be understood that, henceforth, in using the word *predicate*, we mean *the predicate and copula combined.**

348 In grammar, the terms *subject* and *predicate* are used in a more restricted sense than in Logic. In Logic, the *subject* of a proposition is *the entire description* of that which is spoken of: the *predicate* is *all that is employed* to represent the idea which is connected with the subject. Thus in "The father of Charles I. was king of England," the subject is "the father of Charles I.;" the predicate is "king of England." But in grammar, the single noun *father* is called the subject, and *king* the predicate, the words connected with *father* and *king* being treated as enlargements of the subject and predicate.

---

* All abstract sciences labour under the disadvantage of having to employ terms in a rather harsh and arbitrary manner; as, in Algebra, *addition* may be (arithmetically speaking) a *subtraction*, and *multiplication* may be, for example, taking *two-thirds* of a quantity. So in Logic, the terms *predicate* and *copula* involve a little difficulty. In the proposition, "The earth is a globe," it would be said that the predicate (*praedicatum* or *thing asserted*) is *a globe*, that is, *what we assert* of the earth is, *a globe*. This mode of speaking requires a technical meaning to be put upon it before it has any sense. More strictly in accordance with the meaning of the language, it should be said that *what we assert*, or the *thing asserted* about the earth is, its *being a globe*. The grammatical use of the word predicate, as it is explained in the text, is in strict accordance with its real meaning. Again, with regard to the copula, although for logical purposes it is necessary to throw propositions into a form in which each term is *substantive* in its nature, and the two terms are connected by some finite form of the verb *be*, it is demonstrably wrong to say that the copula of every proposition is a part of the verb *be* (*is, are, was, &c.*) For "Time flies" is a perfect proposition *in its present form*, and yet involves no part of the verb *be* either expressed or understood. It is true that the proposition will assume a different shape when reduced to its technical logical form; but if that form involves any element that does not exist in the original proposition, it is plain that it is not its exact equivalent. Again, the so-called *copula* in Logic is really more than a copula, or *link* by which two ideas are connected. If we have a finite form of the verb *be* (and without a finite form there can be no predication), we may ignore, but we cannot eliminate, either the root-meaning of the verb, or the *idea of time*. *Is* and *are* involve the notion of present time as essentially as *was* and *were* that of past time. This little difficulty, however, is quietly swallowed by logicians who tell us that the copula, as such, has no relation to time. The fact is that technical logic ought to have some abstract sign for the copula, something like = in mathematics, and not the verb *be* at all. Now if we put together the two facts that there may be a perfect proposition without the verb *be*, and that when that verb is used there is no proposition unless the verb *be* is in a *finite form*, the inference is plain that the real copula consists of those inflections by which a verb assumes a finite form. This justifies the mode in which the matter is stated in the text, and which, while it differs somewhat from what is generally set down in grammars, will be found to introduce a little more harmony between grammatical theory and grammatical practice.

349 Whenever we speak of anything, we make it a separate object of thought. A word that can stand for anything which we make a separate object of thought is called a *substantive*.

350 It follows therefore that the *subject* of a sentence must be a *substantive*.

351 An adjective is not the *name* of anything. It does not stand for a separate object of thought. An adjective therefore can never be the subject of a sentence.

352 Substantives may be arranged in the following classes:—

1. Nouns.
2. The Substantive Pronouns (see § 131).
3. The Infinitive Mood (see § 187).
4. Gerunds, or Verbal Nouns (see § 200).
5. Any word which is itself made the subject of discourse, every word being *a name for itself*.

353 The only part of speech by means of which we can make an assertion is the verb (see § 173). The essential part of every affirmation respecting a subject of discourse is a finite verb (*i. e.* a verb in some one of its *personal* forms, not the infinitive mood or participle).

354 The subject and the verb are the cardinal points of every sentence. All other words in a sentence are attached directly or indirectly to one or other of these two. There cannot be a complete sentence without a subject and a verb (§ 344), and a complete sentence may be formed containing nothing but a subject and a verb.

355 When a sentence contains only one subject and one finite verb, it is said to be a *simple* sentence.

When a sentence contains not only a principal subject and its verb, but also other clauses which have subjects and verbs of their own, the sentence is said to be *compound*.

The subject of a compound sentence may be an entire clause.

356 The subject of a sentence stands for some object of thought: the predicate denotes some fact or idea which we connect with that object, and the union between the two is effected by the copula. But this union may be viewed in more ways than one.

1. When it is our intention to declare that the connexion which is indicated between the subject of discourse and the idea denoted by the predicate does exist, the sentence is *affirmative;* * as, "Thomas left the room."

---

* A *negative* sentence is only a particular variety of affirmative sentence. If we deny that John is here by saying, "John is not here," we *affirm* that John *is not here*.

2. When it is our wish to know whether the connexion referred to subsists, the sentence is interrogative; as, "Did Thomas leave the room?"

[It is in this way that relative pronouns come to be used interrogatively. When we say, "Who did that?" it is equivalent to saying, "Name to me the person who did that." *Who did that*, is in each case a clause describing a person; but when used *relatively*, it is used with the intention of declaring that the description does apply to some person already named; when used interrogatively, it implies a wish to know the person to whom the description applies.]

3. When we express our *will* that the connexion between the object of thought described by the subject, and that which is expressed by the predicate should subsist, the sentence that results is called an imperative sentence; as, "Thomas, leave the room."

4. When we express a *wish* that the connexion may subsist, the sentence that results is called an optative sentence; as, "May you speedily recover."

In some imperative sentences the *will* is so weakened as to become simply a *wish;* as, "Defend us, O Lord." "Sing, heavenly muse." The *grammatical* force of the sentence, however, is not altered by this.

357 In all the above-named kinds of sentences, the *grammatical* connexion between the subject and the verb is the same. It is sufficient, therefore, to take one as a type of all. The affirmative sentence is the most convenient for this purpose.

RELATION OF WORDS TO ONE ANOTHER.

358 The modes in which the various words of a sentence are related to each other may be classed as follows:—1. The Predicative Relation. 2. The Attributive Relation. 3. The Objective Relation. 4. The Adverbial Relation.

359 1. **The Predicative Relation** is that in which the predicate of a sentence stands to its subject. In the sentence, "The boy ran away," the verb *ran* is in the predicative relation to the subject *boy*. In the sentence, "The ball is round," not only the verb *is*, but the adjective *round*, which belongs to the predicate, is said to be in the predicative relation to the subject *ball*.

360 2. **The Attributive Relation.** When we speak of anything, and connect with it the idea of some attribute that it possesses, or some circumstance respecting it, *assuming* the connexion, but not *asserting* it, the word or phrase by means of which the attribute is indicated, is said to stand in the *attributive* relation to the word which denotes the thing

spoken of. Thus in "Wise men sometimes act foolishly," the adjective *wise* stands in the attributive relation to the noun *men*. The attribute which it denotes is *assumed* to belong to the men, but it is not *asserted* of them. If we say "The men are wise," then *wise* is in the predicative relation to *men*. If we say, "Socrates was wise," *wise* is in the predicative relation to *Socrates*. If we say "Socrates was a wise man," then *wise* stands in the attributive relation to the word *man*.

361 As an attribute can only belong to a thing, it is only to substantives that words can stand in the attributive relation.

362 This attributive relation may be held by—

1. An adjective or participle; as, "*A large apple, many men*;" "the soldier, *covered with wounds*, still kept his ground."

2. By a noun in apposition to the substantive; as, "*John Smith, the baker*, said so."

3. By a substantive in the possessive case; as, "My *father's* house;" "*My* mother;" "*John's* book;" "The man *whose* house was burnt down," &c.

4. By a substantive preceded by a preposition; as, "The inventor *of this machine*;" "The uncle *of that boy*;" "The trees *in the garden*;" "A horse *for riding*;" "A mistake *to be avoided*." [N.B. In its grammatical relations the infinitive mood is a substantive. The infinitive mood in the preceding sentence is, *be avoided*.]

5. By an adjective clause.

362* Strictly speaking, adverbs cannot be attached to nouns. Nevertheless we find such phrases as, "*The house here* belongs to me." "*The church there* is a fine one." These constructions are in fact *elliptical*, a word or phrase denoting *being* is to be supplied: "The house (*being*, or *which is*) here," &c. (just as, in Greek, οἱ νῦν ἄνθρωποι is οἱ νῦν ὄντες ἄνθρωποι). As the mention of a thing presupposes its *being*, the omission of that which indicates this idea is very easy. Adverbs used in this way may be said to be in the *quasi-attributive* relation to the noun.

363 Adjectives must always be either in the attributive, or in the predicative relation to some substantive expressed or understood. Hence the rule of syntax, that "An adjective must always qualify (or agree with) some substantive expressed or understood."

364 When a word is in the attributive or predicative relation to a substantive, it must agree with it in number, gender, and case, if it is capable of expressing those distinctions by its form; as, "*This man*;" "*These men*;" "*He is the testator*;" "*She is the testatrix*;" "*Romulus and Remus were the founders of Rome*." One application of this principle is that the verb *be* takes the same case after it as before it.

365 Words which stand in the attributive relation to a substantive should (in English) be placed next it, except when the attributive is qualified by an adverb or adverbial phrase.*

366 3. **The Objective Relation.** When a verb, participle, or gerund denotes an action which is directed towards some object, the word denoting that object stands in the *objective relation* to the verb, participle, or gerund. Thus, in "The dog bites the boy," *boy* is in the objective relation to *bites*. In, "Seeing the tumult, I went out," *tumult* is in the objective case to *seeing*. In, "Hating one's neighbour is forbidden by the Gospel," *neighbour* is in the objective relation to the gerund *hating*.

367 As an action can be exerted only upon a *thing*,† it is only a *substantive* that can stand in the objective relation to a verb, participle, or gerund. An adjective can never be the object of a verb.

368 When an infinitive mood is used after another verb, it stands to the latter in the objective relation, whether preceded by *to* or not.

369 The objective relation is not indicated by prepositions. except in the case of the infinitive mood. In declinable words the objective relation is indicated by the use of the objective case.

370 The objective relation is expressed by the grammatical rule, that "transitive verbs, with their participles and gerunds, govern nouns and pronouns in the objective case."

In compound sentences an entire clause may be in the objective relation to a verb, participle, or gerund.

371 Grammarians generally include, under the head of the objective relation, the relation of a substantive to a preposition by which it is governed. Thus, in "He went to London," *London* would be said to be in the objective relation to *to*. This is objectionable, as the relation is not really the same. It would be better to invent a new name for it, and call it the *postpositional relation*. Practically it is sufficient to say that the substantive is *governed* by the preposition.

372 4. **The Adverbial Relation.** When a verb or adjective is used to point out some attribute of a thing, or make some assertion respecting it, it is often necessary to *qualify* the

---

* The following sentence, therefore, is faulty:—"The country—beyond which the arts cannot be traced of civil society or domestic life." (Johnson: *Rasselas.*)

† That is, what we can make a separate object of thought.

meaning of the verb or adjective; that is, to point out the conditions of manner, time, place, degree, or circumstance under which the verb or adjective is applicable. The words that are used with the verb or adjective to point out these conditions are said to stand to it in the *adverbial relation.*

373 This adverbial relation may be sustained—1. By an adverb (see § 259); as, "He fought *bravely.*" "I set out *yesterday.*" "He is *very* industrious."

2. By a substantive preceded by a preposition; as, "He is sitting *on a stool.*" "He is fond *of reading.*" "He killed the bird *with a stone.*"

As a verb in the infinitive mood is virtually a substantive, we frequently get adverbial adjuncts consisting of a verb in the infinitive preceded by *to*. *E. g.* "This coat is too good *to give away.*" Here *to give away* is in the adverbial relation to the adverb *too.* "He is a foolish man *to throw away such a chance.*" Here *to throw away*, &c. is in the adverbial relation to *foolish.*

3. By a noun (qualified by some attributive word) used in the sense of an adverb; as, "He arrived *last night.*" "We see him *every day.*"

4. By substantives in the objective case, before which some such preposition as *to* or *for* may be understood, and which in Latin, Greek, or German would be in the dative case; as, "Give *me* (i. e. *to me*) the book. "I will sing *you* (i. e. *for you*) a song." "Do *me* (i. e. *for me*) the favour," &c. This use of the objective case may be called the *adverbial adjective.* It is, perhaps, under the head of the *adverbial relation* that we should class such anomalous passive constructions as, "He was taught *his lesson.*" "He was paid *his bill.*" "He was promised *a new coat,*" &c., where an objective case seems to be governed by a passive verb. The accusative case in Latin is often used adverbially to define or limit the range within which the meaning of the verb is applicable. That the above are not examples of the proper *objective* relation is evident.

5. By a substantive (accompanied by some attributive adjunct) in the nominative absolute; as, "*The sun having risen,* we commenced our journey." "*He being absent,* nothing could be done."

6. By an adverbial clause.

374 Adverbs themselves admit of limitation or qualification as regards *degree;* as, "He writes *very badly.*" "He will be here *almost immediately.*"

375 When a noun stands in either the predicative or the attri-

butive relation to another substantive, it may have words standing to it in the adverbial relation; as, "Napoleon, lately Emperor of the French."

376 It appears, therefore, that words may stand in the adverbial relation to any words which are themselves in the predicative, attributive, or adverbial relation to other words.

377 Words or phrases which stand in the adverbial relation to others are called adverbial adjuncts. The greater part of them are included in the following classification:—

1. *Adverbial adjuncts of Time.*—Now, then, when, yesterday, last year, &c.

2. *Adverbial adjuncts of Place.*—Here, where, whither, in the house, yonder, &c.

3. *Adverbial adjuncts of Manner.*—Well, slowly, thus, as, so, perhaps, probably, in which way, &c.

4. *Adverbial adjuncts of Degree.*—Very, almost, much, more, most, &c.

5. *Adverbial adjuncts of Cause.*—Therefore, wherefore, whereby, on this account, &c.

6. *Adverbial adjuncts of Consequence.*—As, "He that sweareth *to his own hurt*," &c. "*To his eternal disgrace* he broke the compact," &c.

SUBJECT AND PREDICATE.

378 As both the subject and the verb of a sentence are spoken of the same thing (the subject naming or denoting it, and the verb making some assertion respecting it), they must agree with each other in those points which they have in common, otherwise there would be a mutual contradiction. The points which they have in common are *number* and *person*.

379 Hence the rule that "A verb must agree with its subject* in number and person."

380 The subject of a verb in English is always put in the nominative case.

381 Thus the predicative relation is indicated partly by the

* It is common to say that a verb must agree with its *nominative case* in number and person. This mode of speaking is incorrect. It confounds a *substantive* with a *case*. A *case* of a substantive is a certain *form* of it; but it is obviously nonsense to talk of a verb agreeing with *a form* of a substantive. In the sentence, "I wrote the letter," *I* is not a *nominative case*, but a *substantive in the nominative case*. Through this mischievous habit of treating *nominative case* as synonymous with *subject*, beginners in Latin, when parsing dependent sentences, are constantly betrayed into the absurdity of speaking of the subject of the dependent verb as being in the *accusative* case because it is the *nominative* to the verb in the infinitive mood.

subject of the verb being in the nominative case, and partly by the verb indicating by its inflection the same number and person as the substantive which is its subject.

382 There is, however, an exception to this rule. The relation of the verb to the subject is often modified to suit the *sense* of the words rather than their *form*. Hence a noun in the singular number which denotes a *multitude* (as *crowd*, *senate*, *army*, *flock*), may have its verb in the plural number, when the idea to be kept in view is not the *multitude viewed as one whole*, but the *individuals* of which the multitude is composed. As, "The multitude were of one heart and one mind." But we should say, "The army *was led* into the detile," because we then speak of the army *as a whole*.

383 The verb is put in the plural number when it has for its subject two or more nouns in the singular coupled by the conjunction *and;* as, "John and Thomas were walking together."

384 In English every finite verb must have a subject in the nominative case expressed or understood. It is only in the case of the imperative mood that the subject can be understood. Such a sentence as, "That is the man whom I heard was ill," is faulty because the verb *was* is left without a subject; the relative pronoun, which ought to be the subject, being wrongly put in the objective case.

Subject.

385 The subject of a sentence may be simple, compound, or complex.

386 The subject of a sentence is *simple* when it consists of a single substantive; as, "*I* love truth;" "*men* are mortal;" "*Cæsar* conquered Gaul." (See § 352.)

387 The subject of a sentence is *compound* where it consists of two or more substantives coupled together by the conjunction *and;* as, "Cæsar and Pompey were rivals." "You and I will travel together." *

---

* Many grammarians insist that in cases of this kind we are to regard the sentence as a contraction of two co-ordinate sentences joined by *and*. This explanation might do very well for such a sentence as, "John and William are eleven years old;" that is, "John is eleven years old and William is eleven years old;" but it is simply absurd when applied to such a sentence as "Two and three make five," or, "He and I are of the same age." What is the sense of "He is of the same age and I am of the same age"? Be it observed, *we have no right to alter the phraseology of the predicate*. In any case it is a mistake to attempt to push *grammatical* analysis beyond the natural limits of *verbal expression*.

Similar remarks apply to the case of two *objects of a verb*, or two nouns after a preposition, when they are coupled by the conjunction *and;* as, "He drank a glass of brandy and water."

388 The subject of a sentence is *complex*, when it consists of a phrase or quotation; as, "'England expects every man to do his duty,' was Nelson's watchword."

389 The subject of a sentence is said to be *enlarged*, when it has any attributive adjunct attached to it (*see* § 360, 362); as, "*This tree* is dead." "*The man* told a lie." "*A horse* has just passed." "*Good men* love virtue." "*Edward the Black Prince* did not succeed his father." "*John's coat* is torn." "*The defenders of the city* were slain." "*The brave old man* died maintaining his innocence." "*The general, having reviewed his troops*,* advanced to meet the enemy."

Predicate.

390 The predicate of a sentence is either simple or complex.

391 The predicate of a sentence is simple when the notion to be conveyed is expressed by a simple tense of a finite verb; as, "Virtue *flourishes*." "Time *flies*." "I *love*."

392 Many verbs do not make complete sense by themselves, but require some other word to be used with them to make the sense complete. Such verbs are *be, become, grow, call, be called, think, deem*, &c. To say, "The horse is," "The light becomes," or "I think the man," makes no sense. It is requisite to use some other word (either a substantive or an adjective) with the verb; as, "The horse *is black*." "The light *becomes dim*." "The danger *becomes imminent*." "William the Norman *became King of England*." "I *think* the man *insane*." "I *believe* the prisoner *to be guilty*." "I *wish* you *to go away*." "I *command* you *to stay*." "I *dare* you *to strike me*." Verbs of this kind are called *Verbs of incomplete Predication*, and the words used with them to make the predication complete are called † the *complement of the predicate*.

393 The predicate of a sentence is complex when it consists of a verb of incomplete predication accompanied by its complement.

394 When a verb of incomplete predication is passive or intransitive, the complement of the predicate stands in the predicative relation to the subject of the sentence; as, "He is called John." "The wine tastes sour." "He feels sick."

395 The complement of the predicate in these cases is spoken of

---

* Observe, that when a participle is in the attributive relation to a substantive, it may have words in the objective or adverbial relation to itself.

† In this work (and, I may add, in a passage in Arnold's English Grammar, which I had not noticed before writing the above. C. P. M.)

the subject, and must therefore agree with the subject in all that they can have in common. Hence the rule that the verbs *be, become, feel, be called*, &c., take the same case after them as before them.

396 When the verb is transitive, the complement of the predicate usually stands in the attributive relation to the object of the verb; as, "He dyed the cloth red." "She called the man a liar." But this is not the case when the complement of the predicate is a verb in the infinitive mood.

397 A predicate is enlarged when the verb has words standing to it in the *objective* or the *adverbial* relation.

a. Enlargement by means of an object. "He struck *William.*" "He fears *God.*" "He called *Henry* a liar."

b. Enlargement by means of an adverb or adverbial phrase.—"The boy runs *fast.*" "I arrived *yesterday.*" "He walked *across the field.*" "He sits *on a chair.*" "The book was given *to me.*" "He hopes *for* * *success.*"

Of course these two modes of enlarging a predicate may be repeated, or combined; as, "Give *me the book.*" "He walked *ten miles yesterday.*"

398 Adverbs and adverbial phrases thus used are called *adverbial adjuncts* to the predicate. (See § 271.)

399 The object of a verb, and the complement of a predicate, may be enlarged by words standing to them in the objective, the attributive, or the adverbial relation.

a. Enlargement of the Object.—"I see *a tall* man." "He forsook *the* home *of his fathers.*" "I have begun to study *German.*"

b. Enlargement of the Complement of the Predicate.—"He feels *very* tired." "I am thought *a very rich* man." "I esteem him *a very wise* man." "He became *a great* general."

---

* Some writers consider that in such cases as these the preposition should be taken with the verb (*hope for, despair of*), and the noun that follows be considered as in the objective relation to the compound phrase, *hope for*, &c. This is objectionable—1st, because it is unnecessary; 2nd, because no amount of conjuring can make *hope for, despair of*, &c., anything but a separate verb and a separate preposition; and, as *a preposition must govern something*, the objective case that follows must be governed by the preposition; 3rd, because there is no reason why a few phrases like the above should be separated from a variety of others which are their grammatical equivalents. "*To despair of success,*" "*to despair about success,*" "*to despair with respect to success,*" are constructions which (as far as the above analysis is concerned) are grammatically equivalent.

COMPOUND SENTENCES.

400 A Compound Sentence is one which contains more than one subject and finite verb, the different clauses being joined together by connective words; as, "He is happy, but I am not." "I shall never be happy again if you leave me." "I am sure that he will succeed."

401 There are two relations in which the separate clauses or sentences of a compound sentence may stand to each other; namely, 1. The Co-ordinate Relation; 2. The Subordinate Relation.

I. CO-ORDINATE CLAUSES.

402 The clauses of a compound sentence are co-ordinate, when, as regards their *logical* force, they are independent of each other, being separate propositions which are linked together, and stand in the same relation to the entire sentence. They are either simply *coupled* together (as "You are rich, and your brother is poor"), or coupled and at the same time *opposed* to each other (as, "He is not clever, but he studies hard"). In the former case they are said to be in the *copulative* relation to each other, in the latter case in the adversative* relation.

403 Co-ordinate clauses are always joined together by the co-ordinative conjunctions. (See § 287.)

Examples.—"John is clever *and* Richard is industrious." "The horse ran away, *and* his rider was thrown." "They toil not, *neither* do they spin." "They are not rich, *nor* are they industrious." "*Either* you are mad, *or* you are drunk." "Not only was he the cleverest boy, *but* he was also the most industrious."

Contracted Sentences.

404 When co-ordinate sentences contain either the same subject, the same predicate, the same object, or the same adverbial adjunct to the predicate, it often happens that the portion which they have in common is expressed only once. In this case the compound sentence is said to be *contracted*.

* Some grammarians set down a third relation in which co-ordinate sentences may stand to each other, namely, the *causative* (as, "He is upright; therefore his friends trust him." "He is extravagant; consequently he is poor.") In these sentences, however, the words *therefore, consequently*, &c., are not conjunctions at all, but simple adverbs. Clauses thus related are of the kind here called *collateral*. They do not form a compound sentence at all.

405 *Examples.*—"Neither I nor you have seen that;" *i. e.* 'Neither I [have seen that], nor you have seen that." "Both John and his brother were there;" *i. e.* "Both John [was there] and his brother was there." In these contracted sentences the predicate is expressed only once.

"He stole a purse, and was convicted of the theft;" *i. e.* "He stole a purse, and [he] was convicted of the theft." "Religion purifies and ennobles the soul;" *i. e.* "Religion purifies and [religion] ennobles the soul." In these contracted sentences the subject is expressed only once.

"Carbonic acid is gaseous and poisonous;" *i. e.* "Carbonic acid is gaseous and [carbonic acid is] poisonous." Here the subject and the verb of incomplete predication *is* are expressed only once.

"He rode away in anger and in haste;" *i. e.* "He rode away in anger and [he rode away] in haste." Here the common subject and predicate are expressed only once.

"He reads and writes well;" *i. e.* "He reads [well] and [he] writes well." Here the common subject and the common adverbial adjunct are expressed only once.

406 It has been already remarked (§ 387 note) that a sentence is not necessarily a contracted sentence, because we find co-ordinative conjunctions used in it.

407 It follows, from the principle on which co-ordinate and contracted sentences are constructed, that the co-ordinative conjunctions must always join words and clauses which *stand in the same relation* to the other parts of the sentence. It would make nonsense if we attempted to join an adjective to a noun (unless the latter be used *attributively* or *predicatively*), or a subject to an adverb, or a verb in the indicative mood to a verb in the imperative mood.*

Collateral Sentences.

408 We frequently find sentences side by side, which have a connexion with each other as regards their sense and use, but have no *grammatical* link of connexion between them (that is, no conjunction, relative pronoun, or relative adverb). Such sentences cannot be treated as forming one compound sentence, though the complex idea that they suggest to the mind is the same as if they did. For example: "I came. I saw. I conquered." "Fear God. Honour the king."

* Young letter-writers constantly forget this rule at the close of their epistles, where such combinations as "I have no more to say, and believe me yours truly," are very frequent.

"Sometimes the linnet piped his song,
Sometimes the throstle whistled strong."

"The way was long, the wind was cold;
The minstrel was infirm and old."

"So he spoke, so I replied." "This is foolish, that is wise." "I was robbed of all my money; for that reason I was unable to proceed." "I believed, therefore have I spoken." "He is virtuous; consequently he is happy."

Such sentences as those placed side by side in the above examples may be called *collateral* sentences.

409 A proper consideration of the nature of collateral sentences will enable us materially to thin the usual lists of conjunctions.* A word is not a conjunction because it *refers* us to something that precedes. Simple demonstratives do this. Such words as *therefore*, *consequently*, *likewise*, *also* (i. e. *all so*, = *just in that manner*), *nevertheless*, *notwithstanding*, are not conjunctions, but demonstrative adverbs. (See § 292.) It has been before explained (see § 266, 285) that there is a difference between a *conjunction* and a *connective adverb*.†

410 We frequently have a series of sentences which are partly collateral and partly co-ordinate.

Examples.—

"He stay'd not for brake, and he stopp'd not for stone;
He swam the Esk river, where ford there was none."

"The Lord shall endure for ever. He hath prepared his throne for judgment, and he shall judge the world in righteousness."

411 Collateral sentences may be *contracted* in the same way as co-ordinate sentences; as, "A true friend advises justly, [a true friend] assists readily, [a true friend] adventures boldly, and [a true friend] continues a friend unchangeably." "The serenity of the sky, the various fruits which cover the ground, the discoloured foliage of the trees, and all the sweet but fading‡ graces of inspiring autumn, open the mind to

* Tables of conjunctions will be found in some grammars in which the simple adverbs *also*, *likewise* (*in like manner*), *moreover*, *further*, are classed with *and*, as copulative conjunctions; the relative adverbs *where*, *whence*, *as*, &c., classed with *that*, *though*, and *because*, as continuative conjunctions; *as if* treated as a single conjunction, although the *as* and the *if* in reality belong to different clauses, and so on. A classification which takes in relative adverbs as conjunctions should also take in relative pronouns.

† There is another mode of showing that words like *therefore*, *accordingly*, &c., are not conjunctions. It will be easy to see that *one clause of a sentence does not admit of being joined to another by more than one conjunction or connective word at once.* (A phrase like "The house which I built, *and in which* I live," is not a case in point, because the conjunction *and* joins the one relative clause to the other, but the relative pronoun *which* connects its clause with the *antecedent*.) From the nature of the case, such a repetition would be unmeaning. Nevertheless *therefore*, *nevertheless*, *accordingly*, &c., may be used without difficulty after *and* or *but*.

‡ Those who insist upon finding a contraction wherever there is a co-ordinative conjunction which joins two *words* only, will find it difficult to deal with this pair of attributives.

benevolence, and dispose it for contemplation." This, at full length, will run, "The serenity of the sky opens the mind to benevolence, and the serenity of the sky disposes it for contemplation. The various fruits which cover the ground open the mind to benevolence, and the various fruits which cover the ground dispose it for contemplation. The discoloured foliage of the trees opens the mind for benevolence, and the discoloured foliage of the trees disposes it for contemplation; and all the sweet but fading graces of inspiring autumn open the mind to benevolence, and all the sweet but fading graces of inspiring autumn dispose it for contemplation."

II. SUBORDINATE CLAUSES.

412 Compound sentences may contain clauses which are *subordinate* to the principal clause.

In sentences of this kind the various clauses have not the same relation to each other, or the same *logical force*.

One clause constitutes the *principal sentence*, to which the subordinate clauses are attached by means of connective words (see § 285), namely, *relative* pronouns, relative adverbs and subordinative conjunctions.

413 Subordinate clauses are of three kinds; Substantive Clauses, Adjective Clauses, and Adverbial Clauses.

Substantive Clauses.

414 A Substantive Clause is one which, in its relation to the rest of the sentence, is equivalent to a substantive. It is generally either the subject or the object of the verb in the principal clause. Thus in the sentence, "I know that he did this." The clause, "*that he did this*," is the object of the verb *know*. In "He asked how old I was," the clause "*how old I was*" is the object of the verb *asked*. In "When I set out is uncertain," the clause "*when I set out*" is the subject of the verb *is*.

415 When a substantive clause is the subject of the verb of the principal clause, the sentence is commonly formed by using the word *it* as the *grammatical* subject of the principal verb, and putting the substantive clause after the main clause. In this case the substantive clause is *in apposition* to the subject of the main verb. As, "*It* is not true *that he died yesterday*."

416 There are other cases in which a substantive clause is found in apposition to a noun; as, "Hence appears the *impossibility that he should succeed*."

417 It is to *verbs* that substantives and substantive clauses most commonly stand in the objective relation. This is because verbs are more commonly transitive in their meaning than any other class of words. But

this transitive character belongs quite as much to participles and gerunds as to verbs, and belongs also, in some degree, to other adjectives and nouns, which take after them, as an object, not indeed a substantive, but a substantive clause. Thus: "There is no *proof that he did this.*" "I am *sure that this is so.*" "I do this in the *hope that he will deserve it.*"

418 Substantive clauses may even be governed by a preposition; as, "In that he himself hath suffered being tempted, he is able also to succour them that are tempted" (Heb. ii. 18). This construction, however, is obsolete, except after the preposition *but* (see § 282); as, "I should have forgiven him, but that he repeated the offence.

419 Substantive clauses always begin either with the conjunction *that* or with an interrogative word.

Adjective Clauses.

420 Adjective Clauses are clauses which stand in the attributive relation to substantives. In their most natural form they begin with a relative pronoun. Thus in the sentence, "Look at the exercise which I have written," the clause "*which I have written*" qualifies the noun *exercise*. In "The man with whom you dined yesterday is dead," the clause "*with whom you dined yesterday*" qualifies the noun *man*.

421 A substantive governed by a preposition frequently denotes an idea for which an adverb may stand equally well. Thus *near me* = *here*, *in that place* = *there*, *at which time* = *when*. Hence adverbs are often employed in cases in which a preposition and a pronoun would be the proper words to use. In Latin *unde* often means *from whom*, as well as *whence*. In this way we often get adjective clauses commencing with a relative adverb, instead of a relative pronoun; as, "Autumn is the time *when fruits ripen*," for "*the time at which*," &c. "That is the house *where I dwell*," for "*the house in which*," &c. In their natural and proper use, clauses beginning with *when*, *where*, *whence*, *why*, &c. are *adverbial* clauses: they answer most simply to adverbs, to which they may be placed in *apposition*. Thus: "There, where a few torn shrubs the place disclose." "Then shall I not be ashamed, when I have respect unto all thy commandments."

Adverbial Clauses.

422 Adverbial clauses are clauses which stand in the adverbial relation to verbs, adjectives, and other adverbs, just as though they were replaced by single adverbs. Thus: "He was writing a letter when I arrived." Here the clause "*when I arrived*" indicates the time at which the action expressed by the verb *was writing* took place. The clause "*when I arrived*" is therefore in the adverbial relation to the verb *was*

writing. The sense and construction may be represented by a single adverb. "I arrived. *Then* he was writing." So, "He still lay *where he had fallen*: i. e. "He had fallen [somewhere]: he still lay *there*." "I give you this *because I love you*:" i. e. "I love you; therefore I give you this."

423 Adverbial clauses admit of the same classification as ordinary adverbial adjuncts. That is to say, we have

1. Adverbial clauses relating to Time.
2. Adverbial clauses relating to Place.
3. Adverbial clauses relating to Manner.
4. Adverbial clauses relating to Degree.
5. Adverbial clauses relating to Cause.
6. Adverbial clauses relating to Consequence.
7. Adverbial clauses relating to Condition.

1.—Adverbial Clauses relating to Time.

424 Clauses of this kind begin with the relative adverbs which denote time (see § 267). As, "Every one listens *when he speaks*." "I was glad *when he had finished*." "He read *while I wrote*." "He punished the boy *whenever he did wrong*." It must be observed that the relative adverbs which introduce such clauses not only connect the adverbial clause with the principal clause, but themselves qualify the verb of the clause which they introduce.

425 It is usual to consider the words *before, after, since, ere*,* &c., as conjunctions in such sentences as, "He left the meeting before I did." "He never spoke after he fell." "He has left the country since you saw him." In the present state of the language there is no great objection to this. We shall then have another class of adverbial clauses relating to time, beginning with conjunctions, and not with adverbs.† The true nature of such sentences, however, has been already explained. (See § 289.)

426 With *after* and *since* the time of the action spoken of in the dependent clause *precedes* that of the action spoken of in the main clause; as, "He was punished after he was convicted." "He has repeated his offence since he was punished." The introduction of a negative does not alter this logical relation between the two actions; as, "He has not repeated his offence since he was punished."

427 With *until, ere, before*, the time of the action referred to in the subordinate clause *succeeds* the time referred to in the principal clause; as, "He went away before I arrived." "He will go away before I arrive;" or even with a negative, "He will not go away before I arrive."

---

* German *eher*.

† It must be observed that the words *after, before*, &c. in such cases do not qualify the verbs of the clauses which follow them.

2.—Adverbial Clauses relating to Place.

428 Clauses of this kind are introduced by the relative adverbs *where*, *whither*, *whence*, &c. As, "He is still standing *where I left him.*" "*Whither I go* ye cannot come." "*Whithersoever I went* he followed me." "Let me alone, that I may take comfort a little before I go whence I shall not return." The relative adverbs connect the dependent clauses with the main clause, and at the same time qualify the verbs of the dependent clauses themselves.

3.—Adverbial Clauses relating to Manner.

429 Adverbial clauses relating to manner are introduced by the relative or connective adverb *as*. E.g. "He did *as he was told.*" "It turned out *as I expected.*" Here the dependent clauses qualify the verbs of the main sentence, while the adverb *as* refers to the manner of the action spoken of in the dependent clauses themselves. It must be remembered, however, that clauses beginning with *as* are generally elliptical. At full length the above would be, "He did as he was told *to do*" (where *as* indicates the idea of manner with relation to the verb *to do*). "It turned out as I expected *it to turn out*" (where *as* indicates the idea of manner with relation to the verb *to turn out*).

430 When clauses beginning with *as* come after the words *such*, or *same*, they must be regarded as standing in the adverbial relation to those adjectives, indicating the kind of *such* and the kind of *same* that are meant, just as in such a phrase as "He is the same in character," the words *in character* form an adverbial adjunct to the adjective *same*. (Compare the note on § 267, and the examples of analysis of sentences given further on).

431 Clauses beginning with *as* frequently come after the adverb *so* or the demonstrative *as*. In this case they must be regarded as standing in the adverbial relation to the adverbs *so* and *as*, defining the meaning of *so* more particularly, just as in such phrases as "*just so*," "*almost so*," &c. The clauses are usually very elliptical. When *as* answers to *so* or *as*, it qualifies a word (expressed or understood) expressing the same sort of idea as is expressed by the word which the *so* or *as* qualifies. This is best seen by the Latin usage. It is not uncommon to find such sentences as the following: "Qui se oppido munitissimo tamdiu tenuit *quamdiu* in provincia Parthi fuerunt" (Cic. *Fam.* xii. 19)—"Who kept himself in a very strongly fortified town *so long as* the Parthians were in the province." We see from the Latin that the relative adverb *as* (answering to *quam*) really qualifies the word *long* understood ("as long, *as* the Parthians kept themselves *long*, &c.) So again: "Nemo orator *tam multa* ne in Graeco quidem otio scripsit, *quam multa* sunt

nostra" (Cic. *Orat.* 30).—"No orator has written *so many* things, *as* our writings are *many*." "Tam magis illa fremens, et tristibus effera flammis, quam magis effuso crudescunt sanguine pugnae" (Virg. *Æn.* vii. 788). In English we render *tam magis—quam magis* by *so much the more—as*; but the Latin shows that the *as* really qualifies the word *more* understood. The same principle is illustrated by such correlatives as *tantus—quantus*, and *talis—qualis*. If *tantus* means *so great*, *quantus* (though rendered only by *as*) must really mean *as great*.

4.—Adverbial Clauses relating to Dgeree.

432 Clauses of this kind are introduced by the adverbs *than*, *the* (§ 270), and *as*.

As *degree* is an idea which attaches not to actions (*per se*), but to attributes of things, and to the mode or manner of actions, adverbial clauses denoting *degree* are always attached to adjectives or adverbs. They are almost always elliptical. (See note, § 267).

433 *E. g.* "He is not so (*or* as) tall as I thought" (*i. e.* as I thought *he was tall*). Here the clause "as I thought [he was tall] qualifies (or is in the adverbial relation to) the adverb *so*, and the relative adverb *as* at the beginning of the adverbial clause qualifies the adjective *tall* understood.

"He is taller than his brother;" *i. e.* "He is taller than his brother [is tall].* Here the clause, "than his brother [is tall]" qualifies the adjective *taller*, denoting the *degree* in which *taller* is asserted of the subject of the sentence, and the relative adverb *than*, which denotes the degree in which *his brother* is *tall*, is in the adverbial relation to the adjective *tall* understood.

"I love study more than ever [I loved it]." Here the adverbial clause "*than ever [I loved it]*" qualifies the adverb *more* in the principal clause. It will follow also from what has been already said (§ 431) that the word *than* really qualifies some word understood denoting degree, and corresponding to *more*, the clause in full being "*than ever [I loved it much]*."

"The more I learn, the more I wish to learn." Here the adverbial sentence "*the more I learn*" qualifies the demonstrative adverb *the*, which in its turn qualifies the adverb *more* in the principal clause; the word *more* in the adverbial clause being itself qualified by the relative adverb *the*. (See § 270, and the note on § 267.)

---

* That we must understand the adjective *tall* as well as the verb *is*, will easily be seen if it be considered that every clause or subordinate sentence must have a predicate as well as a subject. If then we ask what is predicated of *his brother*, the answer obviously is, *being tall*.

5.—Adverbial Clauses relating to Cause.

434 Clauses of this kind begin with the conjunctions *because* and *for*.

E.g. "I love him because he is good." Here "*because he is good*" is an adverbial clause qualifying the verb *love*.

"He could not have seen me, for I was not there." Here "*for I was not there*" is an adverbial clause qualifying the verb *could*.

6.—Adverbial Clauses relating to Consequence.

435 Clauses of this kind commonly stand in the adverbial relation to the adverb *so* expressed or understood. They bear a close resemblance to those which denote manner and degree. *E.g.* "He ran so fast *that he was out of breath*." Here the adverbial clause "*that he was out of breath*" defines more particularly the meaning of the adverb *so* which qualifies *fast*. It therefore stands in the adverbial relation to it.

"Is thy servant a dog [so] *that he should do this?*" Here the adverbial clause qualifies or defines more exactly the adverb *so* understood.

436 Adverbial clauses relating to *purpose* come also under this head. *E. g.* "He labours *that he may become rich*." Here the adverbial clause qualifies the verb *labours*. "I will not make a noise, *lest I should disturb you*." Here the adverbial clause qualifies the verb *make*.

437 *Consequence* implies the *actual* connexion between a contingent event and that on which it depends. *Purpose* implies that the connexion is not *actual* but *intended*.

438 It has been already remarked (§ 409) that sentences beginning with such adverbs as *therefore*, *consequently*, &c. do not come under the head of dependent sentences at all. They are *independent* sentences, collateral with the sentences that precede them.

7.—Adverbial Clauses relating to Condition.

439 Clauses of this kind begin with the conjunctions *if*, *unless*, *except*, *though*, *although*, and the compounds of *ever* (*however*, *whoever*, *whatever*, &c.)*

---

* Sentences of this kind present considerable difficulty, because the practice of the best writers is not quite uniform or consistent, and common usage tolerates in some cases a departure from what is required by the principles of grammatical construction.

440 In adverbial clauses of *condition*, the principal sentence is called the *consequent clause* (*i. e.* the clause which expresses the *consequence*); the subordinate sentence is called the *hypothetical clause* (*i. e.* the clause which expresses the *hypothesis*, *supposition*, or *concession*).

441 To understand sentences of this class, it is necessary to examine the different varieties of hypothesis and consequence.

442 Suppositions or hypotheses may be made respecting two sorts of events:—

1. Events which are certain in themselves, but which may be spoken of by us without our knowing whether they occurred or not.

2. Events which are contingent or uncertain in themselves, and not merely as regards our knowledge of them.

Of course, in order that an event may be certain in itself, it must be either present or past.

443 With respect to events present or past, and therefore certain in themselves, we may make two kinds of supposition:—
1. Suppositions that may be consistent with the actual fact.
2. Suppositions contrary to the actual (known) fact.

444 1. When a supposition is made about an event which is certain in itself, but of which we speak without knowing whether it occurred or not, making a supposition that may be consistent with the fact, the indicative mood is used in the hypothetical clause whenever the form of the hypothesis (whether it be affirmative or negative) implies that the supposed case may be consistent with actual fact.

445 It follows, also, that in such cases the indicative (or imperative) mood must be used in the consequent clause, because the *consequent event* cannot be spoken of as less certain than the event on which it is affirmed to depend.

446 *Examples.*—"If the prisoner committed the crime, he deserves death. If he did not commit it, all the witnesses have sworn falsely." "If he is at home, I shall see him." "If your exercise is finished, bring it to me." "If you have read the book, return it to the owner." "He has arrived by this time, unless he has met with some accident." "He deserves our pity, unless his tale is a false one."*

447 In like manner *concessive clauses* (*i. e.* clauses in which

* This is the present usage; but in old-fashioned English it is common to find the subjunctive mood in hypothetical sentences of this kind. *E. g.* "If I have done this, if there be iniquity in my hands", &c. "If it be so, our God is able to deliver us." (*Daniel* iii. 17.) "If it be thou, bid me come to thee on the water." (*Matt.* xix. 28)

something is *granted*) beginning with *though* or *although*, which relate to what *actually is* or *was the case*, have the indicative mood; as, "Though he was there, I did not see him." "Although he is rich, he is not contented."

448 When a supposition is made which is contrary to some known fact, present or past, the subjunctive mood is used both in the hypothetical and in the consequent clause, the past indefinite tense* of the subjunctive being used in the hypothetical clause with reference to present time, and the past perfect with reference to past time. In the consequent clause the future subjunctive (or *conditional*, as it is sometimes termed) is used after a supposition referring to present time, and the future perfect subjunctive (or *conditional perfect*) after a supposition relating to past time.

Examples.—"If he were present (which he *is* not), I would speak to him." "If he had confessed his fault (which he *did* not *do*), I should have forgiven him." "If he were not idle (which he is), he would make rapid progress." "If our horse had not fallen down (which he did), we should not have missed the train."

449 In old-fashioned English and in poetry we also find the past perfect subjunctive used in the consequent clause, instead of the future perfect subjunctive (or conditional perfect); as, "I *had fainted* unless I had believed to see the goodness of the Lord."

450 Clauses expressing a *wish* contrary to the fact have also the subjunctive mood. Thus: "I wish that he *were* here (which he is not)." "Would that this had never happened (but it did happen)."

451 Suppositions with regard to the future have reference to events which are uncertain in themselves. Strictly speaking, therefore, we should expect to find the indicative mood inadmissible in such sentences. Nevertheless, usage sanctions its employment in some.

452 Suppositions with regard to the future are of two kinds:—

453 1. In making a hypothesis we may at the same time imply that the matter will be decided, one way or the other, before the time referred to in the consequent clause. In strictness, the present tense of the subjunctive mood should be used in

* It seems anomalous to have a *past* tense in any mood referring to *present* time; but the idiom is found in French, German, Latin, and Greek. In French and Greek we even have a past tense of the indicative mood used in sentences of this kind. (The verb *be* is of great value as a criterion for the *mood* in English.)

the hypothetical clause, and the future indicative (or the imperative mood) in the consequent clause. *E. g.* "Though he *slay* me, yet will I trust in him." "Though hand *join* in hand, the wicked shall not go unpunished." "If this *be* granted, the proof will be easy." "If thy right eye *offend* thee, pluck it out." In all these cases a supposition is made with regard to what is still future.

454 As a *general* assertion expressed in the present tense frequently refers to the future as well as the present, we often find the present indicative thus used in the consequent clause. Thus: "Except these *abide* (pres. subj.) in the ship, ye *cannot* be saved." "Except a man *be born* (pres. subj.) again, he *cannot* see the kingdom of God."

455 The usage of modern times, however, in such cases as the above, sanctions the use of the indicative mood in *both* clauses. *E. g.* "If it *rains* to-morrow, we shall be unable to go out." "If he *does* not arrive before next week, he will be too late." "If he *strikes* me, I shall strike him again."

456 The *future indicative* is also allowable in the hypothetical clause, though its use is not very common. *E. g.* "If we *shall say*, From heaven, he will say, Why then did ye not believe him? But if we *shall say*, Of men; they feared the people" (*Mark* xi. 31). "If they *shall enter* into my rest" (*Heb.* iv. 5).

457 2. In making a supposition with regard to the future, we may make a pure hypothesis, without connecting with it the idea that the matter will be decided one way or the other. In this case the subjunctive mood must be used both in the hypothetical and in the consequent clause. As regards the *tense* of the verbs used, we may have, in either clause, either the past indefinite tense of the subjunctive, or the future indefinite tense of the subjunctive. In the hypothetical clause, also, it is not uncommon to find the past indefinite subjunctive of the verb *be*, followed by the infinitive mood.

Examples.—"If he were rewarded, he would be encouraged to persevere." "If he should succeed (*or* if he succeeded) in his endeavours, he would be happy." "If he went (or should go) away without speaking to me, I should be grieved." "If he lost (*or* should lose) his money, he would never be happy again." "He could not (*or* would not be able to) do it if he tried (*or* were to try)." "If it were done, then it were well it were done quickly." "I would not believe it unless I saw (*or* should see) it." "If he were to fail, it would be a great disgrace."

458 In suppositions the conjunction *if* is often omitted. *E. g.* "Had I known this (*i. e.* if I had known this), I would not have come." "Were it not so (*i. e.* if it were not so), I would have told you." "Could I have foreseen (*i. e.* if I could have foreseen) this, I would have acted otherwise."

459 An interrogative or imperative sentence is sometimes used in such a way as to be equivalent to a hypothetical clause. *E. g.* "Is any afflicted (*i. e.* if any one is afflicted), let him pray. Is any merry (*i. e.* if any is merry), let him sing psalms." "Take any form but that, and my firm nerves shall never tremble."

GENERAL RULES OF SYNTAX.

460 The following is a brief summary of the laws of the structure of sentences, and of the functions of the different parts of speech.

461 The primary elements of every sentence are the substantive, which forms the subject of the sentence (see § 345), and the verb, by means of which an assertion is made about that for which the subject stands (see §§ 347, 348, 353, 359, 392).

462 The subject of a sentence is in the nominative case (§§ 380, 381).

463 The verb must agree with the subject in number and person (§ 378).

464 A collective noun in the singular used as the subject of a sentence may be followed by a verb in the plural number (§ 382).

465 If the subject of a sentence consists of two nouns or pronouns united by the conjunction *and*, the verb is put in the plural number (§ 387); but the verb must be in the singular if the two subjects are connected by *or* or *nor*, because all such sentences are contracted.

466 When a verb has two or more subjects of different persons, it is put in the first person, if one of the subjects is of that person. If there is no subject of the first person, but one of the second person, then the verb must be considered as being of the second person. *E. g.* "You and I shall never believe that." "You and your brother are both wrong."

467 The indicative mood of verbs is used when the sentence or clause denotes an action or event which agrees with an objective* reality, either actual or anticipated; as, "He *strikes* the ball." "He *went* away." "He *will return*." "He works so hard, that he *will* soon *finish* the business." "When he *shall appear*, we *shall be* like him." "I am sure that he never *said* that."

The imperative mood is used in commands, exhortations, and prayers.

The subjunctive mood is used when the sentence or clause denotes an event which is conceived of, not as corresponding to any *objective* reality, either actual or anticipated, but as existing only in the mind of the speaker. Thus: "If he *were* here, he *would speak* to me." "If he *had said* so, I *should have believed* him." "He strives that he *may* succeed." "The sentence on the prisoner is, that he *be hanged* to-morrow." (An event *intended* or *desired* exists, so far, only in the mind of the speaker.)

468 A substantive in the nominative case must either be the subject of the sentence, or be in apposition to the subject, or be the complement of the predicate (§ 392),† or be used absolutely (§ 373. 5).

469 A substantive in the possessive case always stands in the attributive relation to some other substantive by which it is said to be governed (§ 360). In such a sentence as "I saw a horse of your father's," it must be carefully observed that a noun is understood, and that the sentence at full length is, "I saw a horse of your father's *horses*." So in "He went to the baker's," we must supply such a noun as *house* or *shop* to complete the construction.

470 A substantive in the objective case is either the object of a verb, participle, or gerund (§ 366), or stands in the adverbial relation to a verb or adjective (§ 373. 4), or is the complement of the predicate when the verb is transitive (§ 396), or comes after a preposition, by which it is said to be governed.

471 The object of a verb should be placed close to the verb which governs it; it should not be separated from the verb by the intervention of any adverbial adjunct.

---

* *Objective* means "having an existence of its own, independent of the thought of the speaker."

† This part of the rule is usually expressed by saying that the verbs *be*, *be called*, *be thought*, *become*, &c., take the same case after them as before them.

472 **A verb in the infinitive mood is constructed like a substantive in the nominative or objective case.**

473 An adjective is always either in the attributive or in the predicative relation to some substantive, expressed or understood (§§ 81, 83, 363, 364).

An adjective cannot qualify any part of speech except a substantive. An adjective cannot be the subject or object of a verb, or be governed by a preposition.

474 Pronouns must agree in gender, number, and person, with the nouns for which they stand, or to which they relate. [N.B. The antecedent of a relative pronoun is sometimes omitted; as, "Who steals my purse, steals trash." "The Son quickeneth whom he will." Also, the antecedent of a relative is sometimes disguised in the form of a possessive adjective pronoun; as, "*Whose* is the crime, the scandal too be *theirs*." This must not be confounded with the cases in which a substantive pronoun in the possessive case is the antecedent; as, "His praise is lost who stays at home" (see § 95).

Even when a pronoun does not mark *person* by its form, it carries on the person of the substantive for which it stands to any verb of which it may be the subject; as, "I *who am* poor am contented." "Thou *who art* rich art unhappy."

The relative does not agree with its antecedent in case. It has its own independent construction in its own clause. Even when its case is the same as that of the antecedent, it is not because it *agrees* with it (in the grammatical sense of that term).*

475 Adverbs can only be used to qualify the meaning of verbs, adjectives, and other adverbs (§ 259).

476 Prepositions govern substantives in the objective case (§ 277), and can govern no other part of speech (§ 279); an infinitive mood being virtually a substantive.

477 Conjunctions are used to join together single words, phrases, or sentences (§§ 285—291). Co-ordinative conjunctions must join words or clauses which stand in the same relation to the other parts of the sentence (§ 407).

* Some grammars state, as a rule, that if no noun come between the relative and the verb, the relative is in the nominative case; that is, is the subject of the verb. Such a rule cannot pretend to be a rule of *syntax*. It could, in any case, be nothing more than a guide for ascertaining the subject of the relative clause. But it is not even accurate. It would *mislead* a beginner in such sentences as "Whose is the crime, the scandal, too, be theirs." "God, in whose hand are all thy ways." "In whom are hid all the treasures of wisdom."

[N.B. There are other connective words which are not conjunctions (§ 285).]

478 Interjections are not integral parts of sentences; they do not stand in any grammatical relation to other words.

479 A noun or pronoun in the nominative case preceded by *O*, is equivalent (in construction) to an interjection. In Latin and Greek the vocative case is used in such instances.

PUNCTUATION.

480 In speaking, the words of a sentence, especially if it be a complex one, are not uttered consecutively without any break. Certain pauses are made to mark more clearly the way in which the words of the sentence are grouped together.

481 In writing, these pauses are represented by marks called *stops* or *points*. *Punctuation* (derived from the Latin *punctum*, a *point*) means "the right mode of putting in points or stops."

482 The stops made use of are, 1. The Comma (,). 2. The Semicolon (;). 3. The Colon (:). 4. The Full Stop or Period (.).*

483 As it is impossible to lay down perfectly exact rules for the introduction of pauses in speaking, so it will be found that in many cases the best writers are not agreed as to the use of stops in writing. All that can be done is to lay down the most general principles.

484 The Full Stop is used at the end of a complete and independent sentence, but not at the end of a sentence which is followed by another *collateral* sentence (§ 408).

485 In simple sentences the comma is inserted:—

1. Before the main verb, when the subject is accompanied by an attributive adjunct, which, with its adjuncts, forms a combination of words of considerable length. As, "The injustice *of the sentence pronounced upon this wise and virtuous man*, is evident." But if the adjunct is expressed briefly, the comma is not used. As, "The injustice *of the sentence* is evident."

2. Before and after any participle (not used as a mere qualitative adjective) or participial phrase; as, "The man, having slipped, fell over the cliff." "The general, having rallied his soldiers, led them forwards." "Undaunted, he still struggled on." "All night the dreadless angel, unpursued, through Heaven's wide champaign winged his glorious way."

3. Before and after any attributive adjunct to the subject which consists of an adjective, or noun in apposition, when these are accompanied by other words standing to them in the attributive, objective, or adverbial relation. *E.g.* "Bacon, the illustrious author of the Novum Organum, declared, &c."

---

* These words (properly speaking) are names not of the *stops*, but of the portions of sentences which they mark off. *Comma* means a *clause; Colon* a *limb* or *member* of a sentence; *Semicolon*, a half *colon; Period*, a complete sentence.

"The soldier, afraid of the consequences of his insubordination, deserted."

4. Before or after a phrase or quotation which is either the subject or the object of a verb. Thus: "Nelson's watchword was, England expects every man to do his duty." "He said to his disciples, 'Watch and pray.'"

5. When the subject of a sentence consists of several substantives enumerated successively without having the conjunction *and* placed between them, they must be separated by commas. Thus: "John, William, James and Henry took a walk together."

6. A comma is inserted after an adverbial phrase consisting of a noun (with its adjunct) used absolutely, or an infinitive mood (preceded by *to*) implying purpose, when it precedes the verb or its subject. As, "To conclude, I will only say, &c." "The man being dead, his heirs took possession of his estate."

7. Other complex adverbial phrases also are frequently followed by commas, when they precede the subject of the sentence; as, "By studying diligently for five hours a day, he mastered the language in six months." Such phrases should be both preceded and followed by commas when they come between the subject and the verb.

8. Nouns used in the vocative (or nominative of appellation) are separated by commas from the rest of the sentence; as, "John, shut the door." "I said, Sir, that I had not done that."

486 In compound sentences:—

1. A substantive clause used as the subject of a verb should be followed by a comma. Thus: "That the accused is innocent of the crime imputed to him, admits of demonstration." "How we are ever to get there, is the question."

If such a clause *follows* the verb (the latter being preceded by *it*), a comma does not usually precede the substantive clause. As, "It is of great importance that this should be rightly understood."

A substantive clause which is the object of a verb is not generally preceded by a comma, unless it is of considerable length. When it is short, it follows the main verb without any break. Thus: "He acknowledged that he had done this." "Tell me how you are." But: "In answer to these inquiries the messenger replied, that he had not been present, when the engagement took place."

2. An adjective clause is not separated by a comma from the noun which it qualifies when it is an essential part of the designation of the thing signified; that is, when the thing or

person signified is not sufficiently indicated by the antecedent noun. Thus: "The man who told me this, stands here." "I do not see the objects that you are pointing out."

But if the designation of the person or thing meant is complete without the relative sentence, so that the latter only extends and defines that designation, then a comma must be introduced. Thus: "We are studying the reign of William Rufus, who succeeded his father A. D. 1087." "I will report this to my father, who is waiting to hear the news."

In accordance with the principle laid down in § 485. 1. an adjective sentence usually has a comma placed after it, when it is attached to the subject of the sentence, and always has a comma after it when it is followed by any adverbial adjuncts of the principal verb. Otherwise it would not be clear whether such adjuncts belonged to the main sentence or to the adjective clause. Thus: "He resisted the man who attacked him, with all his might."

3. Adverbial sentences are generally separated from the main sentence by commas, unless they are very short, and closely connected with what precedes. Thus: "When you have finished your work, tell me." "I will not reward you, unless you deserve it." But: "He ran away as soon as I saw him." "I could not catch him before he escaped."

487 Co-ordinate sentences are generally separated by commas when they are expressed at full length. Thus: "Next day they resumed their labours, and success soon crowned their efforts." "We were very tired, but we could not stop long." "Either he will succeed, or he will perish in the attempt."

488 Commas are also inserted between contracted co-ordinate sentences (§ 404) except when the portions that are expressed are very closely related to each other, and are connected by the conjunctions *and*, *or*, and *nor*. Thus: "We remained there that night, and set out early on the following day." "He searched diligently, but could not find it." But commas are not needed in such sentences as, "The infantry halted and formed a hollow square." "He struck and killed his brother." "He performed his task quickly and well." "Whether he win or lose, does not concern us."

489 Collateral sentences (§ 408) are separated by commas when they are short, and by semicolons when they are of considerable length.

490 When collateral sentences are contracted, commas should be placed between those portions that remain. When a series of contracted sentences are partly collateral and partly co-

ordinate, commas are inserted between the remains of the collateral sentences, but not between those of the co-ordinate clauses, provided these are closely connected together by means of the conjunctions *and* and *or* (see § 488). Thus: "He saw, wooed and won the daughter of the prince." "Early to bed and early to rise, makes a man healthy, wealthy and wise." "He gazed upon the earth, the sea, the sky." "He took leave of his father, his brother and his sister." "He paid his bill, mounted his horse and rode away." "He does not study either Greek or Latin."

491 The above are the chief rules for the insertion of the comma. But a stop may be placed in writing, whenever a pause would be made in speaking for the purpose of rendering the sense more clear. And, *vice versâ*, stops may be omitted in writing where, in reading or speaking, the portions of a sentence, between which some rule would seem to require a stop, are pronounced together without any break.

492 A semicolon is used instead of a comma, when the sense of the passage requires that a longer pause should be made in uttering it than is usually indicated by a comma. No other more exact rules can be given for the use of this stop.

493 The colon represents a longer pause than the semicolon. It may be placed between collateral sentences, when the connexion between them is not very close. It is also frequently placed before a quotation.

494 Besides the stops, some other signs are employed in writing.

495 A note of interrogation (?) must be placed at the end of all direct questions, but not after indirect questions. Thus: "Have you written your letter?" But: "He asked me whether I had written my letter."

496 The note of admiration or exclamation is placed after interjections, exclamations, and after nouns and pronouns used in addresses, when particular stress is to be laid upon them. This mark is also frequently placed at the end of a sentence which contains an invocation.

497 The parenthesis ( ) is used to enclose a clause, or part of a clause, which does not enter into the construction of the main sentence, but is merely introduced *by the way*. Words enclosed within a parenthesis do not require to be separated from the rest of the sentence by any other stop.

498 Double or single inverted commas '—', or "—", are used to mark quotations.

ANALYSIS OF SENTENCES.

1.—SIMPLE SENTENCES.

499 The analysis of a simple sentence is to be conducted in the following manner:—

i. Set down the subject of the sentence.

ii. Set down those words, or combinations of words, which stand in the attributive relation to the subject. These form what are called the *attributive adjuncts* of the subject (see § 360).

iii. Set down the predicate, that is to say, the verb which forms the essential part of every predicate (§ 353).

iv. If the verb is one of *incomplete predication* (see § 392) indicate this, and set down separately the complement of the predicate (§ 392).

v. Set down any words which are in the attributive or adverbial relation to the complement of the predicate.

vi. If the predicate be a transitive verb, set down the object of the verb, or, if the verb is one of incomplete predication, such as *may*, *can*, *must*, &c., followed by a transitive verb in the infinitive mood, set down the object of the dependent infinitive.

vii. Set down those words or phrases which stand in the attributive relation to the object of the predicate, or in the objective or adverbial relation to the object, if the latter is a verb in the infinitive mood.

viii. Set down those words or phrases which are in the adverbial relation to the predicate. These may be called the adverbial adjuncts of the predicate.

Examples of the Analysis of Simple Sentences.

500 "Having abandoned their fortifications, the troops of the emperor began a disastrous retreat."

i. *Subject*, troops.

ii. *Attributive adjuncts of subject.*
1. *Definite article*, 'the'
2. *Preposition and noun*, 'of the emperor.'
3. *Participial phrase*, 'having abandoned their fortifications.'

iii. *Predicate*,* 'began.'
iv. *Object of verb*, 'retreat.'
vii. *Attributive adjuncts of object.* { 1. *Article*, 'a' 2. *Adjective*, 'disastrous.'

501 "The enraged officer struck the unfortunate man dead on the spot with a single blow of his sword."
i. *Subject*, 'officer.'
ii. *Attributive adjuncts of subject.* { 1. *Article*, 'the' 2. *Adjective*, 'enraged.'
iii. *Predicate*, 'struck.'
iv. *Complement of predicate*, *adj.* 'dead' (see § 392).
vi. *Object of verb*, 'man.'
vii. *Attributive adjuncts of object.* { 1. *Article*, 'the.' 2. *Adjective*, 'unfortunate.'
viii. *Adverbial adjuncts of predicate.* { 1. *Adverbial adjunct of place*, 'on the spot.' 2. *Adverbial adjunct of cause*, 'with a single blow of his sword.'

502 "Who are you?" †
i. *Subject*, 'you.'
iii. *Predicate* (*incomplete*), 'are.'
iv. *Complement of predicate*, 'who.'

503 "Beware."
i. *Subject*, 'thou' (understood).
iii. *Predicate* (*incomplete*), 'be.'
iv. *Complement of predicate*, 'ware.'

504 "Alexander, the conqueror of the world, was deservedly called the Great."
i. *Subject*, 'Alexander.'
ii. *Attributive adjunct of subject*, 'the conqueror of the world.'
iii. *Predicate* (*incomplete*), 'was called.'
iv. *Complement of predicate*, 'the great.'
viii. *Adverbial adjunct of predicate*, 'deservedly.'

505 "Give me that large book."
i. *Subject*, 'thou' (understood).
iii. *Predicate*, 'give.'
vi. *Object of verb*, 'book.'

---

* That is, copula and predicate combined (see § 347).

† The construction of an interrogative sentence is most easily seen by looking at that of the corresponding affirmative sentence.

vii. *Attributive adjuncts of object.* { 1. *Demonstrative adjective,* 'that.' 2. *Qualitative adjective,* 'large.'
viii. *Adverbial adjunct of predicate,* 'me' (§ 373. 4).

506 "Do not think me ungrateful."
i. *Subject,* 'thou' (understood).
iii. *Predicate,* 'do think.'*
iv. *Complement of predicate,* 'ungrateful.'
v. *Object of verb,* 'me.'
viii. *Adverbial adjunct of predicate,* 'not.'

[Taking the above sentence as a type, it will be easy to see that in such a sentence as "I wish him dead," *dead* is the complement of *wish,* and *him* is the object of the verb. This last sentence will, in its turn, give us the proper explanation of such sentences as, "I wish him to stay." Here it is best to take *to stay* as the complement of the predicate verb *wish,* and *him* as the object. Some grammarians would make *him* the subject of *to stay* (as though it were equivalent to the accusative case with the infinitive mood in Latin), and say that the object of *wish* is *him to stay.* This is objectionable. In the first place, *to stay* is more than an infinitive mood; it is an infinitive mood *with a preposition before it,* and therefore answers, not to the infinitive mood in Latin, but to the gerund preceded by a preposition (at least as regards its construction). Therefore the idea of a subject before *to stay* is inadmissible, not to say that subjects in the objective case are foreign to the English idiom. In the second place, if *him to stay* could be the object of *wish,* no reason could be alleged why similar phrases should not be the objects of other verbs. Now it would be impossible to use such language as, "*I hope him to stay.*"]

507. "And now, their mightiest quelled, the battle swerved, with many an inroad gored."
i. *Subject,* 'battle.'
ii. *Attributive adjuncts of subject.* { 1. *Article,* 'the.' 2. *Participial phrase,* 'with many an inroad gored.'
iii. *Predicate,* swerved.

---

* When *do* is used as a mere auxiliary, it is better on the whole to treat it as forming, with the dependent infinitive, one predicative notion, in the same way as the compound tenses of verbs. Otherwise, in perfect strictness, *do* should be treated as constituting an incomplete predicate, of which the complement is the dependent infinitive. There is no objection to analysing sentences that contain the verb *do* in that manner.

viii. *Adverbial adjuncts of predicate.*
1. *Adverb*, 'now.'
2. *Noun, with attributive adjunct, in the nominative absolute*, 'their mightiest quelled.'

508 "We will never despair of success."
i. *Subject*, 'we.'
iii. *Predicate* (*incomplete*), 'will.'
iv. *Complement of predicate, infinitive mood*, 'despair.
viii. *Adverbial adjunct of predicate*, 'of success.'

508 *b*. "He gave him a letter to read."
i. *Subject*, 'he.'
iii. *Predicate*, 'gave.'
vi. *Object of verb*, 'letter.'
vii. *Attributive adjunct of object*, 'a.'
viii. *Adverbial adjuncts of predicate.*
1. 'him' (*i. e.* to him).
2. 'to read' (*i.e.* for reading,—*ad legendum*).

509 "I saw a man with a sword."
i. *Subject*, 'I.'
iii. *Predicate*, 'saw.'
vi. *Object of verb*, 'man.'
vii. *Attributive adjuncts of object.*
1. *Article*, 'a.'
2. *Prepositional phrase*, 'with a sword.'

510 "He killed a man with a sword."
i. *Subject*, 'he.'
iii. *Predicate*, 'killed.'
vi. *Object*, 'man.'
vii. *Attributive adjunct of object*, 'a.'
viii. *Adverbial adjunct of predicate*, 'with a sword.'

(NOTE.—In the example in § 509 the preposition *with* denotes a relation in which the *man* stands to the sword. In the example in § 510 the preposition *with* denotes a relation in which the action described by the verb *killed* stands to the sword.)

511 "He found all his wants supplied by the care of his friends."
i. *Subject*, 'he.'
iii. *Predicate*, 'found.'
iv. *Complement of predicate*, 'supplied' (in the attributive relation to *wants*).
v. *Adverbial adjunct of the complement of the predicate*, 'by the care of his friends.'
vi. *Object*, 'wants.'
vii. *Attributive adjunct of object*, 'his.'

(In the phrase "*by the care of his friends*," we may also separate the words "*of his friends*," as forming an attributive adjunct of the noun *care*.)

512 "A man of weak health is incapable of the thorough enjoyment of life."

i. *Subject*, 'man.'

ii. *Attributive adjuncts of subject.*
- 1. *Article*, 'a.'
- 2. *Prepositional phrase*, 'of weak health.'

iii. *Predicate (incomplete)*, 'is.'

iv. *Complement of predicate*, 'incapable.'

v. *Adverbial adjunct of the complement of the predicate*, 'of the thorough enjoyment of life.' (See the note on the last example.)

513 "Nobody but a man of powerful mind can comprehend the entire range of such a subject."

i. *Subject*, 'nobody.'

ii. *Attributive adjunct of subject*,* 'but a man of powerful mind.'

iii. *Predicate (incomplete)*, 'can.'

iv. *Complement of predicate, infinitive mood*, 'comprehend.'

v. *Object of the complement of the predicate*, 'range.'

vi. *Attributive adjuncts of object.*
- 1. *Article*, 'the.'
- 2. *Adjective*, 'entire.'
- 3. *Prepositional phrase*, 'of such a subject.'

514 "Now the bright morning star, day's harbinger, comes dancing from the East."

i. *Subject*, 'star.'

ii. *Attributive adjuncts of subject.*
- 1. *Article*, 'the.'
- 2. *Adjective*, 'bright.'
- 3. *Nouns in apposition*, 'day's harbinger.'

iii. *Predicate (incomplete)*, 'comes.'

iv. *Complement of predicate*,† 'dancing' (standing in the attributive relation to *star*).

viii. *Adverbial adjunct of the predicate*, 'from the East.'

---

* Some grammarians would explain this sentence by saying that *but* is a conjunction, and that we have a compound elliptical sentence. "Nobody can comprehend, &c., but a man of powerful mind can comprehend it." This is awkward, because it involves an assertion which is not made in the original sentence. Nobody would hesitate about the right way of explaining the sentence if the preposition *except* were substituted for *but*. We have before shown (§ 282) that *but* is a genuine old *preposition*. It is therefore better to explain sentences like the above in the manner adopted in the text.

† It is much better to class this example with such phrases as "*looks fine*," "*grows tall*," "*smells sweet*," &c., than to treat *dancing* as an attributive adjunct of the subject, which in the order of ideas it certainly is not.

515 "Thus the native hue of resolution is sicklied o'er with the pale cast of thought."

i. *Subject*, 'hue.'

ii. *Attributive adjuncts of subject.*
- 1. *Article*, 'the.'
- 2. *Adjective*, 'native.'
- 3. *Preposition and noun*, 'of resolution.'

iii. *Predicate*, 'is sicklied.'

viii. *Adverbial adjuncts of predicate.*
- 1. *Adverbial adjunct of place*, 'o'er.'
- 2. *Adverbial adjunct of cause*. 'with the pale cast of thought.'

516 It frequently happens that the attributive adjuncts of the subject or object have in their turn adverbial or other adjuncts of sufficient importance to be worth setting down separately. In that case they may be inserted in the analysis under a heading of their own. Thus:—

"Hence, loathed Melancholy,
Of Cerberus and blackest midnight born,
In Stygian cave forlorn.
'Mongst horrid shapes, and shrieks, and sights unholy."

i. *Subject*, 'melancholy.'

ii. *Attributive adjuncts of subject.*
- 1. *Adjective*, 'loathed.'
- 2. *Participle*, 'born.'

ii.*b*. *Adverbial adjuncts of 'born.'*
- 1. 'Of Cerberus and blackest midnight.'
- 2. 'In Stygian cave forlorn.'
- 3. ''Mongst horrid shapes, and shrieks, and sights unholy.'

iii. *Predicate (understood)*, 'go' (or depart).

viii. *Adverbial adjunct of predicate*, 'hence.'

II. COMPOUND SENTENCES.

a. Co-ordinate or Collateral Sentences.

517 All that has to be done with sentences of this kind is, to analyse each separately, and indicate the link of connexion in the case of those that are co-ordinate. [NOTE.—The conjunction that unites co-ordinate sentences does not enter into the construction of either of them.]

Example.—"The servant neglected his duty, and his master punished him."

A. The servant neglected his duty.
B. His master punished him.

Analysis of A.

i. *Subject*, 'servant.'
ii. *Attributive adjunct of object*, 'the.'
iii. *Predicate*, 'neglected.'
vi. *Object*, 'duty.'
vii. *Attributive adjunct of object*, 'his.'

Analysis of B.

i. *Subject*, 'master.'
ii. *Attributive adjunct of subject*, 'his.'
iii. *Predicate*, 'punished.'
vi. *Object of verb*, 'him.'
Conjunction that unites A and B, 'and.'

b. Sentences containing Subordinate Clauses.

518 When there are subordinate clauses, the analysis of the entire sentence must first be conducted as if each subordinate clause were replaced by some single word. When the relation of the several clauses to the main sentence and to each other has thus been clearly marked, the subordinate clauses are to be analysed on the same principles as simple sentences. Connective words which are not substantives, adjectives or adverbs, do not enter into the grammatical structure of the clauses which they introduce. It will be convenient to mark the subordinate clauses, as they occur, by some letter of the alphabet.

Examples of the Analysis of Compound Sentences.

519 "That he did this, is perfectly certain."
i. *Subject. Substantive clause*, 'That he did this' (A).
iii. *Predicate* (*incomplete*), 'is.'
iv. *Complement of predicate*, 'certain.'
v. *Adverbial adjunct of complement of pred.*, 'perfectly.'

Analysis of A.

i. *Subject*, 'he.'
iii. *Predicate*, 'did.'
vi. *Object*, 'this.'
(The conjunction *that* does not enter into the construction of the dependent clause.)

520 "He inferred from these facts that the intention of the enemy was to retire across the river."

i. *Subject*, 'he.'
iii. *Predicate*, 'inferred.'
vi. *Object of verb, subst. clause*—'that the intention of the enemy was to retire across the river.' (A.)
viii. *Adverbial adjunct of pred.*, 'from these facts.'

Analysis of A.

i. *Subject*, 'intention.'
ii. *Attrib. adjuncts of subj.* { 1. 'the.' 2. 'of the enemy.'
iii. *Predicate (incomplete)*, 'was.'
iv. *Complement of pred.*, 'to retire.'
v. *Adverbial adjunct of the complement*, 'across the river,'

521 "I do not know who did this."

i. *Subject*, 'I.'
iii. *Predicate*, 'do know.'
vi. *Object of verb, substantive clause*—'who did this.' (A).
viii. *Adverbial adjunct of predicate*, 'not.'

Analysis of A.

i. *Subject*, 'who.'
iii. *Predicate*, 'did.'
vi. *Object of verb*, 'this.'

522 "I wish to know who you are."

i. *Subject*, 'I.'
iii. *Predicate*, 'wish.'
vi. *Object of verb, infinitive mood*—'to know.'
vii. *Object of dependent infinitive, substantive clause*—'who you are.' (A).

Analysis of A.

i. *Subject*, 'you.'
iii. *Predicate (incomplete)*, 'are.'
iv. *Complement of predicate*, 'who.'

523 "He would not say where he lived."

i. *Subject*, 'he.'
iii. *Predicate*, 'would say.'
vi. *Object of verb, substantive clause*—'where he lived.' (A).
viii. *Adverbial adjunct of predicate*, 'not.'

Analysis of A.

i. *Subject*, 'he.'
iii. *Predicate*, 'lived.'
viii. *Adverbial adjunct of predicate*, 'where.'

524 "The opinion of the judge was, that the prisoner was guilty."

i. *Subject*, 'opinion.'
ii. *Attributive adjuncts of subject*, 1. *Article*, 'the.' 2. *Prep. and noun*, 'of the judge.'
iii. *Predicate (incomplete)*, 'was.'
iv. *Complement of predicate, substantive clause*—'that the prisoner was guilty.' (A.)

Analysis of A.

i. *Subject*, 'prisoner.'
ii. *Attributive adjunct of subject*, 'the.'
iii. *Predicate (incomplete)*, 'was.'
iv. *Complement of predicate*, 'guilty.'

525 "He informed me yesterday that he had arrived."

i. *Subject*, 'he.'
iii. *Predicate*, 'informed.'
iv. *Complement of predicate, substantive clause*—'that he had arrived.' (A.)
vi. *Object of verb*, 'me.'
viii. *Adverbial adjunct of predicate*, 'yesterday.'

Analysis of A.

i. *Subject*, 'he.'
ii. *Predicate*, 'had arrived.'

526 "I told him that this would happen."

i. *Subject*, 'I.'
iii. *Predicate*, 'told.'
vi. *Object of verb, substantive clause*—'that this would happen.'
viii. *Adverbial adjunct of predicate*, 'him.'

[To understand a sentence like this, we must compare it with others in which such a verb as *tell* is used. If we say, "*I told him my opinion*," it is clear that the object of the verb is "*my opinion*," and that *him* is equivalent to *to him*, and consequently is in the adverbial relation to the verb *told*.]

527 "I convinced him that he was mistaken."

i. *Subject*, 'I.'
ii. *Predicate*, 'convinced.'
iv. *Complement of predicate, substantive clause*—'that he was mistaken.'

[It is easy to see that the construction of the last sentence must differ from that of the one before it. The construction of the former may be explained thus: "This would happen. I told him *that*." But we cannot say, "He was mistaken. I convinced him *that*." This shows that the relation of the substantive clause to the verb is quite different in these two examples].

528 "It is not true that he said that."

i. *Subject*, 'it.'
ii. *Attributive adjunct of subject, substantive clause*—'that he said that.' (A.)
iii. *Predicate* (*incomplete*), 'is.'
iv. *Complement of predicate*, 'true.'
viii. *Adverbial adjunct of predicate*, 'not.'

Analysis of A.

i. *Subject*, 'he.'
iii. *Predicate*, 'said.
vi. *Object*, 'that.'

The introductory conjunction does not enter into the structure of the clause.

529 "The cohort, which had already crossed the river, quickly came to blows with the enemy."

i. *Subject*, 'cohort.'
ii. *Attributive adjuncts of subject*,
  1. *Article*, 'the.'
  2. *Adjective clause*, 'which had already crossed the river.' (A.)
iii. *Predicate*, 'came.'
viii. *Adverbial adjuncts of predicate*,
  1. 'quickly.'
  2. 'to blows.'
  3. 'with the enemy.

Analysis of A.

i. *Subject*, 'which.'
iii. *Predicate*, 'had crossed.'
vi. *Object*, 'river.'
vii. *Attributive adjunct to object*, 'the.'
viii. *Adverbial adjunct to predicate*, 'already.'

530 "I saw the house in which he was born."

i. *Subject*, 'I.'
iii. *Predicate*, 'saw.'

vi. *Object*, 'house.'

vii. *Attributive adjuncts to object*, { 1. *Article*, 'the.' 2. *Adjective clause*, 'in which he was born.' (A.)

Analysis of A.

i. *Subject*, 'he.'
iii. *Predicate*, 'was born.'
viii. *Adverbial adjunct of predicate*, 'in which.'

531 "I know the man to whom he gave the money."
i. *Subject*, 'I.'
iii. *Predicate*, 'know.'
vi. *Object*, 'man.'
vii. *Attributive adjuncts of object*, { 1. *Article*, 'the.' 2. *Adjective clause*, 'to whom he gave the money.' (A.)

Analysis of A.

i. *Subject*, 'he.'
iii. *Predicate*, 'gave.'
vi. *Object*, 'money.'
vii. *Attributive adjunct of object*, 'the.'
viii. *Adverbial adjunct of predicate*, 'to whom.'

532 "He bought a horse with the money which he had saved."

Here the adjective clause, "*which he had saved*," is in the attributive relation to the noun *money*, which (with the preposition *with*, that precedes it) forms an adverbial adjunct to the predicate of the main clause, *bought*.

533 "Where thou dwellest, I will dwell."
i. *Subject*, 'I.'
iii. *Predicate*, 'will dwell.'
viii. *Adverbial adjunct of predicate, adverbial clause*—'where thou dwellest.' (A.)

Analysis of A.

i. *Subject*, 'thou.'
iii. *Predicate*, 'dwellest.'
viii. *Adverbial adjunct of predicate*, 'where.'

534 "He ran so fast, that I could not overtake him."
Principal clause, 'he ran so fast.'
Subordinate adverbial clause (*attached to the adverb* 'so,'

*which it modifies or defines**), 'that I could not overtake him.'

i. *Subject*, 'I.'

iii. *Predicate*, 'ran.'

viii. *Adverbial adjunct of predicate*, 'so fast, that I could not overtake him.' (A.)

Analysis of A.

"That I could not overtake him."

i. *Subject*, 'I.'

iii. *Predicate* (*incomplete*), 'could.'

iv. *Complement of predicate, infinitive mood*—'overtake.'

vi. *Object of verb* "*overtake*," 'him.'

viii. *Adverbial adjuncts of predicate*, { 1. *Adverb*, 'not.' 2. *Adverb*, 'that.'

[The word *that* in this subordinate sentence would usually be called a *conjunction*. But a little consideration will show that it is a conjunctive *adverb*. It refers to the circumstances under which the "*not being able to overtake him*" is predicated of "*me*," and therefore falls under the definition of an adverb (§§ 259, 267, and note on p. 73). The logical connexion of the ideas presented in the above sentence may be indicated by expressing it thus: "He ran so fast (*i. e.* with a certain degree of speed), *and so* I could not overtake him."

535 "He spoke loud, that I might hear him."

Principal clause, "he spoke loud."

Subordinate adverbial clause, "that I might hear him."

i. *Subject*, 'he.'

iii. *Predicate*, 'spoke.'

viii. *Adverbial adjuncts of predicate*, { 1. *Adverb*, 'loud.' 2. *Adverbial clause*, 'that I might hear him.' (A.)

Analysis of A.

i. *Subject*, 'I.'

iii. *Predicate* (*incomplete*), 'might.'

iv. *Complement of predicate* (*infinitive mood*), 'hear.'

vi. *Object of complementary verb* "*hear*," 'him.'

viii. *Adverbial adjunct of predicate*, 'that.'

---

* Subordinate clauses are always attached to *some one word* in the principal clause; and in the case of adverbial clauses, considerable care is often necessary to determine the proper word with which to connect them. To say simply that they are 'attached to the principal clause,' is not a sufficient analysis. An adverbial clause is the expansion of an adverb, and, therefore, like an adverb, must attach itself to some one word.

(The word "*that*" refers to the circumstances under which "*might hear*" is predicated of "*me*."*

536 "He spoke loud, in order that I might hear him."

Here the whole phrase, "in order that I might hear him," forms an adverbial adjunct to the verb *spoke*; but the subordinate clause, "*that I might hear him*," presents a construction quite different from that in the last example. It is no longer an adverbial clause qualifying the verb *spoke*, but an *adjective clause* qualifying the noun *order*. This also confirms the view stated above, that the word *that*, in these instances, is an adverb. An adjective clause never begins with a mere conjunction. (§§ 420, 421.)

537 "He is not so wise as he is witty."

Main clause, "He is not so wise."

Subordinate (*adverbial clause*), "As he is witty."

i. *Subject*, 'he.'

iii. *Predicate* (*incomplete*), 'is.'

iv. *Complement of predicate*, 'wise.'

v. *Adverbial adjunct of the complement*, 'so — as he is witty.' (A.)

Analysis of A.

i. *Subject*, 'he.'

iii. *Predicate* (*incomplete*), 'is.'

iv. *Complement of predicate*, 'witty.'

v. *Adverbial adjunct of the complement, relative adverb*—'as.'

This adverbial clause qualifies the adverb *so* in the main clause, the precise force of which it marks out more distinctly.

538 "He ran away because he was afraid."

Main clause, "he ran away."

Subordinate clause, "because he was afraid."

i. *Subject*, 'he.'

iii. *Predicate*, 'ran.

viii. *Adverbial adjuncts of predicate*, { 1. *Adverb*, 'away.' 2. *Adverbial clause*, 'because he was afraid.' (A.)

Analysis of A.

i. *Subject*, 'he.'

iii. *Predicate* (*incomplete*), 'was.'

iv. *Complement of predicate*, 'afraid.'

* As a general rule, it may be observed that when the event spoken of in the dependent clause is contingent upon that spoken of in the main clause, the connective word which introduces the dependent clause is *adverbial* in its force, and is not a mere conjunction. It always denotes, in such cases, the circumstances under which the predicate of the dependent clause is connected with its subject.

The conjunction *because* does not enter into the construction of the subordinate clause: it does not indicate the circumstances under which *being afraid* is predicated of *him*.

539 "I could not succeed, although I tried my best."

i. *Subject*, 'I.'
iii. *Predicate* (*incomplete*), 'could.'
iv. *Complement of predicate* (*infinitive mood*), 'succeed.'
viii. *Adverbial adjuncts of predicate*, { 1. *Adverb*, 'not.' 2. *Adverbial clause*, 'although I tried my best.' (A.) }

Analysis of A.

i. *Subject*, 'I.'
iii. *Predicate*, 'tried.'
vi. *Object*, 'best' (used substantively).
vii. *Attributive adjunct of object*, 'my.'

The conjunction *although* does not enter into the construction of the dependent clause.

It must be observed that in sentences like the above the adverbial adjuncts which are attached to the verb *could* are not *co-ordinate* adjuncts. The adverbial clause, "although I tried my best," does not connect itself with the verb "could," until the latter has been modified by the adverb *not*.

540 "If you do wrong, you will be punished."

i. *Subject*, 'you.'
iii. *Predicate*, 'will be punished.'
viii. *Adverbial adjunct of predicate, clause*—'if you do wrong.' (A.)

Analysis of A.

i. *Subject*, 'you.'
iii. *Predicate*, 'do.'
vi. *Object of verb*, 'wrong.'

The conjunction *if* does not enter into the construction of the dependent clause.

Analysis of Contracted Sentences.

541 Before proceeding with the analysis of a contracted sentence, the parts omitted must be expressed at full length.

542 "What man, seeing this, and having human feelings, does not blush and hang his head to think himself a man!"

In full,—"What man, seeing this, and having human feelings, does not blush to think himself a man (A); and what man, seeing this, and having human feelings, does not hang his head to think himself a man!" (B.)

Here we have two co-ordinate sentences coupled by the conjunction *and*.

Analysis of A.

i. *Subject*, 'man.'

ii. *Attributive adjuncts of subject*, { 1. 'What.' 2. 'Seeing this;' and 3. 'Having human feelings.'

iii. *Predicate*, 'does blush.'

viii. *Adverbial adjuncts of predicate*, { 1. *Adverb*, 'not.' 2. *Adverbial phrase of cause*, 'to think himself a man.'

The construction of (B) is precisely analogous.

543 "Old and young, in every cottage porch with garlands green, stand still to gaze, and gazing bless the scene."

In full,—"Old (persons), in every cottage porch with garlands green, stand still to gaze (A), and old (persons) in every cottage porch with garlands green, gazing bless the scene (B); and young (persons) in every cottage porch with garlands green, stand still to gaze (C), and young (persons) in every cottage porch with garlands green, gazing bless the scene." (D.)

It then appears that the sentence is made up of four co-ordinate sentences. It will be enough to analyse one of them.

Analysis of B.

i. *Subject*, 'persons' (*understood*).

ii. *Attributive adjuncts of subject*, { 1. 'old.' 2. 'gazing.'*

iii. *Predicate*, 'bless.'

vi. *Object of verb*, 'scene.'

vii. *Attributive adjunct of object*, 'the.'

viii. *Adverbial adjunct of predicate*, { 'in every cottage porch with garlands green.'

544 "I heard the ripple washing in the reeds,
And the wild water lapping on the crag."

---

* It must be observed that in sentences of this kind, although the participle *gazing* is (grammatically) an attributive adjunct to the subject, yet in its *logical* force it is equivalent to an adverbial adjunct to the predicate.

In full,—"I heard the ripple washing in the reeds (A), and I heard the wild water lapping on the crag." (B.)

Here we have two co-ordinate sentences connected by *and*.

Analysis of A.

i. *Subject*, 'I.'
iii. *Predicate*, 'heard.'
vi. *Object of verb*, 'ripple.'
vii. *Attributive adjuncts to object*, { 1. *Article*, 'the.' 2. *Participial phrase*, 'washing in the reeds.' }

ELLIPTICAL SENTENCES.

545 An elliptical sentence is one in which something is omitted which is essential to the complete construction of the sentence, but which is readily supplied in thought, without being expressed in words.

546 Contracted sentences are one variety of elliptical sentences, in which what is common to two or more co-ordinate sentences is expressed only once. In the sentences now to be considered, that which is omitted is not common to two or more clauses.

547 The relative pronoun and relative adverbs are sometimes omitted.

"That is the book I gave you." In full:—"That is the book *which* I gave you."

"That is the house I live in." In full:—"That is the house *which* I live in."

"That is the way I came." In full:—"That is the way *which* (or *by which*) I came." (Here the *which*, or *by which* will be in the adverbial relation to the verb *came*.)

"He left the day I arrived." In full:—"He left the day *that* (or *on which*) I arrived." (In this sentence *the day* is in the adverbial relation to *left; that* (or *on which*) is in the adverbial relation to *arrived;* and the dependent clause *that I arrived* is an adjective clause qualifying *day*.)

548 The commonest (and the most troublesome) elliptical sentences are those which begin with *as* and *than*. In analysing them care must be taken to ascertain *what the predicate really is* in the dependent clause, and what word the adverbs *as* and *than* qualify. (See §§ 267, 429—433.)

549 "He is as tall as I am." In full:—"He is as tall as I am *tall*." (Compare the sentence analysed in § 537.)

i. *Subject*, 'he.'
iii. *Predicate* (*incomplete*), 'is.'
iv. *Complement of predicate*, 'tall.'
v. *Adverbial adjunct of the complement of the predicate*, 'as' (modified by the adverbial clause, '*as I am tall*.') (A.)

Analysis of A.

i. *Subject*, 'I.'
iii. *Predicate* (*incomplete*), 'am.'
iv. *Complement of predicate*, 'tall' (understood).
v. *Adverbial adjunct of the complement* (relative adverb), 'as.'

In the above sentence if we ask what the predicate in the dependent clause is, (or what is predicated of *me*,) the answer is, "*being tall*;" and moreover not *being tall* simply, but *being tall in a certain degree*, which degree is denoted by the relative adverb *as*, which qualifies *tall* (understood) in the adverbial clause, just as the demonstrative adverb *as* qualifies *tall* in the main clause.

550 "He is more industrious than clever." In full:—"He is more industrious than he is clever."

In this sentence two things are predicated of the person spoken of, namely, his being industrious *in a certain degree*, and his being clever *in a certain degree*, and the sentence is so constructed as to draw a comparison between these two *degrees*. It is clear therefore that the adjective *clever* must have an adverbial adjunct of degree attached to it, as well as the adjective *industrious*. The adverbial clause "than he is clever" qualifies the adverb *more* in the main clause, indicating more precisely what degree of *more* is meant.

i. *Subject*, 'he.'
iii. *Predicate* (*incomplete*), 'is.'
iv. *Complement of predicate*, 'industrious.'
vi. *Adverbial adjunct of the complement of the predicate*, 'more—than he is clever.' (A.)

Analysis of A.

i. *Subject*, 'he.'
iii. *Predicate* (*incomplete*), 'is.'
iv. *Complement of predicate*, 'clever.'
v. *Adverbial adjunct to complement of predicate*, 'than.'

551 "When I was a child, I spake as a child." In full:—"When I was a child I spake as a child (speaks)."

i. *Subject*, 'I.'

iii. *Predicate*, 'spake.'

viii. *Adverbial adjuncts to predicate*,
1. *Adverbial sentence of time*, 'when I was a child.' (A.)
2. *Adverbial sentence of manner*, 'as a child speaks.' (B.)

Analysis of A.

i. *Subject*, 'I.'
iii. *Predicate (incomplete,)* 'was.'
iv. *Complement of predicate*, 'child.'
v. *Attributive adjunct of complement of predicate, article* 'a.'
viii. *Adverbial adjunct to predicate*, 'when.'

Analysis of B.

i. *Subject*, 'child.'
ii. *Attributive adjunct to subject*, 'a.'
iii. *Predicate*, '*speaks*.'
viii. *Adverbial adjunct to predicate*, 'as.'*

552 "He has not written so much as I have." In full:—"He has not written *so much*, *as* I have written *much*." (See § 431.)

The adverb *as* does not refer to the *manner* of my writing (*i.e.* it is not an adverb of *manner* qualifying the verb *have written*), but refers to the *quantity* that I have written (*i.e.* it is an adverb of *degree*, qualifying the word *much* understood).

553 "He has lived as many years as you have lived months." In full:—"He has lived *as many* years *as* you have lived *many* months."

In the adverbial clause *as* is an adverb qualifying *many*

---

* Instances may be multiplied endlessly to show that *as* is an adverb and not a mere conjunction. Here it plainly refers to the *manner* of the child's speaking.

It may be taken as a general rule that the relative adverbs *as* and *than* qualify some word (expressed or understood) in the clause which they introduce, of the same kind of meaning as the word qualified by the simple or demonstrative adverb in the main clause.

This principle is most clearly seen in operation in Latin. We frequently find such sentences as this: "Qui se oppido munitissimo tamdiu tenuit, quamdiu in provincia Parthi fuerunt." (*Cic. Fam.* xii. 19.) "Who kept himself in a very strongly fortified town *so long as* the Parthians were in the province." We see from the Latin that the adverb *as* really qualifies the word *long* understood. But it is the common practice in Latin (and the universal practice in English) to omit the word qualified by *quam* (English *as*), when it is already expressed in the main clause; as, "Vixit tamdiu quam licuit in civitate bene beateque vivere." (*Cic. de Off.* ii. 12.) So we often find *eo die—quo die* (on that day on which), where the kind of ellipsis is much the same. (Compare § 431.)

understood, and the whole adverbial clause qualifies the demonstrative *as* in the main clause.

554 "He has written more letters than you." In full:—"He has written more letters than you have written many letters."

It is clear that in the subordinate clause the object of the verb *have written* is not expressed, and yet is requisite to make the sense complete. A transitive verb must have an object (expressed or understood) as well as a subject. And as a comparison is drawn between the *number* of letters written in each case, the object *letters* (understood) must be accompanied by an adjective indicating number, which in its turn must be qualified by an adverb (viz. *than*), to admit of the comparison which is instituted. The whole adverbial clause, "*than you, &c.*" qualifies *more* in the main clause, indicating what degree of *more* is meant. The clause therefore forms an *adverbial adjunct of degree.*

555 "He does not write so well as you." In full:—"He does not write *so well* as you write *well.*" The adverbial idea which is attached to the predicate in the subordinate clause is not the *manner* (speaking generally) of 'your writing,' but the *degree of goodness* that marks 'your writing.' The idea of *goodness* will be expressed by *well*, and the notion of *degree* by the adverb *as* which qualifies *well.*

556 "I would as soon die as suffer that." Here it is clear that the word *as* in the subordinate clause does not mark the *manner* of the suffering referred to, but the *degree of readiness* with which 'I would suffer that.' Therefore *as* must qualify an adverb (marking *readiness*) understood. At full length the sentence is, "I would as soon die as (I would soon) suffer that."

557 "I would rather die than suffer that."

The analysis of the preceding sentence will guide us to that of the one before us. At full length it will be, "I would sooner die than (I would soon) suffer that." Here *than* qualifies the adverb *soon*, and the adverbial clause '*than I would soon suffer that,*' qualifies the adverb *sooner* in the main clause.

558 "He is richer than you suppose." At full length: "He is richer than you suppose he is rich." (See § 554). Here *than* is a relative adverb qualifying *rich* (understood), and the adverbial clause, '*than you suppose he is rich,*' qualifies the adjective *richer* in the main clause, defining more clearly the degree of *richer* that is meant.

i. *Subject*, 'he.'
iii. *Predicate* (*incomplete*), 'is.'
iv. *Complement of predicate*, 'richer.'
v. *Adverbial adjunct of complement*, 'than you suppose.' (A.)

Analysis of A.

i. *Subject*, 'you.'
iii. *Predicate*, 'suppose.'
vi. *Object*, 'that he is rich.' (B.)

Analysis of B.

i. *Subject*, 'he.'
iii. *Predicate* (*incomplete*), 'is.'
iv. *Complement of predicate*, 'rich.'
v. *Adverbial adjunct of predicate*, 'than.'

559 "I am not such a fool as to believe that." In full:—"I am not such a fool as (I should be foolish) to believe that."
i. *Subject*, 'I.'
iii. Predicate, (*incomplete*), 'am.'
iv. *Complement of predicate*, 'fool.'
v. *Attributive adjuncts of complement of predicate*, { 1. 'a.' 2. 'such—as to believe that.' (A.) }
viii. *Adverbial adjunct of predicate*, 'not.'

Analysis of A.

i. *Subject*, 'I.'
iii. *Predicate* (*incomplete*), 'should be.'
iv. *Complement of predicate*, 'foolish' (understood).
v. *Adverbial adjunct of complement*, 'as.'
viii. *Adverbial adjunct of predicate, denoting 'condition,'* 'to believe that.'

560 "He looks as if he knew me." In full:—"He looks as (he would look) if he knew me."

561 "I agree with you in so far as you adopt his opinion."
Here a comparison is instituted between *the extent* to which 'I agree,' and *the extent* to which 'you adopt his opinion.' Each clause therefore involves a word denoting *extent*, qualified respectively by a demonstrative and a relative adverb of degree, by means of which the comparison is effected. At full length therefore the sentence will be, "I agree with you in so far as you adopt his opinion (far)."

562 "He knows that, inasmuch as I have told him." That is to say, the extent to which it is the fact that he knows that, is equivalent to the extent to which it is the fact that I have told him. The relative *as*, therefore, in the subordinate clause qualifies a word (understood) denoting extent, and the whole

adverbial clause qualifies the demonstrative *as* in the phrase *in as much;* the phrase *in as much* being in the adverbial relation to the verb *knows.*

563 "I cannot give you so much as five pounds." In full:—"I cannot give you so much as five pounds (are much)." (In Latin the correlatives *tantum* and *quantum* would be used; and *quantum* shows that the idea of quantity belongs as essentially to the dependent as to the main clause.)

564 "I cannot give you more than five pounds." The analogy of the preceding sentence shows that we must fill up the ellipsis thus: "I cannot give you more than five pounds are much."*

565 "Whether he likes it or not, I shall do it."

This is a contracted elliptical sentence.

Whether is equivalent to *if either* (Latin, *sive,* i. e. *si vel*). At full length we get two co-ordinate sentences.

(A) "If he likes it, I shall do it."
(B) "If he does not like it, I shall do it."

566 "I cannot but believe what you say."

In full: "I cannot (do anything) but (*i. e.* except) believe what you say."

It is best to consider *but* as a preposition (see § 282 *note*). In that case *but believe* forms an attributive adjunct to *anything,* which it limits or defines.

567 "We can but fail if we try."

Here *but* is equivalent to *only.* It is an adverb, qualifying *fail,* which forms the complement of the predicate.

568 *But* sometimes has the force of *unless* or *except.* It must then be regarded as a subordinative conjunction. Thus: "He never sees his son, but he upbraids him." Here "but he upbraids him" forms an adverbial clause of condition, which it is best to regard as limiting, or qualifying, the adverb *never.*

569 "There is nothing born but has to die."

In full: "There is nothing born but that which has to die. Here *but* is a preposition, governing *that* understood; and the whole prepositional phrase, "*but that which has to die,*"

* If it be urged that in Latin *quam* takes the same case after it as before it, and that the English construction must be analogous to the Latin in that as well as other respects, there seems to be no other way of supplying the ellipse than by saying, "I cannot give you more than (I should give you in amount by giving you) five pounds."

forms an attributive adjunct to *nothing*, which it limits or defines.

570 *But* is sometimes equivalent to *that—not*. Thus: "No man is so depraved, but some glimmerings of conscience remain in his soul." Here the subordinate adverbial clause modifies the adverb *so*.

571 "Now that you have finished your task, you may go and play."

Here the adverbial clause, "*that you have finished your task*," modifies (*i. e.* defines more exactly) the adverb *now*, which is in the adverbial relation to the verb *may*. In the adverbial clause itself, *that* is an adverb (of time), and is in the adverbial relation to the verb *have finished*. (See §§ 267, 289).

572 "He died before I reached the house."

A mode of explaining such sentences as the above was suggested in § 289. There is also another mode in which they may be explained. The English idiom permits a substantive sentence to follow a preposition when it begins with *that* (See § 418). The words *before*, *after*, and *since*, may therefore be treated as prepositions governing a substantive clause, the preposition with the clause that it governs forming an adverbial adjunct to the verb of the main clause. This explanation, indeed, is the only one that will suit the word *until*, which is never used as an adverb.*

PARSING.

573 The preceding system of analysis still leaves us with groups of words in many cases, into the mutual relations of which it does not enter. When a minute account of each word of a sentence is given, including not only its syntactical relation to other words, but also its etymological inflections and accidents, the process is termed *parsing*. Two or three examples will show the mode in which it should be performed better than any system of rules.

574 "I told him that I did not know who had taken the red book that lay on the table."

I.—Personal pronoun of the first person, singular number, in the nominative case, because it is the subject of the verb *told*.

told.—Transitive verb: in the active voice, indicative mood, past indefinite tense, first person, singular number; in

* The use of *nachdem* in German corroborates the above view.

the predicative relation to *I*, with which it agrees in number and person.

him.—Personal pronoun of the third person and the masculine gender; in the singular number and objective case, standing in the adverbial relation to the verb *told*, of which it is the indirect object.

that.—Subordinative conjunction, connecting the substantive clause, "*I did not know—table*," with the verb *told*.

I.—Personal pronoun of the first person, in the singular number and nominative case: subject of the verb *did*.

did.—Auxiliary verb, in the active voice, indicative mood, past indefinite tense, first person singular; in the predicative relation to *I*, with which it agrees in number and person.

not.—Adverb of negation, modifying the verb *did*.

know.—Transitive verb, in the active voice, infinitive mood, imperfect tense; depending on the verb *did*.

who.—Interrogative pronoun, in the singular number, third person, and nominative case, being the subject of the verb *had taken*.

had taken.—Transitive verb; in the active voice, indicative mood, past perfect tense, third person, singular number; in the predicative relation to the pronoun *who*, with which it agrees in number and person.

the.—Definite article, in the attributive relation to *book*.

red.—Qualitative adjective, in the positive degree of comparison; in the attributive relation to the noun *book*.

book.—Common noun, of the neuter gender; in the singular number and objective case, standing in the objective relation to the verb *had taken*.

that.—Relative pronoun, of the neuter gender, third person, and singular number, to agree with its antecedent *book*, and in the nominative case because it is the subject of the verb *lay*.

lay.—Intransitive verb; in the active voice, indicative mood, past indefinite tense, third person, singular number, in the predicative relation to *that*, with which it agrees in number and person.

on.—*Preposition*, governing the noun *table*.

the.—Definite article, in the attributive relation to the noun *table*.

table.—Common noun, of the neuter gender; in the singular number, objective case, governed by the preposition *on*.

575 "I will not let you in, unless you tell me who you are."

I.—Personal pronoun of the first person, in the singular number and nominative case; subject of the verb *will let.*

will let.—Transitive verb, in the active voice, indicative mood, future indefinite tense, singular number and first person, having for its subject *I*, with which it agrees in number and person.

not.—Adverb of negation, modifying the verb *will let.*

you.—Personal pronoun of the second person, in the plural number and in the objective case, being the object of the verb *will let.*

in.—Adverb, modifying the verb *will let.*

unless.—Subordinative conjunction, joining the adverbial clause "*you tell me who you are*" to the verb *will let.*"

you.—Personal pronoun of the second person, in the plural number, and in the nominative case, because it is the subject of the verb *tell.*

tell.—Transitive verb, in the active voice, subjunctive mood, present indefinite tense, plural number, and second person, in the predicative relation to *you*, with which it agrees in number and person.

me.—Personal pronoun of the first person, in the singular number and objective case, governed by the verb *tell.*

who.—Interrogative pronoun, in the singular number* and nominative case,† being in the predicative relation to the word *you* (or because the verb *be* takes the same case after it as before it).

you.—Personal pronoun of the second person, in the plural number and in the nominative case, being the subject of the verb *are.*

are.—Neuter (or intransitive) verb, in the indicative mood, present indefinite tense, plural number, and second person; in the predicative relation to *you*, with which it agrees in number and person.

---

* Although *you* is plural, it is singular in sense, and therefore *who* is singular.

† Few mistakes are more frequently committed, even by good writers, than to put a relative or interrogative pronoun in a dependent sentence in the accusative case instead of the nominative. Thus, "Whom say ye that I am?" is ungrammatical, because the interrogative pronoun belongs to the dependent clause, and is in the predicative relation to *I.* It is not the object of the verb *say.* The object of *say* is the whole clause "*that I am who.*" So such a sentence as "The man whom the witness declared did the deed" is an instance of a very common blunder. The relative pronoun in it should be in the nominative case, because it is the subject of the verb *did.* The object of *declared* is not a single word, but an entire clause (with *that* understood); or "the witness declared" may be treated as being parenthetical."

PRACTICAL EXERCISES

ON THE CHIEF

PRINCIPLES AND RULES.

[The following exercises are not sufficiently long or numerous to furnish the pupil with a proper amount of grammatical practice; but they may easily be amplified by the teacher, by means of examples taken from almost any English book.]

The numbers placed at the commencement of each exercise are those of the paragraphs in the Grammar to which they relate.

EXERCISES ON THE NOUN.

22 In the following lists, find out the words which are mis-spelt, and correct them:—

Repelled, inferrence, commited, rubber, defering, offering, confering, visitter, runer, suffering, marvelous, sufferrer.

23, 24 Correct the following:—

Happyly, hastyly, mercyless, merryer, scantyness, naughtyness, moveing, haveing, useing, useable, truely, senseible, fuseible.

Make derivatives from the following words by adding a syllable to them:—

Happy, hasty, love, strike, fuse, repel, rebel, refuse, allot, rap, dip, dig, refit, benefit, forbid, travel.

30, 31 Take a passage from some English book, and make separate lists of the common and proper nouns that occur in it.

33 Make a list of twenty collective nouns.

34 Write down the abstract nouns which correspond to the following adjectives:—

Pure, simple, good, bad, worthy, splendid, just, meek, temperate, large, wide, broad, slow, quick, red, blue, sour, sharp, sweet, distant, near, soft, able, innocent, durable, brilliant, merry, brief.

Write down the adjectives which correspond to the following abstract nouns:—

Nobility, stupidity, fickleness, suppleness, height, depth, acidity, dependence, sleepiness, greenness, rigidity, ductility, sonority, infirmity, patience, condescension, prosperity, wisdom.

38 Take a passage from some English book, and make separate lists of the masculine, feminine, and neuter nouns that occur in it.

Take the list of masculine nouns, and write opposite each the corresponding feminine noun (when there is one).

Make a list of twenty feminine nouns, and write opposite each the corresponding masculine noun (when there is one).

46—55 Take a passage from some English book, and write down separately all the nouns in the singular number that occur in it, and all the nouns in the plural number. Also write down the plural forms of the nouns in the singular, and the singular forms of the nouns in the plural.

Form the plurals of the following words :—

Man, box, gas, grotto, duty, bunch, sheaf, tooth, foot, thesis, effluvium, trick, marquis, hero, lady, brother, colloquy, life, leaf, thief, knife, marble, fancy, goose, calf, cow, deer, sheep, beau, negro, valley, book, arch, toy, blemish, boy, princess, genus, bandit, cherub, species, torch, half, fancy, buoy, envoy, convoy, victory.

65 Take a passage from some English book, and write down :— 1. All the nouns that are in the nominative case. 2. All the nouns that are in the objective case. 3. All the nouns that are in the possessive case. Write down the declension of six of them at full length.

EXERCISES ON THE ADJECTIVE.

81 Make a list of twenty adjectives.

Write down separately the qualitative, quantitative, and determinative adjectives in the following list :—

Long, short, many, more, some, this, white, brown, alluring, two, second, ten, tenth, first, one, each, mine, thine, none, all, few, much, other, black, which, the, great, lovely, fierce, little, sleepy, wicked, just, happy.

83 Make or select ten sentences containing adjectives which are used attributively, and ten containing adjectives which are used predicatively.

107, 111. Form the comparative and superlative degrees of the following adjectives :—

Large, great, high, fierce, lovely, sleek, tame, full, rich, many, happy, handsome, common.

EXERCISES ON THE PRONOUNS.

133—172 Take a passage from some English book, and write out :—1. All the substantive pronouns; 2. All the adjective pronouns (or pronominal adjectives) which are used with the substantives to which they relate expressed; 3. All the adjective pronouns which are used substantively.

Specify also for what nouns those pronouns stand which are substantives, or are used substantively.

In the following sentences, specify to which of the classes marked A—K the pronouns belong. Indicate also whether they are used substantively or adjectively; and in the case of the relative pronouns point out their antecedents :—

Give me that pen. I will give you the money which I owe you. Which is the exercise that you have just written? Show me that exercise. He came to see me each day. I will give each of them an apple. Every one has his own tastes. I will pay the money to any one whom you may send. Neither of them shall have my money. Whoever does that shall be punished. Do you hear what I say? Which of you did this? Whom did your brother see at his father's house? One cannot learn everything. This is very unhandsome conduct on your part. I do not love them; they are selfish. I have not lost my pen, but my brother has lost his, and my sister has lost hers. He is a boy who does not know how to behave himself. Show me the book which you have in your hand. You, who profess such friendship for me, ought not to act thus. I saw him striking his brother. She sings better than her sister. They are tired. Their father has arrived. Give me that book; it is my father's. We are fond of reading. Thou art free. I tell thee it is not so. Will you not believe me when I tell you that your brother has arrived? Whose stick is that? Whosesoever sins ye remit, they are remitted.

State the person, gender, number, and case of the declinable pronouns in the preceding examples.

EXERCISES ON THE VERB.

176 Make a list of twenty transitive verbs. Make a list of twenty intransitive verbs.

177 In the following examples, point out whether the verb is used transitively or intransitively :—

He speaks. He speaks French. He talks too loud. He is talking nonsense. He is eating. He is eating his dinner. He rides to town every day. I ride a black horse. He plays when he ought to work. He plays too eagerly. He plays the flute. He is working a sum. Yeast makes beer work. He strikes the ball. The sound struck upon my ear. The snake twists and turns about. The earth turns round. He has twisted his ankle. He turned the man out of the room. The boy is spinning a top. The top spins round. I smell a rat. The rose smells sweet.

179—183 Show which of the verbs in the following examples are in the active, which are in the passive voice :—

I run. I am walking. He wept. He was killed. The man will be drowned. I shall be travelling at this time to-morrow. They were surprised at the news. He had never heard of such a thing. Such a thing had never been heard of. This will be heard of at home. The man has forfeited my esteem. He is writing a letter. He will be disliked by every one. He must be returning by this time. We had been following the hounds for two hours. Those documents will be destroyed. The man had been insulted. He has impressed the seal on the wax. He is gone. They are fallen.

180 Express the sense of each of the following examples by means of the passive voice of the verbs that are used :—

The man struck the boy. The cat killed the mouse. The soldiers are defending the city. The general had praised the soldiers. We shall refuse your request. They will have lost all chance of success. They will be spending their holidays at home. We have lent the man five shillings. John had been striking Thomas.

191, 193, 195 In the following examples, distinguish the verbs that are in the indicative mood from those that are in the subjunctive mood :—

Oh that it were with me as in days that are past. I could not open the door when I tried. I could not open the door if I tried. Except ye repent, ye shall all likewise perish. If this be granted, the proof is easy. He would not answer me when I called. He would persist in his contumacy in spite of all I could say. If you would lend me fifty pounds, I should be much obliged to you. Though hand join in hand, the wicked shall not be unpunished. I would not go even if they were to send for me. If that really happened, it was a great calamity. If you had the money when he asked for it, you ought to have paid him. If I had the money, I would give it to you. If that was the case, why did you not tell me?

197—200 In the following examples, point out when the imperfect participle is used, and when the gerund :—

I see a man riding on horseback. A man passed by, running at full speed. I like reading. He hates lying. A lying witness ought to be punished. He gained his ends by using false pretences. In keeping thy commandments there is great reward. The officer fell while leading his troops into action. See yonder bark, struggling against the wind and tide. The centre of the group was occupied by a figure holding a globe. We fell in with a ship sailing to America. We arrived there first by taking a shorter route. He is fond of improving his mind. He lives by begging from his friends. He went about, begging from his friends.

Care must be taken to use the gerund, and not the participle, when the action to be denoted is a separate object of thought, and is not regarded merely as an attributive notion. Thus it is incorrect to say, "I have great hopes of the boy improving," because the thing hoped for is not *the boy*, but *the process of improvement*. It must therefore be, "I have great hopes of the boy's improving."

Correct the following :—

I am pleased by you returning the money so soon. He was vexed at me leaving the room. I have great fears of the man dying. He could not answer the letter owing to his servant having mislaid it. I am displeased by you neglecting my orders. He was annoyed by him behaving so rudely. He dreads his father finding out what he has done. He tried to prevent his brother sharing the property with him. I was disappointed at my brother not answering my letter.

203—240 Let the teacher make the pupil conjugate a large number of verbs at full length, and explain carefully of what elements the compound tenses are formed.

Take a passage from some English book, select the verbs in it, and state the Voice, Mood, Tense, Number, and Person of each. [As this is a sort of exercise that should be very frequently repeated, it is hardly worth while to give a few examples, as any English book will furnish as many as may be desired.]

246 Turn each of the following sentences into the negative form:—

I love you. I shall go away. I have finished my task. He returned yesterday. He will return to-morrow. They are coming back. You must do that. He is loved by his friends. He was killed by the enemy. I find this very pleasant. I had thought of leaving. He sent the book back yesterday.

244 Put the following sentences into the interrogative form:—

You are happy. We said so. They are here. We have some money. My brother did that. Your sister sings well. She is pretty. You like music. The man set out yesterday. My father will return to-morrow. The man was surprised at it. I do not understand the question. I am not well. You sent me a letter by post. We received a letter from home. You are not afraid of the danger.

EXERCISES ON THE ADVERB.

260 Select, from some English book, twenty sentences containing adverbs. Point out the adverbs, and specify what words they qualify.

Separate the following adverbs into the classes enumerated in § 271.

Well, now, to-morrow, here, when, where, wherefore, how, therefore, yet, yes, quickly, as, so, quite, all, however, generally, enough, perhaps, often, early, little, twice, very, not, namely, above, whither, then, thither, once, immediately, why, thence, whereon, thus, while, within, that, than, wherein.

262 Arrange in separate classes the simple and the connective adverbs in the preceding list.

272—282 Arrange the prepositions in § 282 in the three classes mentioned in § 278.

277 In the following sentences point out the prepositions and the words that are governed by them, and state in each case

whether the preposition marks the relation of a thing to a thing, of an action to a thing, or of an attribute to a thing.

There is a horse in the meadow. I am fond of music. He rejoices in iniquity. A man on horseback has just passed. He is afraid of the dog. He killed the man with a sword. There is a man with a cocked hat. He is merry without being rude. Those men quarrelled with each other. They bade adieu to each other. Do not stand before me. Do not place yourself between me and the light. He is just in all his dealings. Such a master will be served with readiness. Come away from the window. The book is under the table. I see a book under the table. I see a book lying under the table.

[Continue the exercise by means of examples taken from some English book.]

284 **Distinguish the prepositions from the adverbs in the following examples:—**

He got up behind. There is a garden behind the house. Do not lag behind. I told you that before. He departed before my arrival. I came the day before yesterday. I could not come before. The earth turns round. The earth turns round on its axis. Open that box; there is a book inside. You will find a book inside that box. He repeated that over and over again. I see a picture over the chimneypiece.

EXERCISES ON THE CONJUNCTION.

259—292, 408, 409 **Compare carefully what is said about adverbs and conjunctions, and distinguish the adverbs (that is, the words which indicate or refer to the circumstances or conditions under which a predicate is spoken of some subject of discourse) from the conjunctions in the following examples; and in the case of the conjunctions, distinguish those that are co-ordinative from those that are subordinative.**

Though I am poor, yet I am contented. He is rich; nevertheless he is unhappy. They are poor because they are extravagant. I am sorry that you have not succeeded. He is industrious, and consequently he is successful. The man is neither wealthy nor wise. I believed, therefore have I spoken: we also believe, and therefore speak. Unless you try, you will not succeed. Except ye repent, ye shall all likewise perish. I have heard all your arguments, but still I am unconvinced. However well you do your work, you will never please such a master. I will behave so as to please my parents. I do not care whether you go or stay. If you do that again, I will send you away. Nothing is easier than that. He is so stupid that he can learn nothing. Though hand join in hand, the wicked shall not go unpunished. Tell me why you did that. When did you arrive? He arrived at the same time that I did. Where thou dwellest I will dwell. He is rich, and also generous. As he drew near, he heard music and dancing. He will either succeed or perish in the attempt. He cannot but grieve, for he has lost his best friend.

[Let further practice be given by means of examples made or selected.]

Exercises on the composition and derivation of words may be given by requiring the pupil to produce a certain number of examples of each class.

297—304 Analyze the following compound words, arranging them in the classes denoted by the letters A, B, C, D, E, and showing of what they are composed:—

Breakfast. Salt-cellar. Counting-house. Home-sick. Beehive. Love-sick. Plaything. Sea-sick. Post-office. Busy-body. Hearthstone. Stock-broker. Eavesdropper. Bedfellow. Clergyman. Pickpocket. Gunpowder. Makeweight. Save-all. Daylight. By-word. Foot-stool. First-rate. Godsend. Grandmother. Glow-worm. Milksop. Lily-white. Storehouse. Sweetheart. Turnspit. Horror-struck. Heart-broken. Tale-bearing. Slipshod. Hare-brained. Spendthrift. Blackbird. Club-footed. Upraise. Downstruck. Bow-legged. Up-stairs. Downhill. Therein. Thenceforwards. Herein. However. Whenever. Under-done. Chatterbox. Old-fashioned. New-fangled. Overrun. Underlet. Farewell. Hereafter. Likewise. Nevertheless. Heart-stirring. God-fearing.

EXERCISES ON SYNTAX.

386 Make or select ten sentences having a simple subject.

387 Make or select ten sentences having a compound subject.

388 Make or select ten sentences having a complex subject.

389 (Compare 348, 350, 360—362.) In the following examples, underline the grammatical subject of the verb, and doubly underline those words and phrases which stand in the attributive relation to the subject:—

Bad men are unwise men. Bold measures are the most likely to succeed. Rich men are not always generous. Good and wise advice is often thrown away. The old church has fallen into ruins. The brave soldiers defended their post to the last. Fine, warm weather followed the rain. A rich old uncle left him his property. I, your master, command you to do it. The author of that work must be a very learned man. A stitch in time saves nine. Every finite verb must have a subject. The most difficult tasks are overcome by perseverance. Along thy glades, a solitary guest, the hollow-sounding bittern guards its nest. There the village preacher's modest mansion rose. The palace of the prince was set on fire. A great deal of nonsense has been written on this subject. A messenger has arrived, bringing good news. The laughing children sported round his knee. A horseman, wrapped in a huge cloak, entered the yard. A bird in the hand is worth two in the bush. Alexander the Great, king of Macedon, died at an early age. The rent in his coat was made by an old nail. William the Conqueror was an able but tyrannical ruler.

Make or select twenty sentences containing an enlarged subject, and state in each case of what the enlargement consists.

391 Make or select a dozen sentences containing a simple predicate.

392, 393 Make or select a dozen sentences containing a complex predicate.

In the following sentences underline the verb of incomplete predication, and doubly underline the complement of the predicate:—

He grew rich suddenly. He called the man a liar. They became very poor. The wine tastes sweet. I am not happy. He is called John. He is thought wise. We do not deem the occurrence unfortunate. I believe him to be innocent. We wish him to succeed. That step was deemed imprudent. His friends thought him insane. The number cannot be reckoned. He ought not to say so. The tradesman was declared insolvent. Nothing is more hateful than treachery. Nothing can be more abominable. I wish the boy safe back again. He must do as he is bid. You may play in the garden. You must not touch that. They cannot escape. We judge this course to be expedient. The prisoner was declared guilty.

394, 396 In the above examples, point out those instances in which the complement of the predicate is in the predicative relation to the subject of the verb, and also those in which it is in the attributive relation to the object.

397 In the following examples, point out whether the enlargement of the predicate consists of an object or of an adverbial adjunct:—

He ran across the road. He struck the horse. He walks with a crutch. He set out yesterday. He believes in my honesty. He hopes for the best. I desire nothing better. The severity of the judge overawed the culprit. The prisoners were treated with leniency. He loves to find fault with everybody. He hates learning. He learns rapidly. The boys are playing in the garden. I will do that with great pleasure. I travelled through France with my brother. I rode on horseback. He rides a black horse.

Make a sentence with each of the following transitive verbs, and then enlarge the predicate, 1. With an object; 2. With an object and an adverbial adjunct. Thus: *He loves. He loves his parents. He loves his parents with all his heart.*

Strike. Speak. Love. Stretch. Help. Touch. See. Lead. Draw. Hate. Feel. Slay. Join. Build. Govern. Raise.

399 Take the sentences formed in the last exercise, and enlarge the object in each with two or more attributive adjuncts.

385—399 Analyze the following simple sentences according to the rules given in § 499, and specify to which of the classes enumerated in § 271 the adverbial adjuncts belong.

I know the author of that work. A wise man would have acted differently. The foolish boy threw his ball into the river. Officers of great experience led the expedition. We arrived at our destination in good time. He reached home drenched to the skin. I am tired of writing. Reading aloud tires me. Plenty of exercise is essential to health. Aid slighted truth with thy persuasive strain. Teach erring man to spurn the rage of gain. Downward they move, a melancholy band.

E'en now, perhaps, by cold and hunger led,
At proud men's doors they ask a little bread.

He used a stick to support his feeble steps. No actual survey of the country having been made, it is impossible to state accurately the amount of cultivated land. Did you ever hear a full account of that adventure? Not being acquainted with the facts of the case, I must decline pronouncing an opinion. Virtue and happiness go hand in hand. Full many a flower is born to blush unseen. In coming to a decision on this point, we must be guided solely by the evidence before us. The host himself no longer shall be found careful to see the mantling bliss go round.

Beside yon straggling fence that skirts the way,
With blossom'd furze unprofitably gay,
There, in his noisy mansion, skill'd to rule,
The village master taught his little school.

Analyze also at full length the examples contained in the exercises on §§ 389, 392, 393, 397.

ANALYSIS OF COMPOUND SENTENCES.

A. Co-ordinate Sentences.

1. *Uncontracted Co-ordinate Sentences.*

402 I know that the story is true, but still it is very strange. He is learned, and his brother is rich. They toil not, neither do they spin. Not only did he lose his fortune, but he lost his life also. Leave off making that noise, or I will turn you out of the room. Climb to the top of the hill, and then you will have a fine view. Either he is innocent, or he is the most crafty rogue in the country. The horses started off at full speed, and the carriage was soon dashed to pieces.

2. *Contracted Sentences.*

404, 517, 541. You must either be quiet or leave the room. Neither John nor his brother was present. He wrote the exercise quickly, but well. He pursued, but could not overtake the retreating enemy. The man left the house, but soon returned. He is a good writer, but a bad speaker. They are poor, but honest. You may go and play in the garden. The larynx, or rather the whole of the windpipe taken together, besides its other uses, is also a musical instrument.

Marathon became a magic word,
Which utter'd, to the hearer's eye appear
The camp, the host, the fight, the conqueror's career.

He felt keenly, though he never lamented, the loss of his friend.

Let the rich deride, the proud disdain,
These simple blessings of the lowly train.

He could write and cipher too. You must finish your task, and show it to me before twelve o'clock. They expected either to drive the enemy out of the country, or to compel them to lay down their arms.

In all my wanderings round this world of care,
In all my griefs (and God has given my share),
I still had hopes my latest hours to crown,
Amidst these humble bowers to lay me down;
To husband out life's taper at the close,
And keep the flame from wasting by repose.

B. Sentences containing Subordinate Clauses.

1. *Sentences containing Substantive Clauses.*

414—419, 518—528 Analyze the following sentences:—

Tell me how old you are. I know that your story cannot be true. It is scarcely to be expected that he will succeed in that attempt. Confess that you did wrong, and I will forgive you. The opinion of all sensible men was, that the undertaking was unwise. It is my opinion that you ought to adopt a different plan. I cannot tell you how sorry I am for your misfortune. I wish to know when this message was delivered. The thought that so many innocent persons suffered through his folly, is very distressing. 'Tis true; 'tis pity; and pity 'tis 'tis true. I wish to know how you are.

2. *Sentences containing Adjective Clauses.*

420, 421, 529, 530, 531, 532, 547 Compare these paragraphs before analyzing the following sentences:—

That is the man who stole the purse. This is the house in which I was born. He that is down need fear no fall. They that will be rich fall into temptation and a snare. Blessed is he whose transgressions are forgiven, and whose sin is covered. Youth is the time when hope and ambition are strongest.

Along the lawn, where scatter'd hamlets rose,
Unwieldy wealth and cumbrous pomp repose;
And every want to opulence allied,
And every pang that folly pays to pride.
Ill fares the land, to hastening ills a prey,
Where wealth accumulates, and men decay.

There is hope for him who repents of his sin. Where is the book I gave you yesterday? This is the only witchcraft I have used. I tried every method I could think of, but none succeeded. I have lost the money you gave me. We can never recover the time we have misspent. He passed his old age in the village where he was born.

3. *Sentences containing Adverbial Clauses.*

422—459, 533—540. Analyze the following sentences, specifying to what word in the main clause the adverbial clause is attached, and to which of the various classes of adverbial clauses (§§ 424—439) it belongs:—

I will tell you the secret when I see you. He still lay where he fell. He was so altered that I did not know him. He is happy because he is contented. While he is here, we shall have no peace. If you do that, you will suffer for it. I must not give you the book, for it is not mine. He will go to ruin unless he alters his conduct. He did not pay me when I called on him, because he had no money; but he said that he expected to get some when he went to town. If this account is true, the man is much to be pitied. Whatever may be the consequence, I will do what I have said. Except ye repent, ye shall all likewise perish. He is not happy, although he is so rich; for his only son has taken to vicious courses. Wherever you go, I will follow you. However dangerous such a course may be, it is the only one that we can adopt. I will walk in the garden until you return. While you are away, I will finish reading this book, which I will return to the owner when I see him. As the tree falls, so it will lie. He left the room that he might not be drawn into the quarrel. The mountain is so high that there is always snow on the top of it.

To them his heart, his love, his griefs, were given;
But all his serious thoughts had rest in heaven:
As some tall cliff that lifts its awful form,
Swells from the vale, and midway leaves the storm,
Though round its breast the rolling clouds are spread,
Eternal sunshine settles on its head.

The higher you climb, the wider will the prospect be (433). She is as good as she is beautiful.

4. *Elliptical Sentences.*

429—433, 548—572. Analyze the following sentences, first carefully supplying the words that are understood:—

He looks as stupid as an owl. He is not so clever as his brother. He is as rich as his brother. He is richer than I am. To prevaricate is as bad as lying. He is not so wise as he thinks. I had rather die than endure such a disgrace. It is not so bad to suffer misfortune as to deserve it.

To me more dear, congenial to my heart,
One native charm, than all the gloss of art.

Better is a dinner of herbs where love is, than a stalled ox and hatred therewith. I will do as you desire. He is not so rich as he once was. He is better to-day than yesterday. A thousand years in Thy sight are but as yesterday when it is passed. He is as fond of sport as ever. She is more captivating than ever. It is better to die than to live in such misery. I am not such a fool as to tell him my secret. It would be better to resign his claims at once than to spend all his fortune in law-suits. Oh, that it were with me as in days that are past! It seems as if we should never get to our journey's end. Even this is better than nothing. This is better than if we had lost everything. He looked as if he could kill me. I'd rather be a dog, and bay the moon, than such a Roman. He told me that wisdom was better than wealth; as if I did not know that before.

5. *Miscellaneous Examples for Analysis.*

Thus to relieve the wretched was his pride,
And e'en his failings lean'd to Virtue's side;
But in his duty prompt at every call,
He watch'd and wept, he pray'd and felt for all;
And as a bird each fond endearment tries,
To tempt its new-fledged offspring to the skies,
He tried each art, reproved each dull delay,
Allured to brighter worlds, and led the way.

The chequer'd earth seems restless as a flood
Brush'd by the wind. So sportive is the light
Shot through the boughs, it dances as they dance,
Shadow and sunshine intermingling quick,
And darkening and enlightening, as the leaves
Play wanton, every moment, every spot.

Either to disenthrone the King of heaven
We war, if war be best, or to regain
Our own right lost: Him to unthrone we then
May hope, when everlasting fate shall yield
To fickle chance, and chaos judge the strife.
The former, vain to hope, argues as vain
The latter.

Had I but served my God with half the zeal
I served my king, He would not in mine age
Have left me naked to mine enemies.

Breathes there a man with soul so dead,
Who never to himself hath said,
"This is my own, my native land?"
Whose heart hath ne'er within him burn'd,
As home his footsteps he hath turn'd
From wandering on a foreign strand?
If such there be, go mark him well;
For him no minstrel raptures swell.
High though his titles, proud his name,
Boundless his wealth as wish could claim;
Despite those titles, power, and pelf,

The wretch concentred all on self,
Living, shall forfeit fair renown,
And doubly dying, shall go down
To the vile dust from which he sprung,
Unwept, unhonour'd, and unsung.

The truth of being and the truth of knowing are one, differing no more than the direct beam and the beam reflected.

We take it for granted that we have a competent knowledge and skill, and that we are able to acquit ourselves properly in our native tongue; a faculty solely acquired by use, conducted by habit, and tried by the ear, carries us on without reflection (see § 387, *note*).

Ye are witnesses, and God also, how holily and justly and unblameably we behaved ourselves among you that believe.

When a man swears to the truth of his tale, he tacitly acknowledges that his bare word does not deserve credit.

See the sole bliss Heaven could on all bestow,
Which who but feels, can taste, but thinks, can know;
Yet, poor with fortune, and with learning blind,
The bad must miss, the good, untaught, will find.
Who wickedly is wise, or madly brave,
Is but the more a fool, the more a knave.

Ring out ye crystal spheres,
Once bless our human ears,
If ye have power to touch our senses so;
And let your silver chime
Move in melodious time;
And let the bass of heaven's deep organ blow.

Look once more, ere we leave this specular mount,
Westward, much nearer by south-west behold,
Where on the Ægean shore a city stands,
Built nobly, pure the air and light the soil;
Athens, the eye of Greece, mother of arts
And eloquence, native to famous wits
Or hospitable, in her sweet recess,
City or suburban, studious walks and shades.

A merrier man,
Within the limit of becoming mirth,
I never spent an hour's talk withal.
His eye begets occasion for his wit;
For every object that the one doth catch,
The other turns to a mirth-moving jest,
Which his fair tongue, conceit's expositor,
Delivers in such apt and gracious words,
That aged years play truant at his tales,
And younger hearings are quite ravished;
So sweet and voluble is his discourse.

Sweet are the uses of adversity,
Which, like the toad, ugly and venomous,
Wears yet a precious jewel in his head.
And this our life, exempt from public haunt,
Finds tongues in trees, books in the running brooks,
Sermons in stones, and good in everything.

EXERCISES IN PUNCTUATION.

485 1. Insert commas (when requisite) in the following sentences:—

The guilt of the prisoner is evident. The credit of this ingenious and useful invention belongs to my brother. The disgrace of having ill-treated and abandoned his wife and family will ever cling to him.

485 2. John having forgotten his master's orders made several mistakes. Unperceived by the enemy they escaped across the ditch. The orator undisturbed by the confusion thus created continued his speech.

485 3. The prisoner conscious that he was innocent maintained a bold attitude. Afraid of being punished for his fault he ran away. Cicero the eloquent leader of the senatorial party was marked for vengeance.

485 4. My maxim is do right and fear nothing. His advice to me was do not meddle with so quarrelsome a person.

485 5. His father brother and sister perished in the fire. All my hopes desires and prayers are directed to that object.

485 6, 7. Before quitting the subject I will make the following observation. This being granted the rest will follow. By incessant application to business his health was undermined. The general in consequence of the information then given determined to attack the enemy at day-break.

486 1. How I gained the money does not concern you. It is not true that I said so. Where I obtained this intelligence must remain a secret.

486 2. I do not believe the story that you have just told me. I cannot respect a man who has been guilty of such meanness. The man who told you that has deceived you. I am not an admirer of Hume's history which is disfigured by much prejudice and party spirit. Every one has heard of William the Conqueror who defeated the Saxons at Hastings. It is impossible to admire so egotistical a writer whose sole aim is to display himself.

486 3. He left the room that he might not witness the dispute. I will try my best lest I should fail. No one should expect to be rewarded if he does not use his best endeavours. I will not give you the book unless you promise to take care of it. He was so tired that he fell asleep as soon as he lay down.

488 He called immediately on his benefactor and thanked him for his generosity. I will either come myself or send my brother. He will neither give nor lend the book.

489 I came I saw I conquered. I believe it therefore I say so. He has dealt kindly towards me consequently I am his debtor.

490 He saw pursued and soon overtook the runaway. He trained the child wisely kindly and well. He is fond of painting drawing and music. I am pleased by your diligence obedience and progress.

Additional exercises can easily be given by dictating passages from some English book.

EXAMPLES OF MISTAKES FOR CORRECTION.

He said he had broke his leg.
They have wrote their exercises badly.
He has forsook his children.
He has not spoke a word.
He was suddenly took ill.
I have chose this book.
He has swam for half a mile.
He has already began Latin.
That author has rose to great eminence.
They have mistook the way.
The river has overflown its banks.
He eat his dinner with a good appetite.
It was said that he had beat his wife with a stick.
The river is froze over.
I have forgot my lesson.
He has trod that path many a time.
He has drank a glass of wine.
They have rang the bell.
He has drove the horse too fast.
I have strove my best.
The horse has fell down.
Between you and I, he is a great fool.
I will not be able to convince you.
I told him that I would be in London the next day.
He says that he shall not come unless you wish it.
He hopes that he will never meet with such a calamity again.
He had promised a large reward to whomever would undertake the risk.
Thou shalt go to all that I shall send thee.
I know what a rugged and dangerous path I am got into.
You were as good preach ease to one on the rack.
He were better be without it.
I had rather be a beggar than to live by such dishonest means.
We can easier walk than ride.
I write agreeable to your request.
How unworthy you have treated me.
All their ungodly deeds which they have ungodly committed.
He is a remarkable fine child.
The simplest points, such as are easiest apprehended.
The coach goes at an extreme slow pace.
He is a tolerable good scholar.
Their requests are seldom and reasonable.

Both those words end the same.
The definite article *the* is frequently applied to adverbs in the comparative and superlative degree.
Verbs neuter do not govern nouns and pronouns.
This offence I shall neither attempt to palliate nor deny (§ 407).
He is not only accused of theft, but of murder also.
The fact is so strange that it almost appears miraculous.
I soon expect to have finished my task.
He took rather a long walk.
He neither loves his father nor his mother.
He either is a fool or else a madman.
You must either be quiet or must leave the room.
He can not only read, but can write also.
He is a wise and a virtuous man.
I saw a black and white man walking together.
This veil of flesh parts the visible and invisible world.
The noun may be either of the singular or plural number.
A dispute arose between the young and old men.
Frequently both the pronoun and verb are omitted.
That word is used both in the literal and figurative sense.
It was preparatory to a future, a better, and perfect revelation.
There was but one only such a bough.
He is a dull and a prolix writer.
He is neither a wise nor witty author.
I had rather die than to live in such misery.
Give me that half the apple.
An articulate sound is the sound of the human voice formed by the organs of speech.
His knees smote one against another.
Who breaks a butterfly upon a wheel?
The Scriptures of the Old and the New Testaments contain a revelation.
Have you read Burke's Essay on the Sublime and Beautiful?
A master mind was equally wanting in the cabinet and in the field.
Hoping that I shall soon hear from you, believe me yours truly (§ 473).
Having failed in this attempt, no further trial was made.
Driven to desperation, a sudden sally was made by the soldiers.
Alarmed by so unusual an occurrence, it was resolved to postpone their departure.
He is so brave that he has no fears for death.
This was the usual punishment of high treason.
This will compensate to you for the loss of your fortune.
I have heard your request, and will consider of it.
I never have and never will indulge so unreasonable a hope.
Man never is, but always to be blest.
Such a course never has and never can lead to happiness.
The judge sentenced the prisoner to be hung.
This sort of mistakes are not uncommon.
Whom do you suppose gave me this watch?
Who is there? Me.
Who does this book belong to?
Who are you speaking of?
Whom did he say sent me that message?
Whom do men say that I am?
Who do men take me to be?

He feared the enemy might fall upon his men, whom he saw were off their guard.
You are a much greater loser than me by his death.
A stone is heavy, and the sand weighty; but a fool's wrath is heavier than them both.
Let us make a covenant, I and thou.
Let you and I take a walk together.
Let the elders that rule well be counted worthy of double honour, especially they who labour in the word and doctrine.
The sons of false Antimachus were slain; he who for bribes his faithless counsels sold.
It is not me you injure.
I perceive it is not the person whom I supposed it was.
Who was the letter from?
That will do well enough for you and I.
These kind of mistakes are very common.
I have left off troubling myself about those kind of things.
Every one must judge of their own feelings.
Let each esteem other better than themselves.
Every body trembled for themselves or their friends.
Let none of you imagine evil in your hearts against his neighbour.
She fell to laughing like one out of their right mind.
Your levity and heedlessness, if it continue, will prevent all substantial improvement.
Even a rugged rock or barren heath, though in themselves disagreeable, contribute by contrast to the beauty of the whole.
This book is one of the best that has been written.
I am not the first that have been wretched.

> What art thou? Speak, that on designs unknown,
> While others sleep, thus range the camp alone.

Each of these authors afford instruction.
Neither of these two senses are confined to this signification only.
Each in their turn like Banquo's monarch stalk.
Every mountain and island were moved out of their places.

> Praise from a friend, or censure from a foe,
> Are lost on hearers that our merits know.

And dost thou open thine eyes upon such an one, and bringest me into judgment with thee?
I am afraid of the man dying before a doctor can come.
The fact of me being a stranger to him does not justify his conduct.
He told me a long story about John having stolen a shilling.
A purse with ten shillings were stolen.
Is that John or James's book?
It is true what I told you in my letter.
He is not in the position he once was.
The audience was astonished at his eloquence.
That is seldom or ever the case.
Her brother is much older than her.

APPENDIX.

CONSTITUENT ELEMENTS OF THE ENGLISH LANGUAGE.

The English language is made up of words and forms derived from various sources, the chief of which are the Saxon, Celtic, Danish, Latin, French, and Greek languages. The structural elements of English, and most of the words in common use, are of Saxon origin, derived from the language spoken by the Anglo-Saxons. The settlements of the Danes introduced some Scandinavian elements, and the Norman Conquest introduced Norman French, which was the language formed by the amalgamation of the Scandinavian tongue of the Norsemen with the corrupted Latin of which the language of France chiefly consisted. The union of Norman French with Anglo-Saxon gave rise to the modern English language. A great many Latin elements found their way into the language through the Norman French; and others, together with some Greek terms, were introduced more directly by ecclesiastics in connexion with religious matters. Since the amalgamation of Anglo-Saxon and Norman French, many direct importations have been made of Latin and Greek words (especially in the departments of science and philosophy), and also of French, German, Spanish, and Italian words, with a few from more barbarous languages.

For further details, and more extensive information on this subject, the learner is referred to Latham's "Handbook of the English Language," and Craik's "Outlines of the History of the English language."

A List of the principal Latin Words from which Derivatives are formed in English.*

Acer (*sharp*), acidus (*sour*), acerbus (*bitter*); acrid, acerbity, acrimony, acid.

Acuo (*I sharpen*); acute, acumen.

Aedes (*house*); edifice, edify (*literally, to build up*).

---

* In most cases only a few samples of the English derivatives are given.

Aequus (*level*); equal, equation, equator, adequate, equity, iniquity, equivocate, equinox.
Aestimo (*I value*); estimate, esteem. Aestus (*tide*); estuary.
Aeternus, i.e. aeviternus (*of endless duration*); eternity, eternal.
Aevum (*age*); coeval, primeval. Agger (*heap*); exaggerate.
Ager (*field*); agriculture.
Ago (*I set in motion, drive, do*); agent, act, agile, agitate.
Alacer (*brisk*); alacrity.
Alius (*other*), alter (*other of two*); alien, alibi, alter, alternate.
Alo (*I nourish*); alimony, aliment. Altus (*high, deep*); altitude, exalt.
Ambitio (*going round, courting favour*); ambition, ambitious.
Ambulo (*I walk*); amble, somnambulist (i.e. *sleep-walker*).
Amo (*I love*), amicus (*friend*), amor (*love*); amour, amorous, amicable, amiable.
Amoenus (*pleasant*); amenity. Amplus (*large*); ample, amplify.
Ango (*I choke*), anxius; anxious, anxiety, anguish.
Angulus (*corner, bend*); angle.
Anima (*breath*), animus (*mind*); animate, animal, magnanimous, animosity.
Annulus (*ring*); annular. Annus (*year*); annual, anniversary.
Anus (*old woman*); anile. Aperio (*I open*); April, aperient, aperture.
Apis (*bee*); apiary. Appello (*I call*); appellation, appellant, appeal.
Aptus (*fitted*), apto (*I fit*); adapt, apt.
Aqua (*water*); aqueous, aquatic, aqueduct.
Arbiter (*umpire, go-between*); arbitrate, arbitrary.
Arbor (*tree*); arbour. Arca (*chest*); ark. Arcus (*bow*); arc, arch.
Ardeo (*I burn*); ardent, ardour, arson. Arduus (*steep*); arduous.
Arena (*sand*); arena, arenaceous. Argentum (*silver*); argent.
Argilla (*clay*); argillaceous. Arguo (*I prove*); argue, argument.
Aridus (*dry*); arid, aridity. Arma (*fittings, arms*); arms, arm, armour.
Aro (*I plough*); arable, earing. Ars (*skill*); art, artist, artifice.
Artus (*joint*), articulus (*little joint or fastening*); articulate, article.
Asinus (*ass*); asinine. Asper (*rough*); asperity, exasperate.
Audax (*bold*); audacious, audacity. Audio (*I hear*); audience, audible.
Augeo (*I increase*); augment, auction, author, authority.
Aurum (*gold*); auriferous.
Auspex (*one who takes omens from birds*); auspicious, auspices.
Auxilium (*help*); auxiliary.
Avarus (*greedy*); avarice, avaricious. Avidus (*eager*); avidity.
Avis (*bird*); aviary. Auris (*ear*); aurist, auricular.
Barba (*beard*); barb, barbed, barber. Beatus (*blessed*); beatitude.
Bellum (*war*); belligerent, rebel. Bene (*well*); beneficent, benediction.
Benignus (*kind*); benign. Bestia (*beast*); beast, bestial.
Bini (*two by two*); binary. Bis (*twice*); bissextile, bisect.
Blandus (*coaxing*); bland. Brevis (*short*); brief, brevity.
Caballus (*horse*); cavalry.
Cado, *sup.* casum (*I fall*); cadence, ac-cident, oc-casion, casual.
Caedo, caesum (*I cut*); suicide, regicide, incision, concise, cement (*i.e.* caedimentum).
Calamitas; calamity. Calcitro (*I kick*); recalcitrant.

Calculus (*pebble*); calculate. Calx; chalk, calcine.
Callus (*hard skin*), callosus; callous. Campus (*plain*); camp, encamp.
Candeo (*I burn or shine*), candidus (*white*); candid, incandescent, incendiary, candle, candour.
Canis (*dog*); canine. Canna (*reed or tube*), canalis; canal, channel.
Canto (*I sing*); chant, incantation.
Capillus (*hair*); capillary. Carmen (*song*); charm.
Capio (*I take*), captus (*taken*); captive, capacity, accept, conception, recipient, anticipate.
Caput (*head*); cape, capital, captain, chapter, decapitate, precipitate.
Carbo (*coal*); carbon, carboniferous. Carcer (*prison*); incarcerate.
Caro, carnis (*flesh*); carnal, incarnate, charnel-house.
Carpo (*pluck*); carp. Carus (*dear*); charity.
Castigo (*restrain*); castigate, chastise. Castus (*pure*); chaste.
Casus (*falling*); case. Causa; cause.
Caveo, cautum (*I take care*); caution.
Cavus (*hollow*); cave, cavity, excavate.
Cedo (*I go*); cede, precede, proceed, cession.
Celeber (*frequented*); celebrate, celebrity.
Celer (*quick*); celerity. Celo (*I hide*); conceal.
Censeo (*I judge*); censor, censure. Centum (*hundred*); cent, century.
Centrum; centre, concentrate, centrifugal.
Cerno, cretum (*I distinguish*); discern, concern, discreet, secret.
Certus (*resolved*); certain, certify. Cesso (*I loiter*); cease, cessation.
Charta (*paper*); chart, charter, cartoon.
Cingo (*I gird*); cincture, succinct.
Circum (*round*), circus (*a circle*); circle, circulate, circuit, circumference.
Cista (*box*); chest. Cito (*I rouse*); citation, excite.
Civis (*citizen*); civil, civic, city (*from* civitas).
Clamo (*I shout*), clamor; claim, exclaim, clamour.
Clarus (*bright*); clear, clarify. Classis; class, classic.
Claudo, clausum (*I shut*); close, enclose, exclude, preclude.
Clemens (*mild*); clemency, inclement.
Clino (*I bend*); incline, recline, declension.
Clivus (*sloping ground*); declivity. Coelebs (*bachelor*); celibacy.
Coelum (*heaven*); celestial. Cogito (coagito—*I think*); cogitate.
Cognosco (*I examine, know*); recognize, cognizant.
Colo, cultum (*I till*); culture, cultivate, colony.
Color; colour. Columna; column.
Comes (*companion*); concomitant, count.
Commodus (*convenient*); commodious, commodity, incommode.
Communis; common, community. Contra (*against*); counter.
Copia (*plenty*); copious. Copulo (*I join together*); copulative.
Coquo, coctum (*I boil*); cook, decoction.
Cor, cordis (*heart*); cordial, concord, record. Corona; crown.
Corpus (*body*); corps, corpse, incorporate, corporeal, corpulent.
Cras (*to-morrow*); procrastinate.
Credo (*I believe*); creed, credulous, incredible, credit. Creo; create.
Cresco, cretum (*I grow*); increase, accretion, crescent.

Crimen (*charge*); crime, criminal. Crispus (*curled*); crisp.
Crudus (*raw*), crudelis; cruel, crude. Crusta; crust.
Crux (*cross*); crusade, crucify, excruciate.
Cubo, cumbo (*I lie*); succumb, recumbent.
Cubitus (*a bend, elbow*); cubit. Culpa (*fault*); inculpate, culpable.
Culter; coulter. Cumulus (*heap*); accumulate.
Cupidus (*eager*); cupid, cupidity.
Cura (*care*); curator, curious, procure, secure.
Curro, cursum (*I run*); concur, discursive, current, curricle, succour, course.
Curvus (*bent*); curve. Custodia (*guard*); custody.
Damno; damn, condemn. Debeo, debitum (*I owe*); debt, debit.
Debilis (*weak*); debility. Decem (*ten*); December, decimal, decimate.
Decens (*becoming*), decor, decorus; decent, decorous.
Densus; dense, condense.
Dens, dentis (*tooth*); dentist, trident, indent.
Desidero (*I long for*); desire, desiderate.
Deus (*God*); deity, deify, deodand (*to be given to God*).
Dexter (*right*); dexterous, dexterity.
Dico, dictum (*I say*); contradict, predict, diction, dictate.
Dies (*day*); diary, diurnal.
Digitus (*finger*); digit, digital. Dirus; dire.
Dignus (*worthy*); condign, dignity, dignify.
Disco (*I learn*); disciple, discipline.
Divido; divide, division. Divinus; divine.
Do, datum (*I give*); dative, addition, date.
Doceo (*I teach*); docile, doctor, doctrine.
Dolor (*grief*), doleo (*I grieve*); dolorous, condole.
Domo (*I tame*); indomitable. Dono (*I present*); donation, condone.
Domus (*house*); domicile.
Dominus (*master*); dominate, dominant, domineer.
Dormio (*I sleep*); dormant, dormitory, dormouse.
Dubius (*doubtful*); doubt, dubious, indubitable.
Duco, ductum (*I lead*), dux (*leader*); conduct, duke, adduce, seduce, educate.
Duo (*two*); dual, duet, duel.
Durus (*hard*), duro (*I harden*); endure, durable, indurate.
Ebrius (*drunken*); ebriety, inebriate. Edo (*I eat*); edible, esculent.
Ego (*I*); egotist. Emo (*I buy*); redeem, exempt.
Eo, ivi, itum (*I go*); exit, initial, transit, perish.
Equus (*horse*), eques (*horseman*); equine, equerry, equitation.
Erro (*I wander*); err, error, erroneous, erratic, aberration.
Esca (*food*); esculent. Examino (*I weigh*); examine.
Exemplum; example, sample. Exerceo; exercise.
Expedio (*I set free*); expedite, expedition.
Experior (*I try*); experiment, expert, experience.
Faber (*mechanic, engineer*), fabricor; fabricate.
Fabula (*little story*); fable, fabulous. Facetus (*clever*); facetious.
Facies (*make* or *appearance*); face, facial, superficial.

Facilis (*easy*); facile, facility, difficulty, faculty, facilitate.
Facio (*I make, do*); fact, faction, affect, infect, defect, deficient, benefactor, manufactory, perfect.
Fallo (*I deceive*); false, fail, fallible.
Fama (*report*); fame, infamous. Familia; family, familiar.
Fans (*speaking*), fatum (*what is spoken or decreed*); infant, fate, fatal.
Fanum (*temple*); fane, profane, fanatic. Fastidium (*loathing*); fastidious.
Fatuus (*tasteless, silly*); fatuous, infatuated. Faveo; favour.
Febris; fever, febrifuge, febrile. Fecundus (*fertile*); fecundity.
Felis (*cat*); feline. Felix (*happy*); felicity.
Femina (*woman*); feminine, effeminate.
Fero (*I bear*); fertile, infer, defer, circumference; *part.* latus; dilate, translate.
Ferox; ferocious, ferocity. Ferrum (*iron*); ferruginous.
Ferveo (*I boil*); fervent, fervid, effervesce.
Festus (*solemn, joyful*); festive, feast. Fibra; fibre.
Fides (*faith*), fido (*I trust*); fidelity, confide, perfidy, defy.
Figo, fixum (*I fasten*); fix, crucifix. Filius (*son*); filial, affiliate.
Findo, fissum (*I cleave*); fissure, fissile.
Fingo, fictum (*I shake*); fiction, figure, feign.
Fendo (*I strike*); offend, defend, fender.
Finis (*end*); final, finite, finish, confine, define, infinitive.
Firmus; firm, confirm, affirm. Fiscus (*treasury*); fiscal, confiscate.
Flaccidus; flaccid. Flagellum (*scourge*); flagellation.
Flagitium (*disgrace*); flagitious. Flagro (*I burn*); flagrant, conflagration.
Flamma; flame, inflammation. Flo, flatum (*I blow*); inflate, flatulent.
Flecto (*I bend*); deflect, inflect, flexible, circumflex.
Fligo, flictum (*I strike*); afflict, conflict, profligate.
Flos, floris (*flower*); flora, florid, floral, effloresce.
Fluo, fluxum (*I flow*), fluctus (*wave*); flux, fluxion, influence, superfluous fluctuate, fluid.
Fodio, fossum (*I dig*); fosse, fossil.
Folium (*leaf*); foliage, folio, exfoliate, trefoil.
Fons; fount, font, fountain. Forma; form, reform, inform.
Formido (*fear*); formidable. Fors, fortuna; fortune, misfortune.
Fortis (*strong*); fort, fortify, fortitude, fortress.
Frango, fractum (*I break*); fragile, frail, infringe, infraction, refraction, refractory, fragment, fracture.
Frater (*brother*); fraternal, fratricide. Fraus, fraudis; fraud.
Frequens; frequent. Frico (*I rub*); friction.
Frigus (*cold*); frigid, refrigerate. Frivolus; frivolous.
Frons; front, affront, frontispiece. Frugalis; frugal.
Fruges, fructus (*fruit*), fruor (*I enjoy*); fruit, fructify, fruition.
Frustra (*in vain*); frustrate. Fugio (*I flee*); fugitive, refuge.
Fulgeo (*I lighten*); refulgent. Fulmen (*thunderbolt*); fulminate.
Fumus (*smoke*); fumigate, fume.
Fundus (*bottom*); found, foundation, fundamental, profound.
Fungor (*I discharge*); function, defunct. Funus; funeral.
Fur (*thief*); furtive. Futilis; futile.

Garrio (*I prattle*); garrulous.
Gelu (*ice*); gelid, congeal, jelly, gelatine. Gemma; gem.
Gens (*race*), gigno (*root* gen, *I beget*); genus (*kind*); gentile, generate, generation, gender, degenerate, general, gentle, genteel.
Germen (*bud*); germinate.
Gero, gestum (*I bear*); gesture, suggest, belligerent, vice-gerent.
Glacies (*ice*); glass, glacial, glacier. Glans (*kernel*); gland, glandular.
Gleba (*clod*); glebe.
Globus (*ball*), glomero (*I make into a ball*); globe, conglomerate.
Gloria; glory.
Gradus (*step*), gradior, gressum (*I walk*); grade, degrade, digression, congress, transgress.
Grandis (*large*); grand, aggrandize. Granum; grain.
Gratia; grace, gratuitous, ingratitude. Gratus; grateful, gratitude.
Gravis (*heavy*); grave, gravitation.
Grex (*flock*); gregarious, congregate. Guberno (*I pilot*); govern.
Habeo, habitum (*I have*); have, habit, prohibit.
Habito (*dwell*); habitation, inhabit.
Haereo (*I stick*); adhere, adhesion, hesitate.
Haeres *or* heres (*heir*); inherit, hereditary.
Halo (*I breathe*); exhale, inhale. Haurio, haustum (*I draw*); exhaust.
Herba; herb, herbaceous. Hibernus (*wintry*); hibernate.
Histrio (*actor*); histrionic. Homo (*man*), humanus; human, homicide.
Honestus; honest. Honor; honour, honourable, honorary.
Horreo (*I shudder*), horror, horridus; horror, horrid, horrify, abhor.
Hortor; exhort. Hortus (*garden*); horticulture.
Hospes (*guest*); hospitable, hospice, host. Hostis (*enemy*); hostile.
Humeo (*I am wet*); humid, humour.
Humus (*ground*); exhume, humble, humiliate.
Ignis (*fire*); ignite, igneous. Ignoro; ignore, ignorant.
Imago; image, imagine. Imbecillis (*weak*); imbecile. Imbuo; imbue.
Impero (*I command*), imperium; empire, emperor, imperious, imperative.
Index, indico (*I point*); indicate, indicative.
Inferus (*low, placed underneath*); inferior, infernal.
Ingenium (*talent, disposition*); ingenious.
Ingenuus (*native*); ingenuous, ingenuity. Insula (*island*); insular, insulate.
Integer (*whole, sound*); integral, integrate, integrity.
Intelligo (*I perceive*); intelligent, intellect. Invito; invite.
Ira (*anger*); ire, irate, irascible. Irrito (*I provoke*); irritate.
Irrigo; irrigate. Iterum (*again*); reiterate.
Iter, itineris (*journey*); itinerant.
Jaceo (*I lie down*); adjacent.
Jacio, jactum (*I throw*); eject, reject, object, adjective, conjecture, subject.
Jocus; joke, jocular. Jubeo, jussum (*I order*); jussive.
Judex; judge, judicious, adjudicate, prejudice.
Jugum (*yoke*); conjugal, conjugate, subjugate.
Jugulum (*collar-bone*); jugular.
Jungo, junctum; join, joint, juncture, conjunction, injunction.
Juro (*I swear*); conjure, jury, perjury.

Jus (*justice*), justus (*just*); just, unjust, injury, justify, jurisdiction.
Juvenis (*young*); juvenile, junior. Labor; labour, laborious, laboratory.
Labor, lapsus sum (*I slide*); lapse, elapse, collapse.
Lac, lactis (*milk*); lacteal, lactic. Lacero (*I mangle*); lacerate.
Lacrima (*tear*); lacrimose. Lacus; lake.
Laedo, laesum (*I dash* or *hurt*); lesion, elide, elision, collision.
Lamentor ; I lament. Langueo, languidus; languid, languish.
Lapis, lapidis (*stone*) ; lapidary, dilapidate. Largus ; large.
Lassus (*weary*); lassitude. Lateo (*I lie hid*) ; latent.
Latus (*broad*) ; latitude. Latus, lateris (*side*) ; lateral, equilateral.
Laus, laudis (*praise*) ; laud, laudation, laudable.
Lavo (*I wash*) ; lavatory, lavation, lave. Laxus (*loose*); lax, relax.
Lego (*I send* or *depute*) ; legate, allege, legacy.
Lego, lectum (*I gather, choose*) ; collect, select, elect, recollect, lecture, college, legion.
Lenis (smooth) ; lenity. Lentus (*flexible*); relent.
Levis (*light*), levo (*I lift*); levity, alleviate, relieve, elevate.
Lex, legis (*law*) ; legal, legitimate, legislate.
Liber (*free*); liberal, liberate, deliver. Liber (*book*) ; library, libel.
Libo (*I pour*); libation. Libra (*balance*); deliberate, libration.
Licet (*it is lawful*) ; licence, illicit. Lignum (*wood*) ; ligneous.
Ligo (*I tie*); ligament, religion, league, allegiance, oblige.
Limen (*threshold*); eliminate. Limes, limitis (*boundary*) ; limit.
Linea; line, lineal. Lingua (*tongue*); linguist, language.
Linquo, lictum (*I leave*) ; relinquish, relict, delinquent.
Liquor, liquidus; liquor, liquid, liquefy.
Litera; letter, literal, illiterate. Lividus (*dark blue*); livid.
Locus (*place*), loco (*I place*); locate, local, locomotion.
Longus; long, longitude, elongate.
Loquor, locutus (*I speak*), loquax; elocution, loquacious, colloquy, eloquent. Lucrum (*gain*); lucrative, lucre.
Ludo, lusum (*I play*) ; elude, prelude, illude, illusion, ludicrous.
Lumen (*light*); luminous, illuminate. Luna (*moon*); lunar, lunatic.
Luo, lutum (*I wash*); dilute, ablution, diluvial.
Lustrum (*purification*) ; lustre, lustrous, lustration, illustrate.
Lux (*light*); lucid, elucidate.
Machina ; machine. Macula (*spot*) ; immaculate.
Magister (*master*) ; magistrate, magisterial.
Magnus (*great*), major (*greater*); magnitude, majesty, majority, mayor.
Malus (*bad*); malice, malignant, maltreat, malady.
Mamma (*breast*) ; mamma, mammalia.
Mando (*commit, enjoin*); mandate, command, commend, remand.
Maneo, mansum (*I remain*); mansion, remain, remnant, permanent, imminent.
Manus (*hand*); manual, manufactory, manuscript, maintain, manacle, emancipate, manumit. Mare (*sea*); marine, maritime, mariner.
Mars ; martial. Massa ; mass, massive.
Mater (*mother*) ; maternal, matricide, matron, matrix, matriculate, matrimony. Materia (*timber, stuff*) ; matter, material.

Maturus (*ripe*); mature, immature, premature.
Medeor (*I heal*), medicina; remedy, medicine, medical.
Medius (*middle*); mediator, mediocrity, immediate.
Mel (*honey*); mellifluous. **Melior** (*better*); ameliorate.
Membrum; member, membrane.
Memor (*mindful*), memini (*I remember*); remember, memory, memorial, memoir, commemorate, comment. **Mendax** (*lying*); mendacious.
Mendicus (*beggar*); mendicant, mendicity.
Mendum (*fault*); amend, mend, emendation.
Mens, mentis (*mind*); mental, vehement. **Mereo, meritum** (*I deserve*); merit.
Mergo, mersum (*I plunge*); immerse, merge, emergency. **Merus**; mere.
Merx (*wares*); merchant, commerce, mercer, market.
Metior, mensus sum (*I measure*); immense, mensuration, measure.
Migro (*I change my abode*); migrate.
Miles, militis (*soldier*); military, militia.
Mille (*thousand*); mile, millennium, million.
Minister (*servant*); minister, ministry.
Minor (*less*), minuo (*I lessen*); diminish, minor, minority, minute.
Mirus (*wonderful*); admire, miracle.
Misceo, mixtum (*I mix*); miscellany, promiscuous.
Miser (*wretched*); miser, miserable, misery, commiserate.
Mitigo; mitigate.
Mitto, missum (*I send*); emit, admit, permit, promise, mission, missile.
Modus (*measure*); mode, mood, model, moderate, modest, modulation.
Mola; mill-stone, meal, molar, immolate, emolument (*the miller's perquisite*).
Mollis (*soft*); emollient, mollify, mollusk.
Moneo, monitum (*I warn*); admonish, monument, monster, monitor, money (*what is distinguished by a mark or token*).
Mons, montis; mount, mountain, surmount, dismount, promontory.
Monstro (*I show*); demonstrate. **Morbus** (*disease*); morbific, morbid.
Mordeo, morsum (*I bite*); remorse, morsel.
Mors, mortis (*death*); mortal, mortuary. **Mos, moris** (*custom*); moral.
Moveo, motum (*I move*); mobilis, momentum; move, motive, moment, mobility, emotion. **Mula**; mule.
Multus (*many*); multitude, multiform, multiple, multiply (plico-plex).
Mundus (*world*); mundane.
Munio (*I fortify*); munition, ammunition, muniment.
Munus, muneris (*gift, share*); remunerate, immunity.
Murus (*wall*); mural, intramural.
Musa (*muse*); music, amuse, museum. **Mutilus** (*maimed*); mutilate.
Muto (*I change*); mutable, mutation, commute, transmute.
Narro; narrate, narrative. **Nasus** (*nose*); nasal.
Nascor, natus sum (*I am born*); nascent, natal, native, nation, cognate, nature, natural.
Navis (*ship*); naval, navigate, navy. **Nauta** (*sailor*); nautical, nautilus.
Necesse; necessary, necessitude, necessity.
Necto, nexum (*I tie*); connect, annex. **Nefas** (*wickedness*); nefarious.
Nego (*I deny*); negation, renegade. **Negotium,** (*business*); negotiate.
Nervus (*string*); nerve, enervate. **Neuter** (*not either*); neuter, neutral.

Niger (*black*); negro. Nihil (*nothing*); annihilate.
Noceo (*I hurt*); innocent, noxious, innocuous.
No-sco, notum (*I know*); no-men (*name*), no-bilis (*noble*); noun, name, nominate, nominal, noble, ignoble, ignominy, note, notation, notion, notice. Non (*not*); non-entity, non-age.
Norma (*rule*); normal, enormous. Novem (*nine*); November.
Novus (*new*); novel, innovate, renovate, novice.
Nox, noctis (*night*); nocturnal, equinox.
Nubo (*I marry*); nuptial, connubial. Nudus (*naked*); nude, denude.
Nullus (*none*); nullity, nullify, annul.
Numerus (*number*); numeral, enumerate.
Nuntio (*I announce*); nuncio, announce, renounce, renunciation.
Nutrio (*I nourish*); nutritious, nutriment, nurse.
Nympha; nymph. Oblivio (from liv-idus); oblivion.
Obliquus; oblique. Obscoenus; obscene. Obscurus (*dark*); obscure.
Occulo, occultum (*I hide*); occult.
Occupo (*I lay hold of*); occupy, occupation.
Octo (*eight*); octave, octavo, October.
Oculus (*eye, bud*); ocular, oculist, inoculate.
Odium (*hatred*); odious, odium.
Odor (*smell*), oleo (*I smell*); odour, odorous, redolence, olfactory.
Officium (*duty, business*); office, officious. Oleum (*oil*); oleaginous.
Omen; ominous, abominate.
Omnis (*all*); omnipotent, omnibus (*for all*).
Onus, oneris (*load*); onerous, exonerate. Opacus (*shaded*); opaque.
Opinor (*I think*); opine, opinion. Optimus (*best*); optimist.
Opto (*I desire*); option, adopt. Opus, operis (*work*); operate.
Orbis (*circle*); orb, orbit, exorbitant.
Ordo, ordinis (*order*); ordinate, ordain, ordinary.
Orior, ortus sum (*I rise*); orient, origin, abortive.
Oro (*I speak*); orator, oracle, adore, inexorable.
Os, oris (*face*); oral. Osculor (*I kiss*); oscillate.
Ovum (*egg*); oviparous, oval.
Paciscor, pactus sum (*I make an agreement*); pact, compact.
Pagina; page. Pagus (*village*); pagan, peasant.
Pallium (*cloak*); pall, palliate.
Pallor (*paleness*); palleo, (*I am pale*); pallor, pallid. Palma; palm.
Palpo (*I stroke*); palpable, palpitate.
Palus (*stake*); pale, palisade, impale.
Pando, pansum and passum (*I spread*); expand, expanse, compass, pace.
Pango, pactum (*I fasten*); compact, impinge.
Panis (*bread*); pantry. Par (*equal*); parity, peer, compare.
Parco, parsum (*I spare*); parsimony. Pareo (*I appear*); apparent.
Pario (*I bring forth*); parent, viviparous.
Paro (*I prepare*); impair, repair, prepare, compare, comparative.
Pars, partis (*part*); partition, impart, party, particle, participle, parse, particular, bipartite. Pasco, pastum (*I feed*); pasture, repast, pastor.
Pateo (*I lie open*); patent.
Pater (*father*); paternal, patron, patrimony, patrician, patristic.

Patria (*country*); patriot, expatriate.
Patior, passus sum (*I suffer*); patient, passion, passive.
Pauper (*poor*); pauper, pauperism. **Pavio** (*I ram tight*); pave, pavement.
Pax, pacis (*peace*); pacific.
Pecco (*I sin*); peccant, impeccable, peccadillo.
Pectus, pectoris (*breast*); pectoral, expectorate.
Peculium (*private property*); peculiar, peculation.
Pecunia (*money*); pecuniary, **Pellis** (*skin*); peltry.
Pello, pulsum (*I drive*); compel, repel, repulse, pulse, pulsation.
Pendeo (*I hang*), **pendo, pensum** (*I hang* or *weigh*); depend, expend, pension, pensive, recompense, pendulum, compensate, perpendicular, pensile. **Pene** (*almost*); peninsula.
Penetro (*I pierce*); penetrate.
Penuria (*want*); penury, penurious. **Perdo** (*I lose*); perdition.
Persona (*mask*); person.
Pes, pedis (*foot*); pedal, pedestrian, impede, expedite, biped.
Pestis (*plague*); pest, pestilence.
Peto, petitum (*ask, seek*); petition, compete, repeat, appetite.
Pingo, pictum (*paint*); depict, picture, pigment, Picts.
Pilo (*I steal*); pillage, compile. **Piscis** (*fish*); piscatory.
Pius (*dutiful*); pious, piety, pity, expiate.
Placeo (*I please*); placid, placable, complaisant, pleasant.
Plango; com-plain, plaint. **Planta**; plant, plantation.
Planus (*level*); plane, plain, explain.
Plaudo (*I clap*); applaud, applause, plaudit, plausible.
Plebs (*commonalty*); plebeian.
Plecto, plexus (*I weave*); complex, perplex.
Pleo (*I fill*), **plenus** (*full*); plenary; complete, replete.
Plico (*I fold*); implicate, apply, application, comply, reply, supplicate, suppliant, duplicity, double, complex, pliable, surplice, accomplice.
Ploro (*I weep*); deplore, explore. **Pluma**; plume.
Plumbum (*lead*); plumber, plummet.
Plus, pluris (*more*); plural, surplus.
Poena (*fine*); penal, punitive, punish, repent, penance, penitent.
Polio; polish, polite.
Pondus, ponderis (*weight*); pound, ponderous, preponderate, ponder.
Pono, positum (*I place*); impose, repose, deposit, compound, position, component. **Pons** (*bridge*); pontoon.
Populus (*people*); popular, depopulate, public, publish.
Porcus (*hog*); pork.
Porta (*door*); portal, portico, porthole.
Porto (*I carry*); export, portable, support. **Portus**; port.
Possum (*I can*); possible, potent.
Post (*after*); posterity. **Postis**; post. **Postulo** (*I demand*); postulate.
Praeda (*plunder*); predatory, depredation, prey.
Pravus (*crooked*); depraved.
Precor (*I pray*); deprecate, precarious (*depending on entreaty*).
Prehendo (*I grasp*); apprehend, apprehension.
Premo, pressum (*I press*); express.

Primus (*first*); prime, primitive, primeval, primrose.
Princeps (*prince*); principal, principle. Pristinus, pristine.
Privo (*I deprive, make separate*); deprive, private, privacy, privy.
Probo (*I approve, make good*); prove, probe, probation, probable, reprobate.
Probus (*honest, good*); probity. Probrum (*a shameful act*); opprobrious.
Promptus, *from* promo (*ready*); prompt, promptitude.
Pronus; prone. Propago; propagate.
Prope (*near*), proximus (*nearest*); propinquity, proximate, proximity.
Proprius (*one's own*); proper, property, propriety, appropriate.
Prurio (*I itch*); prurient. Pudor (*shame*), pudet; impudent.
Puer (*boy*); puerile. Pugil (*boxer*); pugilist.
Pugna (*fight*), pugno (*I fight*); pugnacious, impugn, repugnance.
Pulmo (*lungs*); pulmonary. Pulpa; pulp.
Pungo, punctum (*I prick*); pungent, puncture, punctuation, expunge, point, appoint. Puppis (*stern*); poop.
Pupus, pupulus, pupillus (*a little boy*); puppet, pupil.
Purgo (*I cleanse*); purge, purgatory.
Purpura; purple. Purus; pure, purify.
Puto (*I cut, calculate, think*); amputate, computate repute, depute, putative. Putris (*rotten*); putrid, putrefy.
Quaero, quaesitum (*I seek*); question, inquire, require, query, quest, exquisite, inquest. Qualis (*of which kind*); quality, qualify.
Quantus (*how great*); quantity.
Quatio, quassum (cutio, cussum *in compounds*; *I shake* or *strike*); quash, percussion, discuss.
Quatuor (*four*), quartus (*fourth*), quadra (*square*); quart, quarto, quarter, quadrature, quadrant, quadratic.
Queror (*I complain*); querulous. Quies, quietis (*rest*); quiet, acquiesce.
Quinque (*five*); quintessence. Radius (*rod, ray*); radius, radiate.
Radix, radicis (*root*); radish, radical, eradicate.
Rado, rasum (*I scrape*); erase, razor, abrade.
Ramus (*branch*); ramification.
Rapio, raptum (*I snatch*); rapid, rapture, rapine, rapacious, ravish, ravage, raven, ravenous. Rarus (*thin*); rare, rarefy.
Ratio (*reckoning, calculation, proportion*); reason, ratiocination, rational, ration. Ratus (*reckoned, fixed*); ratify, rate.
Rego, rectum (*I make straight*); regular, direct, erect, regent, regimen, regiment, rector, rectify.
Rex, regis (*king; not the same root as the last*); regal, regicide: Regnum; reign, regnant, interregnum.
Reperio (*I find*); repertory. Repo (*I creep*); reptile.
Res (*thing*); real, republic. Rete (*net*); retina, reticule.
Rideo, risum (*I laugh*); deride, risible, ridicule, ridiculous.
Rigeo (*I am stiff*); rigid, rigour.
Rigo (*I water*); irrigate, irriguous. Ritus; rite, ritual.
Rivus (*brook*), rivalis (*having the same brook in common*); river, rival, derive, arrive, rivulet.
Robur (*oak, strength*); robust, corroborate.
Rodo, rosum (*I gnaw*); corrode, corrosion.

Rogo (*I ask*); arrogate, derogate, rogation, prorogue. Rosa; rose.
Rota (*wheel*); rotate, rotary. Rotundus (*round*); rotund, rotundity.
Rudis (*untaught*); rude, erudite, rudiment. Ruga (*wrinkle*); corrugate.
Ruminare (*to chew the cud*); ruminate. Rumor; rumour.
Rumpo, ruptum (*I break*); rupture, abrupt, eruption, corrupt, bankrupt.
Ruo (*I rush*); ruin. Russatus (*dyed red*); russet.
Rus, ruris (*country*); rustic, rural. Saccus; sack.
Sacer (*sacred*), sacerdos (*priest*); sacred, sacrament, sacrifice, consecrate. sacerdotal, sacristan. Sagax (*knowing*); sage, sagacious, presage.
Sal; salt, saline, salary (*properly an allowance for salt*).
Salio, saltum, *in compounds* sultum (*I leap*); salient, assail, assault. salmon (*the leaping fish*), desultory, exult, insult, saltatory.
Salus, salutis (*safety*); salute, salutary.
Saluber; salubrious. Salvus (*safe*); salvation, salve, salvo, saviour.
Sancio, sanctum (*I consecrate*); sanction. Sanctus (*holy*); saint, sanctify.
Sanguis, sanguinis (*blood*); sanguinary, sanguine, consanguinity.
Sano (*I make sound*); sanative, sanatory.
Sanus (*sound*); sane, sanity, sanitary.
Sapio (*I taste, am wise*), sapor (*taste*); savour, sapient, insipid.
Satelles (*attendant*); satellite.
Satis (*enough*), satur (*full*), satio (*I fill*); satiate, satiety, saturate, satisfy.
Scando (*I climb*); scan, scansion, ascend, descend, condescend.
Scindo, scissum (*I split*); rescind, abscissa, scissors.
Scintilla (*spark*); scintillate.
Scio (*I know*); science, prescience, omniscience, conscious.
Scribo, scriptum (*I write*); scribe, describe, scripture, postscript.
Scrupulus (*a little pebble*); scruple, scrupulous.
Scrutor (*I examine*); scrutiny, inscrutable.
Seco, sectum (*I cut*); sect, section, insect, dissect, segment, secant.
Seculum (*age, world*); secular.
Sedeo, sessum (*I sit*), sido (*I set*), sedo (*I settle*), session, sedentary. sedulous, sediment, assess, possess, preside, subside, assiduous, consider, sedate.
Semi (*half*); semicircle. Senex (*old-man*); senile, senior, senate.
Sentio (*I feel, think*), sensus (*feeling*); sentient, scent, sentence, assent, sense, sensual, sensitive. Septem (*seven*); September, septennial.
Sepelio (*I bury*), sepulcrum; sepulture, sepulchre.
Sequester (*an umpire*); sequestrate, sequestered.
Sequor, secutus (*I follow*), secundus (*following*); sequence, sequel, consequent, persecute, second.
Sero, sertum (*I set in a row*); insert, exert, desert, series, sermon.
Semen (*seed*); seminary, disseminate. Serus; sere.
Servus (*slave*), servio (*I serve*), servo (*I watch or preserve*); serf, servile, servitude, servant, servitor, preserve, observe, deserve.
Sidus (*star*); sidereal.
Signum; sign, signify, signal, resign, design, assignation
Sileo (*I am silent*); silent, silence. Silva (*wood*); sylvan.
Similis (*like*); similar, assimilate, resemble, semblance, simulate.
Simul (*together*); simultaneous. Sincerus; sincere.

Singuli (*one by one*); single, singular. **Sinister**; sinister.
Sinus (*bend*); sine, sinuous.
Sisto (*I stop, I stand*); consist, insist, resist.
Socius (*companion*); social, society. **Sol** (*sun*); solar, solstice.
Solemnis (*annual, festive*); solemn. **Solidus**; solid, solder.
Sollicito; solicit. **Solor**; con-sole, solace.
Solum (*ground*); soil. Connected perhaps with this, is the root *sul* or *sil* in exsul (*exile*); consul (*consul*); counsel. The root is really identical with *sed* or *sid* in *sedeo* and *sido*.
Solus (*alone*); sole, solitude.
Solvo, solutum (*I loosen*); solve, solution, dissolute.
Somnus (*sleep*); somnolent. **Sopor** (*sleep*); soporific.
Sonus; sound, sonorous, consonant. **Sordes** (*dirt*); sordid.
Spargo, sparsum (*I strew*); sparse, disperse.
Spatium; space, spacious, expatiate.
Specio, spectum (*I look*), **species** (*appearance, kind*); special, specious, respect, aspect, spectator, speculate, despise, suspicion.
Sperno (*I reject*); spurn. **Spero** (*I hope*); despair, desperate.
Spiro (*I breathe*), **spiritus** (*breath*); spirit, aspire, conspire.
Splendeo (*I shine*); splendour, splendid. **Spolium**; spoil, spoliation.
Spondeo, sponsum (*I promise, bargain*); sponsor, spouse, respond, response, despond. **Stagnus** (*standing*); stagnant, stagnate.
Stella (*star*); constellation, stellar. **Sterilis**; sterile.
Sterno, stratum (*I throw down, spread*); prostrate, consternation.
Stilla (*drop*); distil. **Stilus**; style. **Stimulus** (*goad*); stimulate.
Stipendium (*pay*); stipend, stipendiary. **Stirps** (*root*); extirpate.
Sto, statum (*I stand*); station, stature, stable, distant, obstacle, superstition, armistice, substance, substantive.
Statuo (*I set up*); statue, statute, constitute. **Strenuus**; strenuous.
Stringo, strictum (*I tighten*); stringent, strain, constrain; strict, strait.
Strangulo (*I strangle*).
Struo, structum (*I pile up*); construct, destroy, destruction, construe.
Studium (*zeal, eagerness*), **studeo** (*I am eager*); study, student.
Stupeo (*I am amazed*); stupid.
Suadeo, suasum (*I advise*); suasion, persuade.
Sublimis (*raised aloft*); sublime, sublimate. **Subtilis**; subtile, subtle.
Sudo (*I sweat*); exude.
Sum (*I am*); root *es*, ens (*being*); entity, present, absent: **Futurus** (*about to be*); future. **Summus** (*highest*); sum, summit, consummate.
Sumo, sumptum (*I take*); assume, consume, consumption.
Super (*above*), **superus** (*upper*), **supremus** (*highest*); superior, supreme, supernal. **Supinus** (*on the back*); supine.
Surgo, surrectum (*I rise*); surge, resurrection, insurrection.
Tabula (*board*); table, tablet, tabular, tabulate.
Taceo (*I am silent*); tacit, reticence, taciturn. **Taedium** (*disgust*); tedious.
Tango, tactum (*I touch*); tact, contact, tangible, contagion, contiguous, attain, pertain, attach. **Taxo**; tax, taxation.
Tardus (*slow*); retard, tardy.
Tego, tectum (*I cover*); protect, integument.

Temere (*rashly*); temerity. **Temno** (*I despise*); contemn, contempt.
Tempero (*I moderate*): temperate, temper.
Templum; temple, contemplate.
Tempus, temporis (*time*); temporal, temporary, tense.
Tendo, tensum (*I stretch*); contend, intend, tense, intense, tension.
Teneo, tentum (*I hold*); tenant, tenure, tenaceous, tenour, retain, contain, content, retinue, tendril, continuous. **Tener**; tender.
Tento *or* **tempto** (*I try*); tempt, attempt, temptation.
Tenuis (*thin*); tenuity. **Tepeo** (*I am warm*); tepid.
Terminus (*boundary*); term, terminate, exterminate, determine.
Tero, tritum (*I rub*); trite, contrition, attrition, detriment.
Terra (*earth*); terrestrial, terrene, inter, terrier, terrace.
Terreo (*I frighten*); terrify, terrible, terror, deter.
Testis (*witness*); testify, testimony, attest, detest, protest.
Texo, textum (*I weave*); text, context, texture, textile.
Timeo (*I fear*); timid. **Torpeo** (*I am numb*); torpid.
Torqueo, tortum (*I twist*); torsion, contort, contortion, torture, torments.
Torreo, tostum (*I parch*); torrid, toast. **Totus** (*whole*); total.
Traho, tractum (*I draw*); **tracto** (*I handle*); treat, tract, contract, attract, tractable, tractate. **Tranquillus**; tranquil.
Tremo (*I tremble*); tremour, tremulous, tremendous.
Trepido (*I am in disorder*); trepidation.
Tres, tria (*three*); trefoil, trident, trinity. **Tribuo** (*I assign*); tribute.
Tribus; tribe, tribune. **Triumphus**; triumph.
Trudo, trusum (*I thrust*); extrude, intrusion. **Truncus**; trunk, truncated.
Tueor (*I protect*); tuition, tutor.
Tumeo (*I swell*); tumid, tumour, tumult, contumely, tomb.
Tuber (*a swelling*); protuberance, tubercle.
Tundo, tusum (*I thump*); contusion.
Turba (*mob*); turbulent, turbid, disturb. **Turpis** (*foul*); turpitude.
Uber (*udder*), exuberant. **Ubique** (*everywhere*); ubiquity.
Ulcus, ulceris (*sore*); ulcer, ulceration.
Ultra (*beyond*), ulterior (*further*), ultimus (*furthest*); ulterior, ultimate, penult. **Umbra** (*shade*); umbrage, umbrageous, umbrella.
Uncia (*a twelfth part*); ounce, inch, uncial, unciary.
Unguo, unctum (*I anoint*); unguent, ointment, unction.
Unda (*wave*), undare (*to rise in waves*); abound, redound, abundant, inundate.
Unus (*one*); union, unity, unit, triune, uniform, universe, universal, unique.
Urbs (*city*); urban, urbane, suburb.
Urgeo (*I press*); urge, urgent. **Urna**; urn.
Uro, ustum (*I burn*); combustion.
Utor, usus sum (*I use*); use, usage, utility, usury, usurp.
Uxor (*wife*); uxorious. **Vacca** (*cow*); vaccine, vaccination.
Vaco (*I am unoccupied*); vacant, vacation, vacate, vacuum, evacuate.
Vado, vasum (*I go*); invade, evade, invasion, wade.
Vagor (*I wander*); vagus (*wandering*); vague, vagrant, vagabond, extravagant.

Valeo (*I am strong*); valid, valour, value, avail, prevail, prevalent, valedictory.
Vallis; vale, valley. Vallus (*stake*); circumvallation.
Vanus (*empty*); vain, vanity. Varius; various, variegate.
Vapor (*steam*); vapour, evaporate. Vas (*pot*); vessel, vascular.
Vastus (*desolate*); vast, waste, devastate.
Veho, vectum (*I carry*); convey, convex, inveigh, vehicle.
Vello, vulsum (*I pluck*); convulse, revulsion.
Velum (*covering*); veil, reveal, develop, envelop. Vena; vein.
Vendo (*I sell*); vend, venal. Venenum (*poison*); venom.
Veneror (*I worship*); venerate, revere.
Venio, ventum (*I come*); convene, venture, convent, advent, prevent, revenue, convenient, covenant.
Venter (*belly*); ventral, ventriloquist. Ventus (*wind*); ventilate.
Verbum (*word*); verb, verbal, proverb.
Vergo (*I incline*); verge, converge. Vermis (*worm*); vermicular, vermin.
Verto, versum (*I turn*); verso (*I turn*); verse, version, convert, divorce, adverse, advertise, perverse, universe, vortex, vertical.
Verus (*true*); verity, verify, aver.
Vestis (*garment*); vest, vesture, vestry, invest.
Vetus (*old*); inveterate, veteran.
Vexo (*I harass*); vex, vexation. Vibro; vibrate.
Via (*road*); deviate, obviate, pervious, trivial.
Vicis (*change*); vicissitude, vicar, vicarious, viceroy.
Vicinus (*neighbour*); vicinity.
Video, visum (*I see*); visible, vision, provide, revise, visage, prudence, providence, survey, invidious, envy.
Vilis (*cheap*); vile, vilify. Villa (*country house*); villa, village.
Vinco, victum (*I conquer*); victor, vanquish, victim, convince, convict.
Vindex (*avenger*); vindicate, vindictive.
Vir (*man*); virtus (*manliness*); virtue, virago, triumvir, virile.
Vis (*force*); violent. Viscus; viscera, eviscerate.
Vita (*life*); vital. Vitium (*fault*); vice, vicious, vitiate.
Vitrum (*glass*); vitreous, vitrify, vitriol.
Vivo, victum (*I live*); revive, vivify, vivacious, victuals.
Voco (*I call*); vox (*voice*); voice, vocal, vocation, invocate, convoke, provoke, vowel, vocabulary. Volo (*I fly*); volatile.
Volo (*I will*); voluntary, volunteer, benevolent, volition.
Volupis (*delightful*); voluptuous.
Volvo, volutum (*I roll*); revolve, volume, revolution, voluble, volute.
Vomo; I vomit. Voro (*I devour*); voracious, devour, carnivorous.
Voveo, votum (*I vow*); vote, votive, votary, devote, devout.
Vulgus (*common people*); vulgar, divulge, vogue, vulgate.
Vulnus (*wound*); vulnerable.

List of the principal Greek Words Derivatives from which have been adopted into English.

'Αγγελος (angelos, *messenger*); angel, evangelist.
'Αγιος (*sacred*); hagiology. Αγωγη (*leading*); synagogue.
Αγων (*struggle*); agony, antagonist. Αδαμας (*steel*); adamant, diamond.
Αηρ (*air*); aeronaut, aerostation. Αθλον (*contest*); athlete, athletic.
Αιθηρ (*sky*); ether, ethereal. Αιμα (*blood*); haemorrhage.
Αινιγμα (*riddle*); enigma. Αιρησις (*choice*); heresy, heretic.
Αισθησις (*perception*); aesthetics. Ακαδημεια; academy.
Ακμη (*point*); acme. Ακολουθεω (*I follow*); acolyte *or* acolyth.
Ακουω (*I hear*); acoustics. Ακροαομαι (*I listen*); acroamatic.
Ακρος (*top*); acropolis. Αλλος (*other*); allopathy.
Αλληλοι (*one another*); parallel. Αλφα (*a*); alphabet.
Αμφι (*on both sides*); amphibious, amphitheatre.
Ανεμος (*wind*); anemometer. Ανθος (*flower*); anthology.
Ανθραξ (*coal*); anthracite. Ανθρωπος (*man*); anthropology, philanthropy.
Αξιωμα (*claim, demand*); axiom. Αρκτος (*bear*); arctic.
Αριθμος (*number*); arithmetic. Αριστος (*best*); aristocracy.
'Αρμονια; harmony. Αρτηρια; artery.
Αρχη (*rule, beginning*); monarch, archangel, architect.
Ασκεω (*I exercise*); ascetic. Αστηρ (*star*); astral, asteroid, astronomy.
Αω (*I breathe*); asthma, atmosphere. Αυτος (*self*); autograph, autocrat.
Βαλλω (*I throw*), βολη, βλημα; hyperbole, parable, emblem, symbol.
Βαπτω, βαπτιζω; baptize. Βαρβαρος (*not Greek*); barbarous.
Βαρος (*weight*); barometer. Βασις (*treading, support*); base, basis.
Βιβλιον (*book*); Bible, bibliopole. Βιος (*life*); biography, amphibious.
Βλασφημια; blasphemy. Βομβυξ (*silk-worm*); bombazine.
Βοτανη (*grass*); botany. Βρογχος (*windpipe*); bronchitis.
Γη (*earth*); apogee, geography, geology. Γαλα (*milk*); galaxy.
Γαμος (*marriage*); bigamy. Γαστηρ (*belly*); gastric, gastronomy.
Γενος (*race*); genealogy. Γιγας; giant, gigantic.
Γλωσσα (*tongue*); gloss, glossary. Γλυφω (*carve*); hieroglyphic.
Γνωμων (*pointer*); gnomon, physiognomy.
Γραφω (*I write*); grammar, telegraph, graphic, paragraph.
Γυμναζω (*I exercise*); gymnastic. Γυνη (*woman*); misogynous.
Δακτυλος (*finger*); dactyl. Δαιμων (*divinity*); demon.
Δειγμα (*pointing*); paradigm. Δεκα (*ten*); decalogue.
Δενδρον (*tree*); dendrology. Δημος (*people*); democracy.
Διαιτα (*way of living*); diet. Διδασκω (*I teach*); didactic.
Διπλωμα (*anything folded*); diploma. Δογμα (*opinion*); dogma, dogmatic.
Δοξα (*opinion, glory*); orthodox, doxology.
Δραω (*I act*); drastic, drama. Δρομος (*running*); hippodrome.
Δυναμις (*power*); dynamics, dynasty. 'Εδρα (*seat*); cathedral.

Εθνος (*race*); ethnic, heathen, ethnology. **Εθος** (*custom*); ethics.
Ειδος (*form*); kaleidoscope, cycloid, &c.
Ειδωλον (*image*); idol. idolatry. **Εικων** (*image*); iconoclast.
Ειρωνεια (*dissimulation*); irony. **Ελαστικος** (*that may be driven*); elastic.
Ελεημοσυνη (*pity*); eleemosynary. **'Ελλην** (*Greek*); Hellenic.
'Εν (*one*); hyphen. **Ενδον** (*within*); endogenous.
Εντερα (*entrails*); dysentery. **'Εξ** (*six*); hexagon.
Εξω (*outside*); exoteric. **'Επτα** (*seven*); heptarchy.
Εργον (*work*); energy, metallurgy.
Ερημος (*solitary*); eremite, hermit.
'Ετερος (*other*); heterodox, heterogeneous. **Ετυμος** (*true*); etymology.
Ευ (*well*); eulogy, euphony. **Εχω** (*I hold*); epoch.
Ζωνη (*girdle*); zone. **Ζωον, ζωδιον** (*animal*); zoology, zoophyte, zodiac.
'Ηγησις (*leading*); exegesis. **Ηλεκτρον** (*amber*); electricity.
'Ηλιος (*sun*); heliacal, heliotrope. **'Ημερα** (*day*); ephemeral.
'Ημι (*half*); hemisphere. **'Ηρως**; hero.
Ηχη, ηχω (*sound*); echo, catechize.
Θεαομαι (*I behold*); theatre, theory, theorem.
Θαυμα (*wonder*); thaumatrope. **Θεος** (*God*); theology, theism, enthusiast.
Θερμος (*heat*); thermometer, isothermal.
Θεραπευω (*I heal*); therapeutics.
Θεσις, θεμα (*placing*); anathema, antithesis, epithet, theme.
Θηκη (*box*); hypothecate, apothecary. **Θυμος** (*mind*); erthymeme.
Ιδεα (*form*); idea.
Ιδιος (*peculiar*); **ιδιωτης, ιδιωμα**; idiom, idiot, idiosyncrasy.
'Ιερος (*sacred*); hierarch, hieroglyphic. **'Ιλαρος** (*cheerful*); hilarity.
'Ιππος (*horse*); Philip, hippopotamus.
Ισος (*equal*); isomorphous, isochronous, isosceles (**σκελος** = leg).
'Ιστορια (*investigation*); history, story. **Ιχθυς** (*fish*); ichthyology.
Καλεω (*I call*); **εκκλησια**; ecclesiastic.
Καλος (*beautiful*); **καλλος** (*beauty*); calligraphy, calotype, calisthenic.
Καλυπτω (*I hide*); apocalypse. **Καθαρος** (*pure*); cathartic.
Κακος (*bad*); cacophonous. **Κανων** (*rule*); canon, canonical.
Καυστικος (*burning*); caustic. **Κεντρον** (*point*); centre.
Κλιμα (*slope*); climate. **Κλιμαξ** (*ladder*); climax, climacteric.
Κλινω (*I bend*); incline, enclitic. **Κοινος** (*common*); epicene.
Κογχη (*cockle*); conchology.
Κοσμος (*world*); cosmical, microcosm. **Κομητης** (*long-haired*); comet.
Κρανιον (*skull*); cranium. **Κρατος** (*strength*); autocrat, democrat.
Κρινω (*I judge*), **κρισις, κριτικος**; critic, crisis, hypocrisy.
Κρυσταλλος (*ice*); crystal. **Κρυπτω** (*I hide*); apocrypha, crypt.
Κυκλος (*circle*); cycle, cycloid, cyclopædia.
Κυλινδρος (*roller*); cylinder. **Κυβος**; cube. **Κυων** (*dog*); cynic.
Κυριακος (*belonging to the Lord*); church. **Κωμος** (*festivity*); encomium.
Κωνος; cone. **Λεγω** (*say, choose*); eclectic.
Λεξις (*speech*); lexicon, dialect. **Λαμβανω** (*I take*); epilepsy, syllable.
Λειπω (*I leave*); ellipse, eclipse. **Λειχην**; lichen.
Λειτος (*belonging to the people*); liturgy.
Λιθος (*stone*); lithography, lithic.

Λογος (*speech, reason*); logic, dialogue, syllogism.
Λυρα; lyre, lyric. **Λυω** (*loosen*); paralysis. **Μαγος**; Magian, magic.
Μακρος (*long*); macrocosm. **Μαθημα** (*learning*); mathematics.
Μαρτυς (*witness*); martyr. **Μελας** (*black*); melancholy.
Μελος (*tune*); melody. **Μεταλλον**; metal.
Μετρον (*measure*); meter, barometer. **Μητηρ** (*mother*); metropolis.
Μηχανη (*contrivance*); mechanics. **Μιαινω** (*I pollute*); miasma.
Μικρος (*small*); microscope. **Μιμος** (*imitator*); mimic.
Μισος (*hatred*); misanthrope. **Μνημων** (*remembering*); mnemonic.
Μονος (*only*); monarch, monogamy, monotheism. **Μοναχος**; monk.
Μορφη (*form*); amorphous. **Μυστηρια**; mystery.
Ναυς (*ship*); nautical, nausea (sea-sickness).
Ναρκοω (*I benumb*); narcotic. **Νεκρος** (*dead*); necropolis, necromancy.
Νεος (*new*); neology, neophyte. **Νευρον** (*string, nerve*); neuralgia.
Νησος (*island*); Polynesia.
Νομος (*law*); antinomian, astronomy, gastronomy.
Νοσος (*disease*); nosology. **Οβελισκος**; obelisk.
Ὁδος (*way*); exodus, method, period. **Οικος** (*house*); economy.
Οικησις (*dwelling*); diocese, oecumenical.
Ὁλος (*whole*); catholic, holocaust. **Ὁμοιος** (*like*); homoeopathy.
Ὁμος (*same*); homogeneous.
Ονομα, ονυμα (*name*); synonymous, patronymic.
Οξυς (*sharp*); oxygen, paroxysm.
Οπτικος (*belonging to sight*); optics, synopsis. **Ὁραω** (*I see*); panorama.
Οργανον (*instrument*); organ. **Ορθος** (*straight*); orthodox, orthography.
Ὁριζω (*I define*); horizon, aorist. **Ορνις** (*bird*); ornithology.
Ορφανος; orphan. **Ορχηστρα** (*dancing-place*); orchestra.
Οστεον (*bone*); osteology. **Οφις** (*serpent*); ophicleide.
Οφθαλμος (*eye*); ophthalmia. **Παλαιος** (*ancient*); palaeography.
Παν (*all*); pantheism, pantomime. **Παν** (*Pan*); panic.
Παθος (*suffering, affection*); pathos, sympathy, pathetic.
Παις (*boy*); paedagogue. **Πανηγυρις** (*assembly*); panegyric.
Παιδεια (*instruction*); cyclopaedia. **Πατεω** (*I walk*); peripatetic.
Παυσις (*stopping*); pause. **Πειρα** (*trial*); empirical.
Πεντε (*five*); pentagon. **Πεντηκοστος** (*fiftieth*); pentecost.
Πεταλον (*leaf*); petal. **Πετρα** (*rock*); petrify, Peter.
Πεπω (*digest*); dyspeptic.
Πλασσω (*I mould, daub*), **πλαστικος**; plastic, plaster.
Πλανητης (*wandering*); planet. **Πλησσω** (*strike*); apoplexy.
Ποιεω (*I make*); poet. **Πολεμος** (*war*); polemic.
Πολος (*bowl, pole*); pole, polar.
Πολις (*city*); polity, policy, metropolis.
Πολυς (*many*); polygon, polygamy, polytheism.
Πομπη (*procession*); pomp, pompous. **Πους** (*foot*); antipodes, tripod.
Πρασσω (*I do*); practice, pragmatical.
Πρεσβυτερος (*elder*); presbyter, prester, priest.
Πρισμα (*something sawn*); prism. **Πρωτος** (*first*); prototype.
Πτωμα (*fall*); symptom. **Πυρ** (*fire*); pyrotechnics, empyrean.
Πωλεω (*I sell*); monopoly.

ʽΡεω (*I flow*), ῥευμα; catarrh, rheum, rheumatic.
ʽΡηγνυμι (*I break*); cataract. ʽΡητωρ (*orator*); rhetoric.
ʽΡις (*nose*); rhinoceros. ʽΡυθμος (*measured motion*); rhythm.
Σαρξ (*flesh*); sarcophagus. Σαρκαζω (*I tear the flesh*); sarcastic.
Σβεννυμι (*I extinguish*); asbestos. Σιφων (*tube*); siphon.
Σιτος (*food*); parasite. Σκανδαλον (*stumbling-block*); scandal.
Σκηνη (*tent, stage*); scene. Σκηπτρον (*staff*); sceptre.
Σκοπεω (*I look*), σκοπος; episcopal, bishop, scope, telescope, microscope.
Σπαω (*I draw*); spasm. Σπερμα (*seed*), σπορα; spermatic, sporadic.
Σπειρα (*coil*); spire, spiral.
Στασις (*standing*); apostasy, ecstasy, system.
Στελλω (*I despatch*); epistle, apostle. Στενος (*narrow*); stenography.
Στερεος (*solid*); stereoscope, stereotype.
Στιγμα (*brand*); stigma. Στιχος (*line*); distich, acrostic.
Στρατος (*army*); strategy. Στροφη (*turning*); catastrophe, apostrophe.
Συκος (*fig*); sycophant. Σφαιρα (*ball*); sphere.
Σφυζω (*I throb*); asphyxia. Σχημα (*form, make*); scheme.
Σχιζω (*I divide*); schism. Σχολη (*leisure*); school, scholar.
Ταφος (*tomb*); epitaph. Ταξις (*arrangement*); syntax.
Τονος (*stretching, pitch*); tone, tonic, monotony.
Τομη (*cutting*); atom, epitome, entomology.
Τευχος (*implement, book*); pentateuch.
Τηλε (*far off*); telescope, telegraph.
Τοπος (*place*); topography, topic. Τροπος (*turning*); tropic, trope.
Τυπος (*shape*); type. Τυραννος; tyrant.
ʽΥγρος (*moist*); hygrometer.
ʽΥδωρ (*water*); dropsy, hydrate, hydrostatics, hydrogen, hydrophobia.
ʽΥμνος; hymn, anthem. ʽΥπνος (*sleep*); hypnotic.
ʽΥστερος (*womb*); hysteria, hysterical.
Φαγω (*I eat*); sarcophagus.
Φαινω (*I show*); phenomen on, phantom, phase.
Φαρμακον (*drug*); pharmacy.
Φερω (*I bear*); phosphorus, metaphor.
Φημι (*I say*); emphasis, prophecy. Φθογγη (*voice, vowel*); diphthong.
Φθισις (*wasting*); phthisic. Φιλος (*fond of*); philosophy, Philip.
Φλεβς (*vein*); phlebotomy.
Φλεγμα (*inflammation, slimy humour*); phlegm.
Φοβος (*fear*); hydrophobia. Φραγμα (*fence*); diaphragm.
Φρασις (*saying*); phrase. Φρην (*mind*); phrenology.
Φυσις (*nature*); physics, physiology. Φυτον (*plant*); zoophyte.
Φωνη (*voice*); phonetic, phonography. Φως (*light*); photography.
Χαος (*empty space*); chaos. Χαρακτηρ (*something engraved*); character.
Χαρις (*thanks*); eucharist. Χειρ (*hand*); chirography, chiromancy.
Χιλιοι (*thousand*); kilogramme.
Χιμαιρα (*a fabulous monster*); chimerical. Χολη (*bile*); melancholy.
Χονδρος (*cartilage of the breast*); hypochondriac.
Χορδη (*string*); chord. Χορος (*dance*); chorus, choir.
Χρονος (*time*); chronology. Χριω (*I anoint*); Christ, Christian.
Χρωμα (*colour*); achromatic. Χυμος, χυλος (*juice*); chyme, chyle.

Χωρος (*place*): chorography. Ψαλλω (*I play the lyre*); psalm.
Ψευδος (*falsehood*); pseudonym. Ψυχη (*soul*); psychology.
Ωδη (*song*); ode, monody, parody. Ων, οντος (*being*); ontology.
῾Ωρα (*hour*); horology, horoscope. Ωσμος (*thrusting*); endosmose.

The above list does not include a large number of scientific terms employed in botany, medicine, zoology, &c.

The following table of the Greek alphabet is inserted for the use of those who are unacquainted with the Greek character:—

Α, α = a. Β, β = b. Γ, γ = g. Δ, δ = d. Ε, ε = ĕ. Ζ, ζ = z. Η, η = ē. Θ, θ = th. Ι, ι = i. Κ, κ = k or c. Λ, λ = l. Μ, μ = m. Ν, ν = n. Ξ, ξ = x. Ο, ο = ŏ. Π, π = p. Ρ, ρ = r. Σ, σ = s. Τ, τ = t. Υ, υ = y. Φ, φ = ph. Χ, χ = ch. Ψ, ψ = ps. Ω, ω = ō.

CPSIA information can be obtained
at www.ICGtesting.com
Printed in the USA
LVHW041003020323
740706LV00008B/822

9 783375 149109